Spirits Of The Once Walking

Copyright © 2002 Barbara Lakey

All Rights Reserved

ISBN 1-928857-05-1

Published 2002

Published by A.M.F. Limited, 3039 38th Avenue South, Minneapolis, MN 55406. ©2002 Barbara Lakey. All rights reserved. No part of this publication may be reproduced, stored in a retrieval system, or transmitted in any form or by any means, electronic, mechanical, recording or otherwise, without the prior written permission of the author.

Manufactured in the United States of America.

The characters and events in this book are fictitious. This is a work of fiction. Characters, places, and events are the products of the author's imagination or are used fictitiously. Any similarity to real persons, living or dead, is coincidental and not intended by the author.

Booklocker.com, Inc.
2002

Spirits Of The Once Walking

DISCARDED

babs lakey

an Elsie Sanders novel
Third in a Series of Psychological Suspense Novels

Spirits Of The Once Walking

To my always friend, Lynner, from Flipper

Chapter One

THE LAST WEEK OF NOVEMBER, 1993

I snorted, woke with a start.

No one had been able to observe me as I dozed. The car was on idle, tinted windows steamed for privacy. Good. The wind chill was fifty-some below zero. Lucky for me my Jaguar had perfect temperature control; I had not frozen to death. Slick-drool had bubbled from my lips, then, slipped down my chin. I wiped the saliva with one finger that looked a puffy white in this light. Although the light was dim I could see a disgusting blotch on my Italian seersucker jacket. Yes, it was too cold for the jacket, but when I wore it I felt rather delicious. I envisioned my soul in a type of metempsychosis, doing its tango into the stiff but dapper body of an old sepia-toned daguerreotype photograph that hung in my office at the treatment center I owned. I morphed in and out of that old photograph.

Rather than cold, I felt cool.

The habitual passion with which I catered to my feelings could be likened to the slick workings of a modern-day vending machine …slip in the coins…press the button. *Kachung.* Instant gratification.

And feelings were my business.

I fancied that man in the faded tin-type—sporting a neat mustache not unlike my own, standing rigid, but deep inside his bowels he was charged—Ever-ready. The only things missing in that photograph were the faded eyes. Those windows-to-the-soul that had once gleamed bright were vacant. Empty holes gaped at the viewer.

This shipment of dope was primo. The good shit always made me nod off for a few minutes. How fortunate I'd had the good sense to hit the power door-locks before I lit up. In this neighborhood you had to worry about being robbed, car-jacked, or God-knows-what.

I turned the defrosters on high and extended my wrist, giving it a shake. The Rolex lost three seconds every twenty days—a damn irritation. It told me that I had slept thirty-three minutes, would be late getting home. Not that I'd be asked to account for my whereabouts, but because I did require dinner at a precise time the Lobster Bisque would soon form a lukewarm crust as it sat on the table in wait of me.

My upper lip curled, incensed to think of that waste of fine French brandy.

How often had I told my dearest wife to add the Cognac right before I sat down to partake?

My 'little woman' was too stupid to grasp the concept of simple obedience.

She would have some weak excuse prepared: she thought she heard my car. I could visualize her head bobbing, shoulder to shoulder, reminiscent of a "why do blondes have shoulder pads" joke. Her whine was so distinctive that the mere memory of it transported me there. I could hear her clearly now. The bonus was the imagined scent of roasted garlic. It gave my nostrils a rush. Perhaps I *could* make it home while the Bisque was still tender, the aromatic Brandy still evident in the dining room air. Salivating, I smacked thin lips while I slipped the small bronze pipe into my briefcase—careful to hold the tinfoil over the ashes.

Waste not; want not.

The Jaguar's defrosters were quiet, discreet, as they cleared the windows. I took in the view without much relish.

Wal-Mart in South Minneapolis on a Friday night. Its parking lot served as an interesting spot for a quick high. I found the goon-parade a form of mild entertainment.

Outside my field of vision, I heard the Salvation Army Santa's bell clang, *cling*-clang. More beggars.

Straight ahead was the same big man that had labored along earlier dragging one leg. He leaned against the yellow post by the driveway. You'd think the freezing wind would have driven the riff-raff under some bridge by now. It was difficult to see the ruddy gimp's features for all the nature-made-smoke; his hacking breath sprayed the raw air. What was he, fifty feet away? His whole body shook while he coughed. *Tubercular.* That's what the tattered form seemed. Icicles collected, resembling a fungus or rare mold that frothed throughout his mustache and beard. The man's tremors made it difficult to read the sign that poked at him leaving a bright red mark on his chin. He clutched the billboard to his chest as if it were a fine wool scarf worn for its warmth, rather than a germ-infested cardboard that read:

> VIETNAM VET
> WILL WORK
> FOR FOOD
> HURRY PLEASE
> HUNGRY

The beggar's performance made me feel like a fancy-man. I slumped in the low slung black car and felt my blood curdle at the sight of such sleaze. My voice filled this luxury-cubbyhole. "Lazy fucking bastard." The words burned, then integrated; they clung to smells of lush leather, fine polished wood, and expensive dope.

"Another leech posing and jiving in hopes some weak-tit will give him a hand-out rather than get himself an honest job."

The Jaguar that encased me was itself surrounded by clouds of its exhaust; a hungry mechanical animal, it did not so much idle as it hummed its mantra of speed. I felt its power as it began to rise to the next level, to pant in readiness, waiting for me, its owner, to give the order to go from 'lounge' to 'lunge'.

That was when I saw her.

Although bundled for the cold she appeared a frail, soft pet—the type I was drawn to—the type that needed me. She read the beggars' sign, then, wonder of wonders, moved right past him.

My eyes took the journey behind her to the corner...prying through my now frost-free windows. Technology, I thought to myself, was it not great? Takes money for the best in anything, but what the hell—money talks, bullshit walks.

The light changed from red to green; her high-booted feet stepped quick to cross the street. I heard the crisp-krack*le*, krack*le*; it sounded as if she were walking on a bed of dry cereal instead of packed snow. The sound made me recall the voice of my mother long ago. "Quiet Randy, I'm watching my serial." *Why does she watch her cereal*, I'd thought? *Why not simply eat it?*

In the car, I laughed out-loud at this foolish childhood memory. Since they were no longer termed serials, but rather soaps, I wondered if children today puzzled at the idea of their mothers enthralled at the sight of a bar of Ivory. My eyes glossed over; I pictured my mother's form. Neighborhood kids taunted me by calling her J-E-L-L-O!

The peacock blue hat, that made my target visible from far away brought me back to the present; it had bobbed almost out of sight. I shrugged—okay, I was mistaken, she wasn't my type.

I tugged on the brim of my soft fedora and prepared myself to leave—to drive in the opposite direction and not give her another

thought, then...I narrowed my eyes into a squint to see better through the traffic. Had she stopped?
She stood a moment...turned...began the trek back.
She was coming back! Yes.
Wait for the light one more time, I thought.
Cross that street one last time.
Last?
Had I thought, last?
I watched, calm as the cool-cuke. Cool, yet my palms were moist, leaving a damp smear on the steering wheel to betray myself.
She stopped directly in front of the bearded lame man. The man too lazy to get a job. Vietnam vet. Just one more name for minority. People like him had no self-control, no pride. My hands dropped their death-grip from the steering wheel and rolled into clenched fists. Rather than cool, my inspection of this scene was a trip aboard an amusement ride—the Mad-Mouse; also like the ride, it was a frantic jerk-off.
I observed as she dug through her pockets; her mittened hands extended green wadded bills, touching the beggar. A sprig of holly, pinned over the right breast of her down-filled coat, broke free, twirling, piggy-back on a gust. It landed next to slimy fast-food remnants and a filthy white sock in the gutter. In *my* eyes it helped justify what I wanted to do to her: she was part of what was wrong with the city—part of the clutter. One of the pigs who cluttered the gutters.
Tears rolled down the panhandler's face—froze on his cheeks. His nose ran; the icicles in his facial hair thickened with snot and I watched, appalled.
I sat in my expensive sports car and longed to add my own spit to those tears. Just then I overheard the worthless piece of slime 'God-blessing' her. That decided it. I slid my Jag into gear. The act was sensual to me. Caressing the solid walnut shift-knob and

she needed. He'd taken too much time. Remembering, angered him. He wanted that time back.

As it turned out they'd had one night together. One sweet night after loving her for all those months—that was all he had to remember. Sam knew Bobbie had fallen in love with him on their one perfect night. He felt no comfort in the knowledge that she had loved him last. Love me now, love me *now,* the words grabbed his mind; he couldn't get away from the sound of them.

He lay back on the bed. His body ached to reach out, find her there; to roll over in the night and feel her soft heat on the sheets and know she was just up in the other room and would return. Was that so much to ask? That body ache did not compare to the pain in his heart. It spun him, clenched his heart tight in its vice... spin-clench, spin-clench. He was trapped. Reach all he wanted, pat those sheets beside him. Bobbie would never be there.

They'd never had a Christmas together.

Never would have one.

Small red beams sprinkled by. Their color highlighted the wet splotches on his black cheeks.

He heard the sound of water running in the bathroom and quickly got out of bed, swiping at his face; he tried to smooth his wrinkled pants by shaking first one leg, then the other.

Why had he let Darwin and Tony talk him into hiring this lady-of-the-night?

Bambi had demurely asked if she could use his 'ladies room' to freshen up. Sam hoped she was freshening 'down' as well as 'up'. Not that she didn't look clean. But she made her living payin' visits to guys just like him, visits just like this one tonight. He grimaced—nervous.

More than likely, she was already plenty fresh and she was taking some time to secure the hundred dollar bill he'd handed over and, then, getting a condom handy and ready for action. Sam glanced in the mirror as he paced in front of it. His bare chest was as damp as if he had stepped out of the shower in the last few minutes.

Why was he fuckin' doin' this? To please his buddies who were only trying to see him get out of his doldrums?

Was she taking a shower? He could hear water continue to run in the bathroom. *The biffy.* That's what the guy's who'd beat the ever lovin' *begora* outta him had called the bathroom. He would always remember that word. And them. The killing family that had killed his Bobbie.

He willed himself to stop pacing, to sit on the edge of his never-made-love-in-bed and take deep breaths.

He inhaled. The smells of Christmas filtered in from the main house.

Holidays. He exhaled.

Oh, what the fuck.

He swung long, lean legs around and lay back again, his arms behind his head; he could feel stress puff out of his pores. He rolled onto his side, his back to his bathroom and the hooker, and stared at his arm. From this angle he could see only a portion of the tattoo. Starting high on his shoulder, it portrayed a demon being crushed in a fist, a fist that turned into a heart as it wound down his muscled arm. Inside the heart was one word in script—Bobbie. Short for Roberta. Over forty and she was his first and only real love. Got to stop this crap, he told himself. If I keep thinking of her, now cold and dead, how will I ever be able to go through with this?

And why was he shook? Like he was about to get laid for the first time. For comin' fast and straight at forty-five his body looked okay—nothin' to be embarrassed about anyway.

He sighed. Maybe a blowjob.

Bambi.

Bambi? Gimme a break, he thought. The name alone was enough to make him shrivel. He knew he wouldn't be able to kiss her as soon as he saw her face. Not that there was anything *wrong* with it. It was a pretty face he guessed... just not her face. Aw, heck. They don't want to be kissed anyway, he thought.

"Oooh, you gorgeous hunk, you," like a magician's pickpocket she'd descended on him without a sound and unzipped his faded jeans; she was practically on top of him before he realized she'd returned, "let's take a look-see at what you've got hidin,' tucked away in there, for Momma."

The sudden feel of soft hands made him jerk. "You ain't my Momma." His voice came out louder than he meant it to; he could see she didn't like it, but intimate touch felt foreign to him. Especially touch that slithered unexpectedly.

"Sure thing, sweets, you're the boss." She raised her eyebrows at him; they were a crown over the mauve eye shadow that glowed in the dim light and matched her see-through blouse. He had thought the service might send someone more high class to this swank apartment—if only because of the ritzy address. Could they tell from his voice he was black?

"It *is* okay if I call you sweets?" Her toe was tapping, legs wide apart and hands, with red dipped nails, posturing on her hips.

He didn't answer right away; words, were day-old oatmeal that caked his throat.

She stopped her appraisal of him, the long scarlet nails traced along the contours of her small breasts. "Why don't you tell me what you have in mind?" Leaning over him she caused her right breast to brush against the side of his chest. He saw her peek out of the corner of her eye to see if the little tit rub got a rise out of him.

The perfume she wore was heavy. This night would not be an exercise in subtlety. If he closed his eyes maybe it would make him dizzy enough to stop his brain and it would be over. Over the hump!

He took his advice, closed his eyes. "Why don'tcha suck me off," the words were a quiet slur. With his eyes closed he could sneak away to a private world and get high on some other image—locked inside himself.

"But hon-buns, you've *paid* for more than that," she was slipping his pants over his narrow hips—anxious to begin her work, in fact, already beginning the game—but wanting to make it clear that his C-note was long gone—hist *o* ry.

His answer, "Keep the change," was barely audible, because while he spoke he felt her cool, wet tongue touch him, encircle him. His sexual drought was really going to end. From close proximity he heard his cat purring, felt her fur rub against his bare foot, she must have jumped onto the bed to cheer him on.

Bambi's cool tongue and hot, slow-footed lips held him—clamped—all other thoughts were choked-off, gone at last.

In this concentrated state he heard a thump followed by a meow-shriek. *"Wha?"* He could barely speak. The blood in his body was centered under Bambi's expert lips.

"Nothin' sweet-boy, I'm allergic to cats, is all." Bambi had kicked the tabby to the floor. Her lips went quickly back to work.

 Hot blood gushed to his head. He shoved at her as he stood. "Get out." He spat the words as if she'd done something terrible. "Yeah. An', by the way, I ain't no *boy*."

"Whadda' ya' mean?" Bambi backed her body away even as her tone sparred, "Listen here, *babe*." Giving his long, dark body the once over, she was clearly afraid of that gleam in his peppery eyes. "Hey, what's wrong with you? You some kind a' *fag?*" She reached for her aquamarine-blue satin handbag; her slick-dick red plastic hooped earrings gyrated in time to her erratic movements. She was just talking now—throwing words at him—not really caring what he answered, because she was right in front of the door, knew he couldn't catch her in time. She opened the door ready for a quick exit. "No refunds, *boy*." she snapped. That last word was a sharp jab at his jaw. Her Hollywood-smile was gone. The porch light back-lit her face: smudged lipstick went past her lip-line; she could be auditioning for a circus act.

He thought of where those lips had just been. "Go on. Get on out." He was calmer this time, not mean, and his voice was soft when he said it. All the same she scurried. Sam zipped up—couldn't help but notice how fast 'it' had collapsed. His dirigible had been punctured, leaving him this deflated thingamajig. A tiny rubber-suit smeared with red hung comically from his 'little-head.'

He heard his Ma's, "Be sure to wear your rubbers, Samuel."

Right now, he just wanted to get it tucked safely away. Further back, he felt severe cramps. At least his balls still worked. He'd turned plump walnuts into filberts.

He stood at the window, hearing those five-inch black patent leather heels click, click along the cobblestone pathway from his side door, mad at himself for not answering the fag comment. Didn't he owe Darwin and Tony that much?

The neighborhood was as good as it gets in the city, and being a hooker Bambi would be used to taking care of herself, but being the gentleman he was finding himself turning into he needed to see her safely to her car parked at the curb. So, he stayed at the window until she got inside and drove away.

The tabby purred at her protector. He stroked her fur, his voice a monotone. "Yeah, we really showed her, huh Bobbette? A hun' for ten seconds a' wetting my joint."

Was Bambi having herself a good laugh right now? Fuckin'-A she was. She'd be tellin' this story for years.

Damn. Why *did* he do this? Crappola. He knew he wasn't ready. Would maybe never be ready. He'd listened to what his friends tried to tell him. They thought it might be easier with a prostitute; he wouldn't have to pretend to care.

The cat clung to his thigh, batting at him playfully—an attempt to get him out of his funk. "Ouch."

A playful kitty, but heavy on attitude.

"Yeah, okay. Just hang-on there, Bob." He scratched her nose, pulled her ear. "We get you some chow."

She hit the floor rubbing her arched back against his leg while he emptied the small foil bag into her dish. Bobbette cocked her head at him and stood without movement, a statue.

"What?" His voice was on the lowest end of the spectrum; it cracked with such frequency he was often misunderstood. But he'd have made one hell of a blues-man. Robert Johnson look out; that was what Sam's momma used to say.

Well, be it words, or be it moods, Bobbette had no problem deciphering Sam.

She stared at her water dish.

"Oh. Excuse me, ma*dam*." He rinsed the dish and filled it with fresh, cold water.

Daintily, the cat began to dine.

This cat's all I got left a' my lady, he thought, and just that fast, his heart raced back to Bobbie.

He'd wanted to make her Mrs. Sam Bell. Bobbie Bell. Had a nice ring to it. He gulped for air; she was so real to him right this second he could taste her. Yet, all that remained of the woman he called his Bobbette was this cat an' a few memories. He'd named the tabby after her because he could not let go.

Sounds of Bobbette as she nuzzled and batted at her food were interrupted by a voice in his head. "*You can handle one measly shot of Jack, baby, or a slim line of the candy, to numb that awful pain in your brain.*" Samson knew better. Yet he dreamed, daydreams, night-dreams, of booze, cocaine, and his Bobbette. His gut wanted him to believe that either of the first two had the power to make him forget the third. Make him forget? Maybe not, but make his loss melt away if only for a few seconds.

The battle raged inside him.

He pushed at his mind. Forced it on to other things—to thoughts of his friends. Sam was born and raised in Salt Lake City. In those days, the Mormon people believed that if you were black it meant you had committed some hideous crime, murder most likely, in a previous life. They were not cruel in their actions toward blacks, but the result of their belief was worse than cruel. They pitied you as they tried to bring you into the 'fold'.

Minneapolis was a big city, the city without pity.

Just the ticket and much less of an insult.

The first week he hit town Samson got himself a job at Silano's selling used cars. He grinned, thinking of that little swisher Tony being the boss's *wife*. Darwin Silano and Anthony Garcia; the boss and the boss's wife. That would be a marriage made in heaven. Yep, his friends were few, but precious. And there was Elsie Sanders. Sam would do anything for Elsie. She had showed him the way to avenge the murder of his woman.

And helped him do it without regard for her own safety.

They were planning a homecoming of sorts for Elsie this Saturday night. Kind of a surprise dinner-party to end her second week out of jail. They'd all been trying to give her space because she seemed to need it. Whenever he went in search of her she was off on a long walk. She'd been locked-up during the trial.

Well, Sam looked forward to this party; he was anxious to see more of his friends. Mary and Vinny would be coming. He hadn't seen the detectives in weeks. The last time he'd talked to them was at their baby's funeral. That made him feel guilty; he should have made more of an effort to be around for them.

The cop who'd made the most impact on his life was Law. Law and his soon to be wife Georgia, whom they called Gee, wouldn't miss this party. Gee, was the only one of those four that did not work for the police department. Sam had a special feeling for her. She could see inside his soul. She and Elsie were in many ways alike—sisters in another life he'd heard them say.

Sam had felt damn helpless all the time Elsie was in jail. He wasn't alone; demonstrators, people who didn't even know her, had picketed round the clock outside the jail.

Sam saved the newspaper—was it only two weeks ago? It still lay folded under the kitchen chair. Bold front page headlines told the story:

WOMAN AVENGER FOUND NOT GUILTY.

He thought about that awhile. He wasn't sure he liked the term avenger. She was so much more. Of course, who was he to say? Hadn't he just been thinking about how she'd helped him avenge Bobbie's murder?

Semantics.

Had the jury sent a message to the world that we would not stand for it any longer? He remembered a conversation with Elsie after Bobbie's murder. *"People are sick to death of criminals getting off, and knowing that the creeps are laughing at how easy it was, at what fools we all are."* She tossed her head with fervor as she spoke. Sam could picture her in the dark cold car that night. He could *feel* the determination flash from her eyes and pierce his body. In minutes she'd taken him from a man who struggled to live one more hour, to a man who was not only ready to avenge his lost love, but ready to fight to make the whole world a better place.

Well, no one was willing to take the time, risk the danger, or give their own life, to protect the innocent. No one but Elsie. The police tried, Samson knew they did. In many cases they did a damn good job, in others *they* were the problem. The system was broken —the cops weren't the answer anymore.

Anyway, Elsie didn't really kill the bastards. The devil made them do their crimes, Sam thought, and she came along like some avenging angel, (there was that word he didn't like poking its head again) and set them up. She set them up to kill themselves—to let their soulless insides reach out and pluck their lives away. Elsie returned to the devil what was his own. And she forced the devil's hand to do it.

This sting of justice was a fatal sting.
Without Elsie, Sam would be dead, too.

Having your face beat in with a hunk of steel is not pretty. Actually, his nose looked better than ever once the doctor's got through with him. Lucky for him the pricks didn't take their Colt 357 Magnum and drill him. Better that they'd used it as a club. Today he knew it was better, but at the time…. The crunch of his bones, the sight as the red stains spread (his blood) had turned them on. The beating had left his head with nerve damage that would hurt like a bitch for the rest of his days. Yeah, pain was one more thing he had left in life.

My, my, he scowled at himself, self-pity visits. How ugly is that?

All that was left of his family was his old man and he was gone—so long he could be dead. His friends were all he had, but they were plenty. This cozy joint was ready even before he left the hospital. Sure, he paid rent, but at his insistence not theirs. He had to come to terms with his life: Elsie, Dar, and Tony loved him.

So now it would be the four of them who lived in this, what was it, kind of a mansion, here on River Road. Six, if you counted Elsie's beagle-pup Pip, and his own kitty, Bobbette. Sam grinned again: Two gay lovers, one avenger-goddess and her dog, one old used-up used-car salesman and his cat. What a family.

Best he'd ever had.

He listened. What was that noise? Footsteps on the walkway? Surely Bambi hadn't come back for more. The others all used the front entrance. He slipped into loafers and went to the window. "Ka-*rap*." He whispered to himself, tried to stand perfectly still, but knew the visitor had to have seen movement inside.

Sure enough. He could hardly hear the knocking through the heavy door, but the Maggot was relentless, the knocks became thuds—dull, but obvious fist work. Sam opened the door a few inches.

"Are ya' gonna let me in, or keep me freezin' out here?" The familiar voice was hoarse. Not the smooth tones of the last time they had met. But that had been, well, almost a year.

Sam didn't answer—didn't move. His eyes took in the tall, thin figure on the step. Thirty pounds thinner, for sure. Was the shaking from the cold, or was he strung out? Whatever, Sam knew that to open the door to him was to invite trouble.

"What? Don'tcha recognize me, for crissakes?" The shaking hand put his shoulder behind it and gave the door a hard shove.

Sam stepped out of the way; the oak slab banged against the wall-stopper.

"Yeah, I recognize ya' Mag. Come on in." Sam's voice was a quiet, resigned, lets-just-get-it-over-with.

The man he called Mag entered and the cold and ice seemed to stick with him and drop the rooms temperature ten degrees. Sam felt goose-bumps travel his own torso.

Mag looked whiter than Sam remembered. Must not be hitting the tanning-beds as often. The Mag shoved past him and Sam wrinkled his nose. Odor's of gin, cannabis, and more sinister pharmaceuticals, oozed from his pores, clung to his clothing. Inwardly Sam felt like his recently wizened appendage. What more could a body take on in one night?

He'd take off at a run, but he lived here.

"Nice digs. Darwin fix you up, huh?" The man eyed the room like he was casing the joint for a big-time jewel heist. "That's the skinny I hear on the street, you lucky bastard."

"Umhm. So, ah, brush off and leave those boots over here by the door, will ya'? An' watch the carpet. I don't want the place wrecked." Sam leaned back against the doorframe, wanting to keep as much distance between them as possible. "So, what's up? You know where I work. I ain't that hard to find. Why'd you find it necessary to track me down here?"

"Yeah, right." The Mag's expression added, 'you got shit for brains'? "Like I'm gonna walk, big as you please, into Silano's ta' sit and jaw with an old bud. Darwin made it real clear the day he canned me that he ain't fond a' seein' me around." Larry Maggert, or, the Maggot, as the entire crew had learned to call him when they worked with him at Darwin's car dealership, laid out a small mirror and razor blade on the coffee table in front of the sofa where he'd landed.

"Hey! Cut that shit out." Sam's black skin had turned gray. "Look here. I'm clean. Plan to *stay* clean." Without realizing what he was doing, as Sam spoke he strayed toward the sofa, the Maggot, and the drugs.

"Besides, what if Darwin or Tony came home...found you here?" Sam's words said no, but his actions said, well...

"Excuuuse me, Sambo baby." He said Sambo like it was two words, Sam and Bow. "I kind a' thought that when I gave my blood for that transfusion you needed a while back, it made us some kind a' friends, maybe family even." From the gleam in his eye it was easy to see that Maggert got a real charge out of the family idea. "Hey, *relax* will ya'? I came to share a holiday line or two in the spirit of the season—with a friend I thought might be needin' a bit of the ol' spirit."

Sam's face turned to rock. He grabbed his Minnesota Twin's cap, pulled the visor low over dead-calm, 'I-take-my-coffee-black' eyes. "Don't *you* call me Sambo."

The Mag was already standing, stuffing his feet into his rubber boots. He had a short fuse; that was one of his better qualities. With the sudden movement came the smell of Maggert's feet. Sam could easily remember a day when this 'pretty-boy' would have considered it beneath him to wear socks that stunk of decay much less had a hole that exposed a crusty big-toe. Sam held the door open for him, grateful for the breath of cold fresh air.

As the odious man barged by Sam, he tossed a small white packet at the coffee table. "Fuck-you *Mis*ter Bell an' Happy Holidays to *you*. That there's a freebie. *My* blood's in ya' now, so I know you need it." Deep circles under his eyes accentuated the sinister leer. "I notice my blood didn't make your skin any whiter yet, but it won't keep on pumpin' right without a dab a' the cola in it. When you need more you can find me at my new, used-car joint on West Lake Street. Call it Maggert's Machines."

What was this shit? "*You* got your own place?"

"Hey. Why the fuck not? Only a Sam*bo* stays hustlin' for a faggot like Darwin for long. 'Sides, I got to have me some place to run my *real* money through."

The door slammed with a bang. Samson did not move. He was used to having the Maggot call him names, but tonight it made him want to smash that bigoted face into a thousand pieces of meat. Only he couldn't make his body move to run after him. Mag's smell was suspenders for the air inside the apartment. Sam felt gr*eaz*y. It was because of the thought-crime, same as when he woke up after dreamin' about doin' the shit—the blow. He heard footsteps crunch on the packed snow until they reached the street. He thought about how the Maggot's footsteps crunched while Bambi's heels went click, click.

Snow. Why did it have to be snowing?

Even the weather was against him—a reminder for him of *this* snow, *the real snow* that lay on the table in front of him.

He heard the car start. Heard it peal away from the curb and drive off. Sam's eyes were glued to that white packet.

Fucker.

This had been no social call; it was strictly business. The Maggot looked like hell. A short year ago he'd had that thirty pounds on him, his blond hair styled to perfection, you would have thought he was normal, attractive, successful. Now, he'd gone over the edge. Sam knew about that edge; he'd been over it after Bobbie died.

Been there, done that. Promised his good friends never to go there again.

Promised himself.

Fucker.

He knocked off his Twins cap, threw it angrily at the door. Bobbette skittered under the chair, then crept slowly over to inspect the cap that had made him so angry—a nudge first, then wildly she flipped onto her back. With an abandoned frenzy she clawed the cap while it bounced back and forth.

Sam ignored her.

With what seemed a plethora of guilt weighting his body he reached for the packet. It was difficult to move in this room that reeked of his pain. Later, he'd look back, see these next few minutes of his life in slow motion.

But that was later; now, it happened fast.

He opened the packet. No cut in it, no powder. Just rocks—exquisite, hard, creamy, rocks. The good stuff.

This one time couldn't hurt, he thought. And he was alone. No one would know.

He went to the kitchen fast, trying to blank out his brain. All of his paraphernalia had been tossed. Yesterday's garbage. Not a razor-blade in the house. He opened and slammed drawers; utensils clattered to the floor. At least he had a spoon; he could lay the rocks under a dollar bill and crush them with a spoon. He found an old straw from the last time he'd had a chocolate malt at the Lake Street Garage.

Great malts, his mind raced, he laid a rock on the table, laid the bill over it, pressed the bottom of the spoon over the top to smash it to the powder he needed.

His hands shook. His mouth tasted as if he'd licked dust off the floor with his tongue.

He saw, without seeing. Tiny red holiday lights disco'd over his dark skin. They turned it a glorious shade of cinnamon.

He picked up the straw and held it to his nose.

Stopped.

A voice in his head said, *Bobby will know.* She's watching.

Right. Well, shit, it was too late to think about that. He needed her *here*, he needed her *now*, and where was she? Gone.

He leaned down, straw to nose.

"*Don't do it Sambo!*"

He stopped again, his eyes boxed, *jab-jab, jab-jab*, around the room. It'd been *her* voice.

He went to the sofa, fell deep, head back, eyes up toward the ceiling but seeing nothing; tears streamed down his face, down his neck and soaked the collar of his T-shirt. "I can't stand it Bobba. I can't. I hurt. I miss you too much. I need you too much. I can't do it alone. I think about our night—think, how could one night mean so much? But it does, you know it does and you know why. And then I think that if only I'd stayed with you, but I didn't. And so then I think, what *did* happen. Did it hurt you bad, *real bad*? I know it did. And where are you now? *Where are you now, Bobbie?*" Sam sat forward, his head in his hands and cried out-loud. Screams of pain spewed from his soul.

Finally the tears stopped and he stood and walked to the cocaine.

"Just this once, Bobba, I swear it, just this once."

In a nanosecond the shit was up his nose, then, oh, so gratefully, it was a blast to his brain. He knew that soon his memories of Bobbie would be frozen. He could later retrieve them but for now, they would be tucked away, a dim, faded memory, way in the storeroom of his brain.

"Ahhhh," came the throaty moan. His mind flashed back to his non-thought of the discoing Christmas lights. That's why he hated the flashers. They made him feel as if he were in a damn disco bar.

Bobbette, the baseball-cap forgotten, purred louder than the drone that came from his refrigerator and rubbed her tail against his calf.

It was going to be a long time before he noticed her.

Chapter Three

He knew she smelled the dope when she got into the Jaguar. She sniffed and gave him a look. Stupid of him not to have aired it out. Such a small car—wouldn't have taken much.

Her eyes darted—wary.

Now would be the time to use his innate sales ability. His voice flowed. "You were so kind to that lame man. I could not help but notice." He wanted to make her relax and trust him. It would be easier that way.

The mention of the man seemed to help. He kept his eyes on the road, doing his best to exude indifference toward her personal self, and felt the payoff as she sighed and sank back against the plush seat.

To her answering smile he asked, "Your destination?"

"Downtown Minneapolis; the old Ford building. My office is on the seventh floor."

The warm air inside his car was doing its job and she began to chatter as if they were old friends. She was a graphic-designer, liked to work on her computer late at night without the constant phone interruptions. He mentioned that they would take the scenic route along River Road and she barely heard him.

"Did you say you were a veteran? From Vietnam? My daddy died in Vietnam. I never knew him."

Daddy. Sure. He could see it. She was older than he'd first thought. Maybe thirty. But that bloom of innocence that he found so attractive was there. Vietnam. No wonder the drugs weren't more of a signal for her; she was used to them. Likely, her mother had smoked reefer to help get over her loss.

With his peripheral vision he studied her. A graphic-design artist with her own business. Her schooling and her business paid for by hard working taxpayers. And all because her father had been on acid, tripped into a swamp, hit his head and drowned. That was probably closer to the real truth. What a hero.

"What was your name?" He had already forgotten.

"Kandle, with a K, Lauriet. My parents picked out the name before Dad left for Vietnam."

Clear as their bellbottoms—he could see it. The 'parents' hot pre-ship-out night flashed before him.

It is the night before daddy's ship is to sail. They are the perfect hippie couple—all decked out with fringe on their vests and, certainly, bellbottomed trousers. They sat yoga style in a room with no furniture save the oversize pillows on the floor and a big old trunk that was covered with a faded, also fringed, wall-hanging—covered so they could use it as a coffee table. The sound of plastic and glass beads tinkled through the air from time to time—beads hung around her neck and beads hung as a curtain in the doorway. A small cone of incense scented the air and Sonny and Cher sang in the background, "All you need is la...ah...ove." The trunk covered with candles that quivered in the night—if only from the heat passing between their soon to be coupling bodies.

A bong passed back and forth.

Hour after hour of meaningless conversation was followed by some act of rutting that ended in a 'what-if' discussion.

What if we have a baby?

Gazing around the room in their drug-sex induced haze, the two flower children come up with the insipid name of Candle. Only they will be artsy and spell it Kandle. Who can guess what a boys name might have been—who can care?

He brought himself back to the present and the 'morsel' sitting beside him. "What a lovely name, Kandle. I'll bet your mother has a story that goes with the name."

"How did you guess?" Kandle smiled her sweetest smile.

The Jaguar purred on.

Elsie came home early. The time in city jail hadn't left her feeling sociable.

She noted a strange car parked out front, then, as she entered, muted voices from Sam's apartment hummed out at her. She paused; she'd wanted to talk to Samson, felt especially drawn to him tonight, but was too polite to interrupt whatever was going on.

She considered waiting for Darwin and Tony, but they would probably be out for hours. She decided to take some time to think about recent events and headed to her room. She went downstairs through the weight-room, into the sauna, moved the panel, stepped into the tunnel that led to the garages. Each time she opened the secret door to the tunnel she shivered. She knew no one hid in wait of her, still, for an instant the feeling loomed. This *hidden* tunnel with the *hidden* elevator that went upstairs to her *hidden* domicile on what they called the third floor, but was actually the fourth, had once been her secret hideaway. It was no secret now.

The thing she loved most when she first toured this house was what most people called a dumb-waiter; she thought of as the silent butler. She thought it romantic and fitting that it should be what saved her life and ended the life of the monster. That night, almost a year ago, the serial murderer that Minnesotans' dubbed the Eunuch, was found dead at the bottom of the silent butler shaft. Knowing the Eunuch was coming to kill her, she had planted the herbal poison that would make this demon believe demons could fly. The monster dove, with arms, flap-*flap*-flapping, down the shaft. Well, that was the end of her secret hideout. Talk about media. She felt like a blitzed quarterback; they all did. It was matter-of-fact to her now.

The drone of the elevator was loud. She hoped Samson would hear it, realize she was home and visit her when his company left.

She left her lights off; tonight's full moon bathed the lush room with exactly the type of light she wanted—enough for her to strip off her winter outer-layer and boots. Lying on her bed fully clothed she recalled the license plate on the rear of the car she'd seen out front. Dealer plates. But they did not have Silano's logo on the trunk. She went to the window; most of the car was concealed by the thicket of balsam and evergreens that ran along the property. A tall figure moved with a swagger to the car and got inside; the car took off, tires squealing, swerving on the icy street.

Why did that form look familiar? Silano's Chevrolet put their logo on the back of every car, new and used. She didn't know any other car people. Car people—as opposed to *real* people, she smiled. She pictured a jowly face with an old style hood ornament for a nose. "Can ah hep' ya' mam?"

She pulled her quilt over her and closed her eyes—thinking again—always got her into trouble.

After Bobbie's murder Dar and Tony were worried Sam might not make it. Elsie remembered the day they came to visit her in jail. It was obvious the two men were thoroughly enjoying their relationship, more so now that it was out in the open and they could behave like the eccentrics they were—most especially Tony. Well, that day Tony paced and chattered while she and Darwin sat taking it in—taking him in.

"Sam's bashed head is bad enough, we can help with that, but what can we do to make him feel less alone?" Tony's dark eyes were distraught. "The man has always had spunk. You know? *Spunk*. Well, it's gone. Gone, gone. He's aging right before our eyes, letting his heart's pain turn him old. What can we do to make him want to live?" Tony wore a black sweater that zipped to his neck and leather pants. The pitch colored leather paved his slim form; it was amazing he could move back and forth so rapidly, and with such savoir faire.

"Take off that dark cap at least; you look like a rather dashing cat burglar." Darwin slapped him on the fanny, irresistibly drawn to it, Elsie'd thought at the time. "We don't want to get Elsie in any more trouble than she is. But if you're so concerned about Sam why don't we bring him to live with us? We can give him the love and attention he needs. Did you tell Els the dinner story?"

"Oh! Let me tell, let me tell." Tony's black booted feet made an almost soothing rhythm on the concrete. "Well. We had him, Sam that is, stay over for that week between surgeries on his face? He was with us, what Dar, five nights?"

Darwin nodded, and looked amused.

"That last night Sam insisted *he* would make dinner. I mean, the man was in *pain*. I didn't want to ask if he could cook. We played right along, thought it might be therapeutic. He said he'd make pasta something or other, just as if he'd done it all the time. He made me a list of what seemed reasonable ingredients so I went shopping."

Darwin laughed at the memory. "We kept telling him that he didn't have to go to the trouble."

"But he wouldn't hear of anything but this *dinner*. Doing it *his* way. You *know* how he is." The heel clicking stopped, Tony sat next to Elsie, held her hand. "Okay. The short version. We came home from work ready for a feast—even skipped lunch that day. What *were* we thinking?" He gave Darwin's cheek a pat. "'Smells heavenly,' I yell as we walk through the kitchen door. Sam was sitting at the table, head in hands. He'd insisted on making everything from," Tony nudged Darwin—he winked at Elsie to show her it was a joke. "What *is* the word you *old* guys used before everything came *ready* to make?"

Darwin punched him.

Tony ran his nails down Darwin's face, but lightly. "Oh sure, I remember, *scratch*. Sam had to make it from scratch. His damp fuzz-ball head did not move when we entered. The sauce was on simmer and smelled, well, at least, Italian. I went to the stove and lifted the lid. It was a rather darkish yet aromatic water. So, I thought, hmm, let's have a look-see at the pasta. Can't hurt pasta, right? Not so right. There in the center of the pan was a huge blob of, what one might charitably call paste—paste, and the bottom was scorched black. From the looks of him, he'd hopped in the shower while the blob cooked itself." Tony removed his black cap and threw it at Darwin with a wink. "I asked him, tactfully, where he got the pasta. He said he didn't want the thin noodles I'd bought him, wanted them wider, so, he went to the deli and, he said, there were no directions on the package. Of course there *are,* you know. Although the print is very teensy. You cook them for around two or three minutes."

Elsie could picture Sam doing it. "Too much of a chef to read directions, was that it? Of course it sounds like this was more than the difference in time to cook them, he must have forgotten they were cooking. Anyone could do that!"

Tony's eyes sparkled, matching the large diamond in his left ear lobe—a recent present from Dar. "Oh you'd stick up for anyone, but that's why we adore you, Elsie! And right, Samson is a free spirit; that's why we love *him*. Or, maybe he really *is* getting older and needs bifocals. Remember how Law fought them for so long? I've noticed a tiny sparceness—is that a word?—right at the crown of his head. Have you noticed it Dar?"

That was the day they planned the addition for Sam. He needed taking care of and they wanted to be the ones to do it.

This stroll down memory lane made Elsie feel sleepy, still, her mind wandered to her attorney, Eileen.... Eileen had said it was plea time; Elsie responded that she would take her chances with a jury...feeling each day her identity fade more and more away.

Everyday a portion of herself seeped into the prison clothes, the walls of her room, those signs the picketers carried, even all the T.V. news shows. She'd put on thirteen pounds, but she felt she had grown smaller. She fluffed her pillow and pulled her blanket right over her clothes. "Umm." So snug and warm here with friends close-by.

Half listening for Sam on the elevator she fell asleep.

Christmas lights strung from the roof of the house played over her body as she twisted and turned in her sleep. As if connected in some way to the grand piano that sat alone at the far end of the room, the roaming lights played a bloody dirge that splattered their stains over her fair skin in the cool moonlight.

The dream had possessed her nights for months. It took her away right now, always to the same place.

She is playing in fields of sunny yellow with brilliant red poppies; the colors alone are enough to make her laugh and she does, with gayety; she is surrounded by fifteen or twenty small giggling children. The children all call her Momma. This field with these children is her heaven and she loves every second of it. Then, as always happens next, a man appears. He ignores them as he works, chopping at a bottomless pile of wood; his muscular body gleams with sweat from his work and the sun. Elsie feels desire so strong that it constricts her pulse; she sees herself walk through the many children, leaving them to play alone while she runs to this man who seems just beyond reach—she sees this happen but she does not actually do it, she stays where she is. Each muscle on his back and shoulders moves as he splits the wood; she watches each muscle and she aches to touch him, just one touch. Often, in this dream, she will now rise to move slowly in his direction. He'll look at her then, and his eyes are also filled with longing. That moment is vivid, dazzling; all she can see or feel is *him*, this man.

Darkness covers the field.

Her mind is so focused on the man that the dark does not deter her, she continues toward him until she hears a murderous, bloody roar.

This is where the nightmare begins:

The shadows multiply, spreading until they become a pumped-up steroid-spider that covers the sky. Hidden in these black shadows is a monster. With super-human effort she frees herself from the vacuum that is sucking her toward the arms of the man and into what she is certain will soon be a state of euphoria. She hears the small voices scream, her heart begs herself not to veer from her course, yet she turns her head. One of the children is caught between the powerful jaws of a monstrous dung-green beast. The animal flings his head back and forth, its dripping teeth spray blood everywhere. He is a monster-cat about to break the neck of the mouse he has chosen for dinner. But wait! This is not a mouse; it is a child.

This sight sends a message to her brain; she can literally feel it roll throughout her body. She can flee with this man, have the love she yearns to have, and with him have children of her own and live happily ever after. Yes. *She can.* Or, she can forget herself, her needs, run back to save those children.

Why can't she have both? *Why must she choose?*

Her feet are leaden, but she pulls, until, in desperation, she breaks into a run... she is heading toward the children. The beast sees her coming and, with a poof—disappears. In her dream state, instant rainbows fill the sky. The children are safe. She gathers them in her arms and happily begins to walk them all toward the man...she cries out.

He is gone. The man is gone.

A car door slams. The loud metallic echo reaches the third floor, the sound wakes her. The dream is over for now.

Elsie stretches, rotates her neck to try to relieve the crink. What saliva she had left, was curdled; her cracked lips stick together. Her stomach growls. She heads to her kitchen area thinking about a hot bath and a quick sandwich. After that dream nothing could do the trick but comfort food. Bologna and mayonnaise washed down with some ice cold grape soda will hit the spot—make her an eight year old again.

In a semi-daze Elsie bumps the refrigerator door. "Hmm, no mayo, butter will have to do." Amazing—midst the sprouts and tofu is a small packet of bologna and instead of her usual seven-grain—soft, white, Wonder Bread. "Lucky for me that Tony-bud stocked my fridge," the words echo through the still room. Wonder Bread from days of old. Yum. She grins. Wait for me food, she thinks, ravenous, I shall return.

Showered and powdered, Elsie takes her snack to the recliner by the window—the room is still dark. In the background are the muffled sounds of Tony and Dar as they move about the house. The comfort food is doing its job, but hearing her playful friends so soon after her dream brings feelings of intense loneliness. And here, right before her very eyes sits the piano that she can not play, the piano that once belonged to her best friend.

She can't help but remember how this began seven years ago. Elsie rubs her temples; she sees her friends' slaughter, not as if she were looking at a photograph or a film, but in crazed, gut-wrenching colors and Van Gogh-ish whirls and swirls. Just when was it that she came to the realization that the police would never be able to administer justice? Well, whenever it was, that was when she decided on her course of action. Nothing could fill the void inside her soul; her murdered friend Lynn had to be avenged.

She felt satisfaction at having accomplished what she'd set out to do, but guilt at the way she'd done it. To use her body in such a horribly sexual way to lure those monsters! The guilt has lessened now, she's come to terms with the past; she'd been young and using sex was all she knew. Since then, she'd turned her personal life over to justice—to accountability.

Her eyes flutter and close. She can't get what happened earlier tonight—on her walk home—out of her mind. If only she could talk about it—who can she tell?

The lights play hide and seek over her sweet-scented body. The dirge is over; this time they play with whimsy.

Darwin unplugged the ten-foot Christmas tree, leaving only the outside lights for passersby to enjoy.

Together the two men wander around the kitchen area, picking up here, nosing there, then decide to call an end to their evenings' banter and climb the stairs to their bedroom—they exhibit a special harmony that speaks of contentment. The scent of Scotch pine slips into the bedroom behind them.

"Dar." Tony gives him an elbow poke. "I think the old house feels eerie tonight. Is it me?"

Darwin shrugs, yawns.

Tony raises his voice as if louder will get him the attention he craves. "Listen to me, Dar. It's as if *not-so-friendly* spirits are moving about, leaving behind a whirl of kinetic energy. Maybe we have a ghost or two?"

Darwin ignores the question altogether, his mind occupied, but gives Tony a hug. "Lets shower together tonight."

Tony, with flamboyance, kicks his shoes across the room in answer, talk of ghosts put aside. "Honey-babe, I thought you'd never ask."

Darwin can't help but smile. "Hey you. I just want my back scrubbed." They shower together, both exhausted from the hectic week.

Still, neither wants to go right to bed, right to sleep. Tony has his mind on Spirits; as usual, Dar's mind is on what he would consider more important things. Darwin sits on the edge of the bed and Tony climbs behind him, up on his knees. He brushes Darwin's once dark hair to help it dry. He's worn it long for so many years that when he cut it short for the trial it was a shock. In two months it had grown a lot, probably from all the stimulation it got from Tony.

In this cozy room they are one. What in the outside world could be more important to them? Tony tap-tap-taps the brush on Darwin's shoulder. "Okay, what?" Tony asks.

"Hm?"

"Read my lips, I want words. No hm."

"Well." Darwin sighed. It wasn't his nature to talk about feelings. "If you must know, and I'm sure you must, I was picturing the end of the trial—when all the people who had been there day after day gave Elsie a standing ovation. She was a star to them. I've never seen anything like that, have you?"

It was Tones turn to yawn, but he kept brushing the thick, graying hair. "No. Now that you mention it. What did you think of that?"

"Don't know. That's my dilemma. Of course I was pleased for Els. She could be the most moral person I know; it would not have been justice to see her in prison."

"Dear one, why do I hear a but in your voice." Tony flounced onto the blue silk bed-sheets.

"I'm saying I don't know what justice would have been. She's been instrumental in the deaths of so many people! Horrid and evil people, but none-the-less!"

"Dar, *she's our avenger*. Can't you come to terms with the fact that we need someone—an angel put here on earth—to help us? The world has gotten out of hand. Pretend she's from another planet if that's easier to accept. These creeps are after the *babies*. Helpless women and children are their targets—not to mention minority people of all persuasions. Us!" He poked Darwin with the brush handle in the back.

Darwin moaned. He loved having his back rubbed. But Tony was not to be deterred. "They want power; that's what this is all about. Power. It won't stop until we stand up for ourselves. Don't you remember when Clint came to save that town in the Wild West? Taught those average people to protect themselves and their families? Kicked the bad guys out of where-*ever*-county?"

Darwin stared at Tony in the mirror; the red silk robe Tony had carelessly slung over his shoulders set off his damp black curls making him look quite inviting. "You're trying to say that Elsie's our Clint Eastwood?"

Tony yawned, dropped the brush, and fell back on the bed. "Umhm." His body had tumbled over. The 'umhm' was quiet, on the edge of la-la-land.

"Now *you're* doing it." Darwin wasn't used to anything but Tony's undivided attention.

"Hm?" The noise from Tony was muffled, spoken into his pillow.

"Spike? Don't tell me you got me going on this and now you're falling *asleep*? What I really want to know is, when will it be over? Is it over now? Or, will she do it again? And, selfishly, what will that mean for us and *our* lives?" He stood by the bed looking at his love. It was easy to see why he called him Spike. His body jutted this way and that, not much meat on them thair bones. Darwin tugged off Tony's red robe and tenderly covered him before going around to his side of the bed. He crawled under the silky sheets certain he'd be lying awake pondering his ethical dilemma for hours. But when they rolled together and he felt the familiar body against his, it was a signal of peace. He felt fur, followed by a damp nose, under his feet. Spike had managed to sneak Elsie's beagle, Pip, into their bed once again. How does he do that, Darwin wondered?

Content, Darwin drifted.

Later, Tony rolled over on him and as if they were in the middle of a conversation all along, asked, "Dar, did you hear about the Maggot getting his own clip-joint over on East Lake?"

An arm pulled him close, a sleepy voice answered. "Scum rises. Forget him."

Detectives' Mary Johnson and Vince Tonetti had become Mr. and Mrs. Vince Tonetti soon after the close of the Eunuch case—the case that landed Elsie in jail, although she was now deemed not guilty by a jury of her peers. Mary had been pregnant at the time of the wedding.

It was a boy. They did what both had, in a previous existence, sworn never to do, and named him after his dad, so Vinny Junior it was! The joy that quickly spread around to all their friends was short lived.

Vinny clearly remembered her description of how blue the tiny face was that one and only time Mary had been allowed to hold him. The baby had always been in an incubator when Vinny was around. Vinny Junior died of a congenital heart defect. A hole in his heart valve.

Their baby's death left a hole between them.

Both had been workaholics. Now Vinny carried on that suspicious work ethic alone. Mary wanted to have another baby. No—she *existed* to produce another baby. The heated romance that had brought them together was replaced by a whole different hunger. They *had* to have sex.

Vinny worked long hours to make up for Mary's not working. She was still too worn out from the ordeal to return to her job at the precinct—worn out physically and unbalanced mentally. But she found the energy for sex. Only it wasn't what they used to call sex.

This was sex in the biblical sense.

Vinny was having a hard time keeping up, or, keeping *it* up. He sat on the chair beside the bed. He could smell baby powder. He was certain that she was using it on herself to keep the *baby-to-come* always on her mind, and to keep Vinny Junior's memory close. She had some stupid superstition about making the house a place that would seem inviting for a baby. Like the egg and sperm would know this when they met. There was a row of baby-bottles on the kitchen counter collecting dust and grease splatters. She refused to let him put them away. Regardless of how much he tried to avoid the damn things he kept knocking them over; they were in his way. It made them both mad and then, guilty.

Vinny Junior's hooded blue and white bassinet, with the tiny satin bows, was parked against the wall across from their bed. They had a room all fixed for the baby, but she'd chosen to put the baby's basket by the side of their bed—a constant reminder. A few weeks after the funeral Vince put it in the garage, high on the rafters. He came home later that same night to find it back inside. He wondered how in the hell she'd managed to get it down, but he didn't ask.

Some restless nights he'd dream of coming home to find the small white casket resting inside the bassinet.

Vinny looked down at his wife's sleeping face. Dark hair spread over her pillow. Beautiful. But, tired. Her small, barely over five-foot, body made her appear to be a child herself. She'd gotten round with the baby inside her, but that was almost gone. She was his baby, if only that could be enough for her for a while. He felt his life, their lives, slip away; he wanted so much to stop the slide. He worked all the time. Mary had been partnered with Law, Detective Lawrence; so, with her out of work Vinny had taken over her cases with Law, in addition to his own workload.

After work, late every evening, Vinny came right home; they had sexual intercourse. It meant nothing to either of them—other than a potential kid to Vinny and a possibility of filling the hole in her heart, to Mary.

Mary had a book of sexual fantasies. Pre Vinny Junior they read it aloud to one another. They'd pick out the fantasy they wanted to act out. Now, Vince read the book alone to make himself hot so he could perform. His entire life was reduced to performance. What could he do to get through this fucking wall?

He put on his jacket as he walked to the door.

"Honey?" Her voice was sleepy.

"Yeah?"

"Don't forget the dinner for Elsie is Saturday night at Darwin and Tony's. Don't get talked into working."

He listened...hoping to hear some note of excitement or joy at going to see their friends; her voice was flat.

"I'll be there with bells on and my baby by my side." Vinny forced himself to sound light and happy.

No answer. He shouldn't have used the word baby.

He leaned to kiss her forehead, felt the slight jerk of her head at his touch. "See ya, sweetie."

She would come back to him, he knew. She would come back and things would be the way they once were before he became nothing but a sperm donor. She'd come around, and he'd be waiting.

Chapter Four

The smoky, sleek, slowly moving shadow, was a car.
 DEAD END—*that sign just ahead—magically lifted the road they drove on from the center of this metropolitan city and slammed it into the center of Nowhere's-ville.*
 He took the turn down the hill, aiming toward the dead end with deliberation. The sound of her breathing seemed to stop; it made the nervous silence in the small car cloying. He saw her check out the cars in the junkyard that ran beside the road along the river. It was deserted—tombstones of rusty metal—each with its own story to tell. Rats scrambled, but no humans, no one who might help her. Tucked inside any of these rusty old 'buckets,' or even rolled underneath one of them, it would be a long time before anyone found a body.
 Then, there was the river itself—not yet completely frozen— the current was too strong in some spots.
 Was she imagining how her bloated, flesh-hanging, corpse would look after animals or fish had gnawed at her eyes? He could smell her growing terror; it made him want to reach over—stroke her creamy white hand.
 This was the very instant that he understood his destiny. He was to become an artist—this river scene would not be complete without a nude, frozen corpse. Hers.

He felt a chill of excitement. He would kill her. He'd have to. She'd know who he was. Sooner or later his face would appear on the six o'clock news—that happened once every year or two—she would remember this night. Maybe not right away, but someday. She'd remember, and she would talk.

All he wanted was a good fuck. In his day it was called a zipless fuck. But it wasn't in the cards. Her female nature would come into play, and push him into hurting her.

She was talking again.

See? She could never keep her mouth shut. Did he discern a slight whine to her syrup-sweet voice... wondering why they were here, by the river? No doubt. He could not concentrate... no desire to hear her words... looking for a place to park. A place to pump his swollen joint into her liquid hole.

He felt the cold air blast his face before he realized she'd opened the door. And while he was berating himself for not using the drivers control door-lock, his peripheral vision caught her crouch and roll from the car—then away from the road.

Athletic, he thought. Not to mention, strong instincts.

He yanked the emergency brake and ran full out in the direction he'd seen her land. His mind whirled. Too much to think and move, both together.

He stopped running.

What was it she'd said just before she jumped? He hadn't been paying attention—her words were of no consequence. He tried to replay the echo of her voice. "...but I was here recently... never saw these rusty cars before..."

"I don't think they *were* here!"

Forget her prattle. This was to be a first for him. He had thought about killing them often, but this was going to be the real thing. This wasn't the time to make a stupid mistake. What could she say? He'd done nothing wrong. But, he wanted her. It was not over yet. Not over by a long shot.

His eyes surveyed. The lot was barren. Only rusted metal. He could find her if he remained calm... nothing to lose. Hastily, he returned to his glove compartment for a flashlight; the small, but razor-sharp jack-knife was already in his pocket. He flashed his light next to a gutted brown Camero—its door hanging, squeaking with the bitter cold breeze—periwinkle-blue winked at him from the icy ground directly under the rusted door.

Her woolen mitten must have fallen when she made the dive. The shocking blue stocking cap, scarf, and mittens were a matched set—a pre-Christmas gift she'd given herself?

She was here all right... maybe hurt, limping. It was his duty, as a concerned citizen, as the important man that he was, to find this frightened girl.

His confidence returned.

They were, most certainly, alone.

"I can't sleep." Law, Detective Gerald Lawrence, sat in the dark on the loveseat by the window. He thought he'd slipped out of bed without a sound. But there she was in the doorway. Gee could hear hair move, a trait, no doubt, inherited from her ancestors. He noticed how long and beautiful her dark hair was; it touched the bottom of the T-shirt she slept in. Quickly he changed his train of thought. Thoughts about hair would not aid his sleep. He was losing his hair at a rate that he did not find soothing. She slid her round body under his legs and began rubbing his perpetually sore feet. That, he found unbearably soothing. He wriggled his toes over her bare stomach. She never wore bottoms to bed, only special bottoms for special occasions.

"You cannot ignore the implications of the trial." Georgia understood him completely.

They planned to be married in six weeks—New Years Eve—it would be a traditional Native American wedding. They had so much to do; so much ritual was involved in the ceremony. She would still prefer to use her maiden name of Fairbanks. She was proud of her Native American heritage and had many clients who knew her by that name. Deep down he wanted her to take his name. To mark his territory? She'd say that; she'd be right.

"How was I lucky enough to find you, Gee?" The homicide detective knew they were a strange match. The herbalist and the cop. They'd met because of Elsie Sanders. Elsie, and the poisonous herbs she used to set up her *sting-like* executions.

Gee ignored his gratuitous question. "White man's justice is political and ruled by class structure as well. It often goes against the laws of nature." As she spoke, her voice, a melody of lilting tones, vibrated throughout his muscles. His body relaxed under her hands—not from the massage—the song of her words seared straight to his soul.

"Elsie has been your friend, in the past, your love." Her eyes shifted, still not completely comfortable with his past relationship with Elsie. "Inside you, the cop is quarreling with the man who knows that she does, what you as a law enforcement officer, cannot do. And, what she does is *just*." Gee's round face gleamed with love for him, her words flew with wisdom.

He wasn't moving—hypnotized by her voice.

"Is that what worries you so my man? Do you see her out there with her six-gun smoking, blasting those bloodsuckers in cold-blood? As if that would be terrible." Her head bent to kiss his toes. "Even so, that is not how it happens. They come to kill her or someone else. She sets them up. It is a thing of beauty. Really it is!" She laughed—it was a musical sound and it always thrilled him. "What she does is as right as if clouds unfold and the rain dumps out. That is not how the rain comes to us, but if it did, would it not still be rain?"

When Gee said, 'my man', he felt her words thrill his tired body.

"Remember your history, Law. Because we did not speak the white man's language we were spoken to as if we were children, as if those white men were the ones who caused grass to grow, rivers to run. Because we were different they took this country from us with brutality and force. Women and children were butchered; their bodies left for birds and coyotes to devour. They put us on reservations, made jokes about how we were pigs that destroyed the government houses they built for us."

Pigs? Law felt anger quicken his pulse. No one had better express that sentiment in his vicinity.

"*Instead of walls to imprison us we wanted to be free to wander our land until we died. We do not worship clocks like the white man; we are not ruled by time. Like magic they changed paradise into prison. These same men have great-great-grandsons who control our justice system today.*"

Her warm mouth kissed further up, his calves, thighs. "*Think now—people have begun to learn that having 'stuff' is not worth the sacrifice. Even white males are dropping out, learning what we have always known. Learning the importance of family, Spirit and the Earth.*" Her tongue flicked inside his thigh, just once. "*Even their religion is political. God is a white man. What incredible, massive egos. Alternative justice may be precisely what our country needs.*"

He pulled her on top of him, his voice husky. "Me white man."

Her cupid lips kissed his neck. "*Evolution.*"

"Hm?" He knew she was lifting his spirit. How did she do that... make his own problems evaporate?

"Some 'white men' have already evolved; it was inevitable."

"You think?" He filled his hands with her round, soft, flesh.

A few months ago, Elsie had been certain that the rest of her life would be spent behind bars. Walking home this Friday night down River Road gave her a feeling of freedom that made her skin tingle. She didn't know what God she believed in, but she felt that Spirit in everything she saw. The stinging night wind made her cheeks bright red to contrast with her vanilla-caramel hair. Her hair had returned to its natural color while she was in jail, too much effort to keep up the dark dye job, or the curls Tony had insisted on giving her. Thinking back, that disguise hadn't managed to fool Law for a minute.

She'd had plenty of time to consider it all these past months. To realize that this precious freedom would not stay with her forever. She had gone over to the other side. Whatever that meant. Forever the Avenger—never again a normal, real woman. There were too many women and children suffering. The world needed her. There was too much evil.

As she walked along the River Road she turned north toward the dead end, heading to the river. It was nearly Christmas, yet parts of the Mississippi flowed free with icy edges just beginning to show the power weather would have over water. In other areas the entire river was solid ice. The bone chilling cold not only created symphonic patterns with the frozen water, it anesthetized the air. The summer heat and humidity made the city air rancid with the stench of sweating flesh and garbage in various stages of rot and mold. Tonight's clean fresh evening air took her away from the city. She came to this spot as often as she could. Sounds and splash of the water as it made its mark on seemingly immovable rocks put many things in perspective. She thought about her friend Georgia. What Native American woman had long ago knelt on this black dirt to scrub her families' laundry on these exact rocks?

The problem that nagged at her tonight was how to keep her friends safe. Living with them was clearly not the answer; still she wanted to stay.

A noise interrupted her thoughts. An odd, *out-of-place,* sound. She looked to see what was behind her. Was it near those rocks?

Elsie shivered. Was someone here? She wished she had Pip along; he was not much protection, but great company. She turned and scanned the area—a graveyard of old cars and her over active imagination. Strange. She didn't remember the cars being here. She'd come here often even before the trial. Well, they *were* here, and it wasn't the first thing she'd ever forgotten.

It was Sam's state of mind she was considering when she heard the woman's scream. A shriek, shrill with terror, came from behind one of the cars. Without thinking she ran toward the sound, then waited, listening.

Slap-*whoosh*, slap-*whoosh*, the inky water was ominous; even traffic sounds from blocks away unnerved her.

The scream had stopped.

She thought she heard a clack—like the sound of a car door being quietly pushed shut. This noise was very close. Elsie's heart flip-flopped—she held her breath. Was it her imagination? Well she'd hardly imagined the scream.

Ooh! She felt herself being tugged to the ground!

A hand covered her mouth to stifle her cry.

No city lights burned on this dead end street.

He stood the way they'd taught him in Nam—he had not killed since then. He was a ferocious cat, fixed, frozen in motion. His breath, silent as the night. All that moved was his impeccably barbered hair that rose with the wind, then fell neatly into place. It had begun to snow once again; those icy sequins glittered as the moonlight jittered across them. These sparkles that adorned his hair gave his face an undeserved innocence, those that landed on his bare skin sizzled—fried to a crisp from the hell in his soul.

He observed this with a leer.

In all aspects of nature beauty was destined to die when confronted with power. When he finished, Kandle would dissolve as if she were no more than a flake of snow. Sizzle, sizzle, dissolve, equals nothing. She'd be nothing. He thrilled at the idea that her life, her breath, was in his hands. There was no mistake about what he planned to do with it.

She was going to die.

He concentrated on the beat of his pulse and brought it down to slow. The race was never won by speed alone—if speed at all. He allowed his head to move very slightly, searching... this ghost-yard of tin was as deserted as planned. He would hear her steps if she tried to run.

So, it was a game of Chess.

With him in control.

He heard a muffled, scraping sound and pushed the button on his flashlight to off while he crept soundlessly toward the noise.

The hand over her mouth was gentle, the manner intense. Elsie's eyes found her attacker—a small, shivering creature with blood on her knees; black dirt smeared a stark white face that looked to be about twenty.

"There's a man out there." Elsie could barely make out the girl's words whispered close to her ear; they came out in short gasps—nearly hyperventilating. "He's going to hurt me bad...rape me... kill me... there's no time to explain...you must help me."

Elsie could hear something, not footsteps, more like a pressure... it was closer, moving closer. She covered the shivering woman's lips with her own fingers, mouthing, "cooperate." They made a quick change of hats and scarves—the quivering woman was missing one mitten—Elsie pushed the frightened body under a car.

"Don't move. No matter what happens." The wind whistled by, obscuring the sound of her words. She felt for the bottle in her pocket. It hung from a neck-chain—a bottle made for bubbles—for a child's amusement, blowing and chasing bubbles in the sun.

Elsie used it for something else. She felt herself grow fearless with the knowledge of the herbal potion inside the dark bottle. Sensing a presence, she stood tall and came around the side of the old Buick.

Her voice was powerful. "Who are you and what do you want with me?"

His flashlight beam blinded her but she did not shrink back.

The authoritative tone to the words tingled his spine. Not Kandle. This voice did not belong to Kandle. He hesitated, then shot his light to where her head should be. Impulses in time... seemed to happen much slower right now. First, he saw the vivid blue hat and scarf...good, that color sent a message to his brain that said, good. But, what about that voice? His feet moved to shorten the distance. Then, his light hit the face and his feet stopped.

"You!" *he heard his own shock.*

With that word still on his lips, "Beep...beep...beep," *came from his breast pocket. His beeper was the background music to his panic filled voice. His grip came loose on the flashlight—her fervid eyes flashed a light of their own at him—a light he could not bear. He had seen it often on TV.*

Avenger-Woman they called her. She killed men like *him* and got away scot-free.

He heard the metal smash as his flashlight hit rocks and rolled beneath him. He ran to his car, eager to leave the area... to use his cell-phone... to call home and explain why he was late. Not that he cared what his wife thought, but as a cover...always best to have a cover. Gone were thoughts of rape and murder.

Before his car door shut and sealed out the night he heard the same commanding voice. "Well, that was sure easy. Not much of a bogeyman, was he?"

Then laughter! Their laughter made his blood heat 'till it bubbled and shoot to his head...pulsing...pounding.

Claudette Boodles sat on the back-porch and cried. She was afraid of what kind of criminals might be lurking in the bushes that ran all along this east edge of their property.

The back-porch was not heated and she was freezing. Randolph said that there was no need to heat it. She guessed that was true. No one used it except for her and the children. This was the door the children had been instructed and forced to use since they were first able to come in and out of the house on their own. Randolph used the front door. She was allowed to use the front door too, but only if she was *with* Randolph.

They kept the garbage back here until it was time to put it outside for recycling. Randolph did not want anyone to come by and steal *their* cans. Didn't want any thief to make money off of his aluminum; street-people could take it to a scrap yard and receive pretty good money for the aluminum. Claudette tried to explain to him that no one cared; it would not effect their credit from the city, but he was adamant. He was always adamant.

Her teeth chattered and her nose ran; she squatted lower and dug through the trash. She knew it was in here. Her good hairbrush. Her favorite hairbrush. The one Daddy had given her when she had turned sixteen. It was sterling silver and it was beautiful. Claudette was fifty years old now and very little of what she personally owned was beautiful. She slipped on some juice from an old meat wrapper and went over backwards landing on her ass in the smelly pork-chop grease. There! From that vantage point she suddenly spied it. The shiny silver caught her eye; she pulled her treasure out. The precious brush was caked with egg yolk from Randolph's breakfast and the silver had a deep gouge from a jagged pork-chop bone. "Daddy." she whimpered. Claudette cried even harder; her thoughts went back to her wedding night, twenty-seven years ago. Randolph, she'd called him Randy then, had thrown her brush out that night for the first time. It was filthy, he had said. He would not have such a filthy thing in his house. *His house?*

Claudette had spent her wedding night sobbing her heart out in the bathroom of their tiny Minneapolis apartment.

She'd had no warning that this was how he felt. It had come at her out of nowhere. Every night for two years he'd been with her; this same silver hairbrush had been with her, too. She kept it polished and washed it often with care. Evidently not often enough for her husband. She often wondered why he had waited until the night he married her to mention it. She heard the garage door open, heard the soft purr of his car's high-tech motor. Her body flinched as if punched from behind.

Randolph was home.

Chapter Five

The questions have been asked
Who made the world?
Why, God, of course.
And who created sin?
Why, the devil, of course.
And who made the devil?
Why, God, of course.
So who then is the ultimate sinner?
                    -Nostradamus

"Were you really surprised, Elsie?" Tony came around the table to hug her again. It was evident how happy he was to have his *family* together. A sensuous white shirt flared over his slight body making him look like a French poet.

"Really. Yes, I really was." She pulled his head down with both hands to kiss the top of curls that were as black as his bright eyes. "I love these curls," she rubbed her face in them. "I'm glad you decided to go au'natural Italiano, that poufy look wasn't you."

Elsie looked around the long table. These were all friends of circumstance; life had tossed them together. First, Detective Lawrence and his fiancée Georgia Fairbanks. Elsie had been in love with Law, too many years ago to count. In his early fifties, suede vest over a blue work shirt, he still made her heart trill. Now she was equally attached to Gee. Georgia wore a deep indigo caftan that flowed over her slightly roly-poly body. This was one of the few times Elsie had seen her with her long raven hair down, fluid and free. The hair framed and complimented her flawless skin, silken voice, Earth-Mother Spirit. Bringing Gee into their lives was one of the best things Law had done for this group of friends.

Next, Detectives Mary Johnson and Vince Tonetti. They were now Mr. and Mrs. Johnson-Tonetti. How did she get herself close to so many cops? The answer was obvious. She fought against the same thing they did—evil. The Tonetti's first baby died while Elsie was on trial. She hadn't even been able to get out of jail to go to Vinny Jr.'s funeral. She noticed their eyes were tired, strained. But if they were stressed it had to be a temporary; those two had behaved like two rabbits since the day they met. Their love was strong; they would survive.

Tony and Darwin were her best friends. Tony, or Spike, as Darwin called him, was a brother to her, now they both were. Darwin was a nickname—something about Tony thinking he looked like a gorilla. His full name was Clarence Silano. No one ever called him Clarence. In his navy-blue, brass buttoned, double breasted blazer, he didn't look like a Clarence. He looked as rich as he was.

"I'm not sure I like that blazer on you Dar. Makes you look stuffy." Tony smiled when he said it and ran his fingers along the back of Darwin's neck. Darwin, with a flutter of eyelids and a rosy pink color suddenly on his face, removed the jacket.

"On second thought," Tony grinned. "Maybe I love it."

Darwin growled and Tony bit his ear lobe.

Law had to interfere. "Darwin, be a man."

Sure enough the jacket went back on.

It was fun to watch their interaction; they still had it—the love-bug. Tony was right, without the jacket Darwin was transformed into his laid-back self again.

And Sam. Where was he anyway? He was seldom late.

"Darwin, this *is* your anniversary, isn't it?" Elsie asked. "I have it written down so I won't forget."

"Spike and I have been together for five years." Darwin, in his easy-to-listen-to drawl, gave a nod. "That's not the reason for this party though; it's to celebrate your freedom, Els."

"We want to know if you're going to behave yourself now that you're out of the slam—the legal ordeal is over. Can we trust you to be good?" Law's penetrating blue eyes showed concern. He often lapsed into his parental mode with them.

"Let's not interrogate her this early in the evening." Gee stood, her hand rested lovingly on Law's shoulder, and raised her glass. "I want to propose a toast to the gutsiest woman I have ever had the good fortune to meet, to know, to love. May your luck *continue* to be a lady." Hers was a voice they always obeyed, it enthralled them.

They rose; their glasses clinked. "Where's Sam? I have someone coming that I want you all to meet...but especially Sam." Elsie checked her watch.

"What do you mean you have someone coming? If you didn't know about this dinner party, how could you invite a guest?" Tony elbowed her while they laughed. "Well? Who is it?"

"Oh, just a woman I met last evening that I think you'd all like." Elsie twisted her hair round her finger as she spoke, a nervous gesture of hers, not wasted on Darwin.

"*How* did you meet her?" he asked, giving her his suspicious look.

"Hey...compadres!" Saved by the Bell.

Sam Bell came in with a big smile on his face. This was not the usual thing for him lately. Was it genuine? Elsie threw both arms around his neck. Close up she could see that the smile on his Godiva-chocolate face, covered haunted eyes. "Where've you been? I haven't seen you in days. Missed you."

"Ah, sweet Belle." The first poison Elsie had ever used was from the plant, Belladonna. Atropha Belladonna was named after the goddess Atrophos from the trilogy. The goddess whose duty it was to cut the thread of life. Her friends called her Belle on occasion.

"I been around." Sam kissed her neck.

She giggled.

A voice intruded. "Not around selling any cars." Darwin had specifically meant not to mention it. A bit of wine made his lips slip. Sam had not been at work in a week.

"Pour me a glass of somethin' bubbly." Sam handed him his worn leather jacket and went to each of the women in turn and kissed them, then took his seat at the table, ignoring the comments just as Elsie had done. He was the picture of a mountain man tonight, muted red-plaid flannel shirt tucked into faded jeans then stretched over the tall, broad-shouldered body. Mysterious and *very* sexy. He reached across the table and shook hands with Vinny. "Good to see you, man." His voice was deep. "Hope you two are doin' okay."

"What do you mean, *bubbly*?" Darwin frowned.

"I thought you were on the wagon?" Law asked.

Sam held out his glass while Mary filled it with one of Darwin's favorite wines, Château Lafite-Rothschild. Darwin chose it for this evening because he knew Elsie was partial to the delicate herbal aroma and flavor. Her nose, so attuned to herbs, could pick out the rosemary, thyme, and bay leaf.

Sam ignored the questions. "Man, it's somethin' fine seein' you guys. I've been kind of a hermit, ya' know. Havin' you all together like this gives me the chance to say thanks for being so ah, you know, after, ah, after…ah…well, just thanks."

They fussed over Sam for a few minutes; questions about his drinking were set aside. Gee and Tony served salad and filled glasses.

"Before the door chimes Sam, someone's coming tonight to meet you. Ah...um, a friend of mine—a new friend. *No big deal.* I just thought you might hit it off—be friends, too, you know." Elsie talked with her hands and even more when she was excited, or afraid, or like now, nervous. She blushed, too. Maybe Darwin wasn't the only one affected by the wine.

At thirty-three Elsie still seemed an innocent, but a streak of wildness had been added. Her violet, spirited eyes challenged everything. Generally she dressed for comfort, like the jeans and long-sleeved pale pink T-shirt she wore tonight. Her manner was unsettled, as though she had just gotten off a train, or was ready to climb aboard one. She was never at ease, at peace, for long.

Sam walked by Darwin on his way to the bathroom and leaned over. "Sorry boss. I haven't been feeling myself. I'll be a new man tomorrow—make it up to ya'."

"Forget it Sam. Take your time. I've got plenty of peddlers. And I'm not the boss around *here*; I shouldn't have said anything—bad timing."

"Bad, but forgivable." Darwin felt Tony squeeze his hand.

Sam made three more trips to the bathroom before the raspberry torte. Law noticed. He was counting.

Heavy whipped cream laced with a framboise liqueur, topped with toasted hazelnuts, smothered the torte. Everyone at the table was lost in a kind of libidinous trance—raspberry juice and white cream, drip-*slurp*, drip-*slurp*, to sounds of "umm." Everyone except Sam. And he had picked at the roast pheasant, nibbled the asparagus.

"Not hungry, Sam?" Law was determined to force the issue.

"Oh, well, the food's great. I don't have my ol' ravenous appetite back yet, I guess."

"Yeah. I notice you hit the can every chance you get. Got a bug?" The detective's nose was twitching and Sam was his friend.

In his book you took care of friends; their business was your business.

Georgia gave her soon-to-be-husband, a look. "Are we grilling him on his bathroom habits Law dear?"

"Not to change this fascinating subject," Mary stood, weaving slightly. Earlier she had appeared pale, but now her face flushed from the one glass of spirits. Having been pregnant with Vinny Junior and of late trying to get pregnant again, she was no longer used to drinking. "I'd like to make an announcement." She placed her free hand on Vinny's head. "This is news for everyone. I just found this out today and Vinny and I haven't really had time to talk." She stroked Vinny's hair. "I was going to wait and take Vinny aside first, but I wanted to give you—our very *best* friends and the people we love most in life—the news together. Besides, with all this talk of not drinking, well...this will be my last drink for the next nine months."

"Baby-Cakes! Oh Lordie, Hallelujah Baby-Cakes!" Vince jumped so fast he slopped his drink down the front of his pants. The group whooped, yowled and hooted their approval right along with Vinny.

"I haven't had a chance to lose all the weight I gained with Vinny Junior; it all went to my thighs." Mary looked shy, voice soft.

He swung her tiny body around—kissing every inch of her face. "I'll love them stubby little legs till the day I die, I swear it!"

The group went on with congratulations, drinking a special toast to this baby.

Mary and Vinny were caught up in a special celebration of their own. First, he danced her around the room—her ankle length red silk dress, a swirling sunset—while he sang with a husky voice... his throat choked with emotion. *"See the girl with the red dress on, she can do the...tah dah...all night long...whad' I say..."*

They gathered around the couple, clapping, trying to join in the song, not really knowing the words or much caring. This was a day to savor—an event of consequence to all of them. Dancing, Vinny whirled Mary to the sofa where they fell in a heap; the two were lost in their world.

Darwin took charge. "Lets move our party to the den and leave these love-dove's some private time. They can rejoin us later."

Vinny and Mary's heads had disappeared onto the sofa, but, as the group followed Darwin out of the room, they heard the couple's secret whispers and giggles behind them.

Georgia sat down next to Sam. He chattered nervously, happy for his friends, but, in a way, he looked stunned. She understood that any young couple about to have a baby would fill him with longing—but to see them so in love, so happy...

Elsie watched Sam with concern. If only her new friend would hurry and show. It would be a diversion for Sam. The doorbell chimed, and Elsie jumped to her feet. "Why don't I get that, Dar? I'm sure it's my friend." She returned to the room with a striking ash-blonde woman with saucer-emerald eyes; she wore a white Irish linen blouse with just enough lace down the front to be romantic. Under it, dark leggings, with high-heeled cowboy boots made her legs seem like they went on forever.

Elsie placed her hand on the woman's arm. "I'd like you all to meet my new friend, Kandle Lauriet."

Chapter Six

"An' they chased him 'n' never could catch him cause they didn't know what he looked like, an' Atticus, when they finally saw him, why he hadn't done any of those things...Atticus, he was real nice..."

His hands were under my chin, pulling up the cover, tucking it around me. *"Most people are, Scout, when you finally see them."*
- To Kill A Mockingbird - Harper Lee

"I don't believe I have ever known anyone by the name of Candle." Georgia rose to greet the young woman.

"I hate to always say this, but it's spelled with a K. I bet you were thinking C." She shifted to the other leg. The boots were new and pinched her toes. "I mean, that would be the normal thing to think." Her face got red. "Now you're all wondering what does it matter how it's spelled. I sound like a boob."

Elsie, seeing Kandle was nervous, put an arm around her shoulder, gave her a little hug. "We'll find a nickname we all like after we get to know you better."

"Madonna, comes to mind." Sam was on his feet once he realized this was the visitor they'd been waiting for. He felt sucker-punched; there was something about her that was so much like Bobbie. His mind raced. He looked over at Elsie. Had she seen it too? Was that the real reason that this Kandle with a K was here?

The woman's hair was cropped short, but if it had been longer the way Bobbie had worn hers.... What was it about her? Maybe it was those eyes that seemed to know more than her years would suggest she could possibly know. Huh. He could get to know her. Sure. Probably would not have much in common—but you never know. The fact that Elsie liked her was a start.

Kandle seemed to notice that he was at a loss for words and perched on the love seat next to him.

She seemed shy. That relaxed him. She wasn't out scouting for a date. After his very recent sexual attempt and subsequent Bambi-flub he was more reluctant than ever to have anything but a friendship with a woman. To Sam it felt as if that might be his, as Elsie called it, karma. Still, he had this odd lump in the center of his gut. It didn't help to feel Law's eyes prick him. The detective knew he wasn't clean. Sam felt belligerent and, at the same time, shame—real deep shame.

The small talk and introductions continued.

"Elsie thought you and me'd get along, hm?" Kandle checked Sam over.

Tony, who was on his way to get another drink and overheard Kandle, could not resist. "Hon, it's you and I, in fine circles such as this!" He gave his unique giggle and strutted on by talking to himself now, but aloud for all to hear. "I'll be *damned* if they ain't the cutest *dang* couple!"

The couple ignored him. "How, ah, old are you?" Sam was not that good at guessing—better to ask. She could be almost any age.

"Just turned thirty. What you *should* know is that I am, in today's lingo, relationship-challenged." Kandle fidgeted with the lace on the front of her blouse.

Sam sunk further into the soft couch. "Yeah? Me also."

Darwin was talking about something that happened at the dealership today. His animated voice drew their attention. "The man was only in his early sixties...he was a nice, distinguished looking man, dressed in an expensive suit. He drove right off the frontage road that goes in front of Silano's and hit one of our new cars. The first thing I did was move in close enough to smell his breath. He knew what I was doing and broke down. I had to take him to my office."

Tony hadn't gone to work; he'd been home cooking and doing laundry all day. "*Was* he drinking, Dar?"

"Not a drop. It was the saddest thing. He has Alzheimer's disease. He's afraid they're going to take his driver's license; he was piss-your-pants scared."

"Darwin. You *took* his license didn't you?" Law went to the wet-bar to pour himself another brandy. "We can not have people driving the streets that can't remember who and where they are."

"He was *crying*, Law, a grown man, an educated man. We talked until he calmed down. I found out he worked as a big-shot for someplace, oh, maybe it was Control Data. They'd laid him off with full pay." Darwin's distress was evident. "He begged to be allowed to pay cash for a different car, and, of course, the car he damaged, and just leave both of the wrecked cars with us. He wanted his family to think he'd decided to buy a new car—on a whim an' a rainbow, you know, out of the blue."

Georgia put her hand on Darwin's shoulder. "You let him do that, didn't you, Dar?"

He nodded, but answered, looking at her fiancée. "And there are people who would think I did it for the money."

The sound of her voice, and perhaps the accusation that he might consider that Darwin would help this man for the money, had a calming effect on Law. He leaned back and sighed. "Well. We can only hope he doesn't hurt himself or someone else." Here again, was another of life's dilemmas. Law stuck a small chunk of bread into the bowl of baby-shit-green stuff—sitting next to crap-beige stuff—on the coffee table in front of him; everyone had raved about it earlier so how bad could it be? He noticed the room had turned quiet. We're they all listening to him? Time to change the subject. With his mouth full, he said. "Great pumice, Tony." A ripple of laughter caused him to frown.

"Hummus, Law, but thanks."

Law looked embarrassed and could not even respond with his mouth so full and now, dry. He reached for his wine.

"I have an amusing story." Georgia wanted to normalize her man's blushing face, and stop his friends from laughing at him.

"The one we just heard was pretty darn good, Gee. Nice to know we can still pull the hummus over our good friend's eyes." Darwin seldom got the chance to laugh at the detective's expense and didn't want to let him off the hook too easily; they loved to tease him, because he was generally way too serious.

Tony bent over the dish, "I've simply got to have myself a little dab of pumice." He began to hum and sing, "A little dab l' do ya'. You probably remember that *old* saying don't you Law, what was it for, *Brillcrud*?" he giggled, and ran his fingers through the now stern looking detective's hair.

Gee went on as if she hadn't heard them. "At the pain clinic, today I had to call a few people. One of the names was unfamiliar. Kandle, it was you who made me think of it." Gee smiled at her. "The person's name was Karol, with a K? I wasn't sure if it was a man or woman. So, when a woman answered the phone sounding irritated, as if I'd interrupted something, I asked for Karol, let's say, Smith. She said Karol, ah Smith, isn't in. So, I said would her husband happen to be there?" Gee laughed out-loud, and they all waited for her punch line. "She said, 'lady, Karol is a lesbian'. Then, she slammed the phone in my ear. You never know when you are inadvertently stepping on someone's toes."

"Sometimes it ain't all that inadvertent." Sam was returning from the bathroom and had missed the first part of the story about the lesbian. His voice and walk were tainted with an uncharacteristic bluster—out-of-whack; these frequent trips to the bathroom were having an effect. *I'll stand up to Law,* he thought, and anyone else. Who does that pale cop think he *is* anyhow?

"Did something happen to you, Samson?" Gee was concerned and wanted to hear if someone had hurt his feelings.

"A car full a' white boys drove by as I walked ta' the door right here the other day. They hung out the windows yelling 'Porch-monkey go home!'"

Tony, hands on slim hips, was sure Sam had to be joking. "Say it isn't so!"

"I'll say anything you want me to say but it *is* so."

"Speaking of stepping on toes," Kandle said, "would anyone mind if I took off these boots? They're not broken in yet." They assured her they could handle her shoeless.

"You *are* kidding." Tony was still ready to stomp his feet about this.

"Kidding? One thing you white folk could really use is a fuckin' dose a' reality." It upset Sam that Kandle was showing so much concern for her feet and ignoring such open racism. He sniffed and pulled on his nose. He'd been doing that all night.

Elsie frowned. Sam was suddenly not himself. Samson was gentle, seldom bitter, and he almost never swore anymore. *White folk?* Surely he wasn't calling *them* white folk. She observed his legs and feet—they shook to the beat of a drum only he could hear; was his heart racing too, racing with the devil for his next line of nose-dust? First chance she got she was going to find out who it was that visited him the other evening. Something had been bothering her ever since that night. Those dealer plates stood for dealer all right. Dealer of what?

"You got a cold?" Law asked Sam. Pushing, again.

"Law," Elsie looked at Georgia when she talked, avoiding the glare in his eyes. "How's things in the South side precincts? Any particular rash of sex crimes, assaults, rapes, even murders that haven't been on the news yet?"

"What? Are you trying to change the subject, get the heat off your buddy?"

"*My buddy?*" Her voice was a *yowl.* "He's not *your* friend, *too?*" Elsie's eyes scorched him; she looked ready to attack.

"Course he's my friend. Well, do you have a reason for asking?" Chastised, Law rubbed his hands over his face. A gesture that often meant he was getting a headache.

"Kandle with a K." The words came from over Law's shoulder. Vince and Mary were walking, arms around one another, into the room.

"*You* know her?" Law blurted at Vince.

"Yeah. Forgot your last name, sorry." Vinny held out his hand. "This is my wife, Mary." He hugged Mary to him. "And soon to be baby!"

"Happy to meet you Mary, congratulations." Kandle beamed at the happy couple. "Your husband really helped me last night. My last name is Lauriet."

Kandle looked at Elsie. "Do you know *all* the police in town? Vince was on duty last night when you saved my life. The hospital called him to take a statement when I went to have my leg x-rayed. He was kind enough to drive me home. Have you had any luck finding that creep?"

"What?" Tony leapt up. The group went nuts all at once.

"What do you mean Elsie saved your life?" Law's face was red once again. "Vince, what do you know about this? Why didn't I see this report?"

Vinny's answer was drowned out. Everyone talked at once.

Kandle became uneasy. She tugged at Elsie's shirt. "You *knew* I went to the hospital. You called me the cab."

"Are you crazy Elsie? Are you just plain crazy?" Darwin's worst fears were being realized. Elsie saving another life? What was going on?

"Kandle, do you know who this savior of yours is?" Law's face blustered. Gee's soothing voice behind him was not getting through.

"Well, no, but she does look familiar." Kandle's eyes were wide.

"Haven't seen her face on TV?"

"I'm afraid I don't own a television. I like to read."

"Well, *newspapers,* then?"

"Novels. I read mostly mysteries." They hovered around her, closing in on her space. Had she done something wrong? But then, from the back of the group, she heard someone say, "You must have heard talk of the Avenger-Woman. Or try Bite-Woman?"

Kandle stared at Elsie. "Is *that* why he jumped and dropped his flashlight? Why he yelled "*You*!" and then ran? I was too upset at the time to ask what you did, and later I completely spaced it out."

Elsie blew out her lung full of air as she plopped back onto the sofa and watched her friends descend. So many questions—too little time, or so she hoped.

Parked on River Road for what seemed like hours, the rumble of the beast slithered throughout him, penetrating his bones. He felt himself become one with his beast of a Jaguar. He watched the people go inside the large brick and stone mansion. Tonight he was smoking crystal-meth. It made his leg shake now and again. He hated that, and gripped the leg with both hands. It reminded him of that bulldog the neighbors used to have—Morgan was his name. That dog always humped on his leg. But on the plus side, the meth gave his memories *violent* colors. *Tonight was all about memories*, he thought, as he recalled last night:

The laughter coming from the two 'girls' chafed. "Not much of a bogeyman, was he?"

They didn't know he heard that or they'd have felt real fear. Wouldn't they?

He'd called his wife from his cell-phone and told her he had been called back to work—a disturbance only he could attend to. And that, it certainly was.

The chafing festered into a canker sore.

He was a man used to making quick decisions. He turned his car around. Careful now, no need to be seen by anyone. He waited at a distance he felt was safe until he saw them knock on several doors, go inside the last one. Twenty minutes later, he noticed a yellow-cab pull to the curb; the two women came out. Kandle gave her new friend a hug and slid inside the taxi. At least it appeared to be Kandle, he could not be certain from this distance.

The canker sore erupted. He felt castrated by these two bitches.

The woman who appeared to be the Avenger-Woman walked down the street alone. An easy target? Maybe not so easy. Who to follow? The answer seemed plain enough. He should be able to keep a safe distance from the yellow taxi. As he drove his confidence returned. Once again, he held all the cards. He would follow her home. To his chagrin, they were stopping at the Riverside Hospital Emergency. What was *this* shit? Her smile was weary as she paid the driver and walked toward the hospital door... limp...she had a limp. Her jeans were torn and bloody around the left knee. Poor darling Kandle. This close there was no doubt that it was her.

He parked in the nearby lot...where he could still have a perfect view of the door. He had nothing but time. Another taxi would have to take her home. Meanwhile, he took out his bronze pipe, and the plastic bag. Might as well relax. Relax and contemplate his bad luck.

Or good luck.

Now he would have the opportunity to do her right, at her house, with all the amenities of home. She had foolishly told him that she lived alone. He was sure the Avenger had not seen him or his car; he'd shone his flashlight directly into her eyes—smart of him, if he *did* say so himself. In a way he admired what the little *hide* had done, but he was way too smart for her. She was merely a woman. A piece. A hide. And Kandle was too dim-witted to remember much; when he finished with her she would not be a problem. He spotted the cop car right away and killed his engine. The pig was probably a coincidence, but why let exhaust draw attention to his car. Without those clouds he was nothing more than a murky sliver in the shadows.

Christ it was cold. Bitches.

Thirty freeze-fuck-minutes later Kandle came out with the cop. The bastard was giving her a lift home. Fucking moron. Your tax dollars at work. He wrote down the squad car number with stiff red fingers. He'd follow them and have her address, and he'd get the cops name from that police-car number. Spoil his good time; we'll see about that. He'd even the score.

If he couldn't get his rocks off—he could sure get off—getting *even* got him off.

Well, that was then, this was now.

He took one last toke on the pipe and clicked off the projector in his mind. He saw spots of red and purple, stark colors, then, just the black of night. This meth shit made his daydreams come to him in Technicolor.

Time to 'mellowyellow' out.

The party had been going long enough. He'd love to ring the bell, then slice each and every throat. It would be like a trip back to the jungles of 'Nam. A vacation. Well deserved.

Soon people would be leaving. He backed his car almost to the corner—out of sight. Fucking faggots. Fucking cops. Fucking cunts.

Claudette heard the cupboard doors slam, *wham*, bam, as soon as she closed the porch-door behind her. Her face was tear-streaked. She was a mess. He did not seem to notice how she looked anymore.

"I tried to call you from the car. There was no answer here, Claudette. You know that your behavior is unacceptable. I have simple rules for you and your children to follow. Simple." With the last word he threw his briefcase and *kicked* the wallboard. His foot punched in the wall.

His face was a mask. To her, he had worn this mask from day one of their marriage. *Why had he not worn it earlier?* Where was the face under the mask? His eyes bored into her, piercing; she could feel so much pain being wished on her that she nearly cried out her pain.

"What?" she asked. Something must have happened today at the treatment center. Yes. That was it. She knew she had done nothing wrong. Her eyes followed his finger to the refrigerator where his list of rules were posted; it jabbed for emphasis, with each word he uttered, at the neatly typed paper list. She had not broken any of his rules.

"Where is Theodore?" The hatred evident in his tone sickened her.

"He's still working, you know that, to pay his tuition." Was that mouse-like voice really hers?

"I'm proud as a wet-hen to say my son is, what is he now, the assistant-manager? No, the assistant *night*-manager of a Wally's Burger-Heaven."

His sarcasm was a loose metal screw twisting through her flesh and bone.

"And Elizabeth? Where ever could your slut-clone daughter be at this hour?" He walked toward her, pulling his belt off as he walked. "I'm surprised she has managed to drag her lardy-lard-ass out of bed this early."

"She went to the movies with Greta. I wish you wouldn't call her a slut, Randolph. It hurts me." If only he could treat his own daughter half as well as the young women he treated at the center, she thought.

"Hurts *you*? Well, what a coincidence, Claudette. I believe it is time to teach you, you slut, a lesson about hurt."

She began to cry. "No. No, not a lesson, Randolph." She heard the snap of his belt. He liked to crack it... to see her jump in fear.

He took her face in his hand, fingers digging like nails into her cheeks, the Molotov cocktail in his eyes about to detonate and take her with him on a hoof-off to hell. "And in my own home I'll call a spade a spade. Something that seems to be forbidden in public these days."

Pip and Bobbette had just been invited to the party and they were making the rounds. Kandle got the most attention from the black and white beagle, because she was new and needed welcoming. Whereas Bobbette preferred what was old and familiar.

Kandle agreed to go over mug shots in the morning. Satisfied with Elsie and Kandle's explanation of events at the river the party had grown pensive. All they had was an old Sears flashlight with no fingerprints, and the picture in their minds of the sleek dark car, no idea what make or model—which, in itself seemed odd—and that the man used a beeper.

Gee was speaking; her friends, feeling a serene wine induced glow, let her words caress them. They were happy to let Gee lead their minds away from the violence at the river. "Do you have any idea how many questions there are that have no answers? Think about that. It is one of the primary reasons that it is so difficult to find peace—personal peace."

There was a calm about her that they soaked themselves in. "This culture has made our lives a struggle. What about the man Darwin mentioned with Alzheimer's? What if he had been on a horse? Would that not have solved all problems? No small children to run over, no ego to destroy by telling him he cannot drive."

The music of her voice sang to them—each one in its own way—she was the true goddess here. "You think it is laughable Darwin, I feel your heart smile. That sick man could still ride with the wind on the back of a stallion, or better yet an' old work nag. If he fell, he would only hurt himself—a chance I'm quite certain he would choose to take. We would have no worry that the innocent might be maimed. If he were lost, chances are, his horse would return him home to safety."

Law smiled at his woman; love watered his eyes. "You can't be suggesting we go back to horse and buggy days?" Pip licked at his hand, saying, "Pet me." The dog was partial to the detective because he had lived with him for over a month, years ago, right after Elsie's friends' murder.

"I am suggesting that we grew without the time to revel in the miracles that helped us along the way. So fast, our greed enveloped our hearts, and with no thought for the souls of the people, what the children to follow us would inherit, or, what might happen to the earth that feeds us." There was definite moisture in her eyes. "There is no place in this world for diversification; we must all be alike. Yet, we are not. What about that? We do not all worship this American culture that rewards only drive and ambition and looks with disdain on those of us who communicate with our Spirit. We, who can look at a mountain and feel its calm—see emptiness in those competitive eyes. Is it any wonder that as a nation our souls are squeezed tight, that we can find no peace or contentment?"

Kandle's eyes shone. Who *was* this woman? "What can we do?" she asked. Bobbette padded and purred, shedding tiny hairs on Kandle's black tights. Pip noticed the bare toes and began to lovingly lick them. They all laughed when Bobbette pounced on Pip's head.

Gee smiled too, but kept her focus. "It is up to us. Up to *this* group. *Up to the people in this room,* to begin a change. Let each of us begin to save the world. No one else can do it. There are people everywhere like us. We can be the catalyst that will make our collective spirits bloom."

"Brava! Brava!" shouted Sam. He was just returning from another trip to the bathroom. He sniffed as he stumbled and fell back onto the sofa. Kandle was no longer on his faded mind, and he didn't even notice Bobbette. He slid further down, feeling the extreme heat of Law's trained perusal.

Chapter Seven

Randolph Boodles loved his job. He thought about this while he lectured the group. "The bottom-line is that each of us is responsible for our own wellbeing. We must accept responsibility for the choices that we make." Fortunately, he had this bullcrap down—it was mere rote—he could easily guide these darlings while his mind visited an archived museum. Randolph was the director of a halfway house for alcoholics and drug addicts, called Choices. Choices was located in Dundas, a small farm town in southern Minnesota. "...friendship, means risking vulnerability." His voice rang with sincerity. He watched the young, scrubbed faces. First thing they did when they got a kid in was dip them in hot water. This group of girls from ages eleven to fifteen, was his favorite. What could be as wonderful as a young girl straight off the farm, or even one who came from the city once you got her out here to farm country. His mind blinked between the corn fed plump behinds, and the slut-butts the city turned out. Both had merit.

Lola had her hand raised.

"Yes, Lola. You have a question, my dear?" New to the group, Lola had not been what he would term, properly initiated.

Lola's straight blonde hair fell over much of her face; she parted it with her chipped, stubby dark-purple fingernails. "How do we know who can really be trusted to be our friend?" He noticed the defiance in her eyes.

Her twelve-year old body looked ripe to Randolph. He cleared the mucus from his throat, "Eechm," then swallowed it. "You will learn Lola, that to change your life, you must be willing to give away your intimate self, to trust in all of the members of this group." Lola had come from the city, from St. Paul, and her stance told him that she knew exactly what part of her intimate self he referred to. She was a wise one. So much the better; cut the preliminaries. Once they got the message that he was the one with all the power—the one who controlled, not only their world inside, but *when* they would be allowed to return to the real world—there was no such thing as defiance. Lola's developing young breasts seemed to be jutting toward him, begging for his attention. Jut no more, dear Lola, I see them. His wife, Claudette, had once had breasts like that. Pre-children. He cleared his throat again; this country air that brought out his allergies. "We are about to dismiss," he checked his watch. "I have some time. Why don't you have a seat, Lola. You and I can discuss this topic more in depth."

Law's thoughts returned to his baby-brother. It had been a long time. Gee, the most important person in his life, didn't know that he had a brother. How old would he be? Law was fifty-three himself, so...let's see, he talked in silence to himself, that would make Toast, real name was Terrence, forty-nine. The Lawrence brothers. He vaguely remembered some cartoon mice named Gerry and Terry. Did that cartoon influence his Ma at naming time? Silly thought. They were just like their names sounded: good, normal, keep-your-nose-clean, kids. There was a time when they were a close family. Out of the wild blue yonder Toast decided he'd hook up with the Roman Catholic Church, after that their interests set them on different paths. Why did he feel as if he'd just been punched? Law slumped on the sofa. In the early years, after Toast was ordained, he was what one might term a fanatic. Law had already been on the force for several years; he'd seen things that made him doubt the sincerity of the Church. They could help the people no one cared about, but did they do that? Too often, not. So, the letter came as a shock. It came from a person with whom he had lived and loved, but in, what seemed, a previous life.

He read it again.

Dear Gerry,

I hope this letter finds you well and happy. I've kept in touch with Ma and Dad all these years, so I have a good idea as to what your life has been about. Sorry to hear about your marital troubles. I was told that the church excommunicated you because of the divorce. I wish we had talked; I could have spoken to the bishop on your behalf, possibly made a difference. Then again, knowing you, I doubt you'd have accepted any special dispensation, am I right? Well, this is an awkward letter, isn't it? Hard to write. And I suppose, hard to get. So I'll get right to it. I'm leaving the priesthood. Or, I believe that I am. You know yourself how I always had to have my booze. Remember how you used to call me Toast? Said I was always toasted. I find that it has become a problem of great proportion for me. My calling, my prayers, have not saved me from myself.

I am leaving the Chicago diocese in five days for what we call a sabbatical. In my heart I feel it may be something more. I will be entering a treatment facility in your general area—Choices. It is located South of the Twin-Cities, in a small town by the name of Dundas. The name attracted me, and I think that I also wanted to be closer to you. They have no link to the Church, and that seems best, right now. I am as anxious to see you, and to meet your wife-to-be, as I am to get my life in order. After all this time I can only hope that you will feel the same.

I am enclosing Choices' brochure. It contains their phone number, address, and visiting hours.

> Yours in Christ,
> Father Lawrence

P.S. Forgive the pompous signature. I fear my days of using it are numbered.

Law put the letter back in the envelope—preoccupied. Reading about how Toast had kept track of him through their parents made him feel both guilty and glad. Why hadn't he, himself, made an effort to keep in touch with his brother? It occurred to him how lonely he'd felt when Terrence left the family. He was supposed to feel joy, instead he felt abandoned. Becoming a Roman Catholic priest meant that you gave away all your worldly possessions. You became part of a larger family, the family of God. He felt small when compared to the mighty wall of Catholicism. And he was young enough and dumb enough to believe that all this meant that his brother was giving him up, too. Evidently Toast had not seen fit to give up everything, after all. Not the booze, anyhow.

He heard Gee's key in the lock. She'd be surprised to find him home at this early hour. They had much to talk about. Why hadn't he mentioned his brother to the woman who knew all because he told all?

Sam drove the old green Chevette down to West Lake Street and turned into Maggert's Machines. The car was rickety, but he couldn't afford to be recognized, so he'd pulled it off the used car lot last night before leaving Silano's. Said he might have a buyer and wanted to make sure it wouldn't break down on their way home if he sold it. They were happy to see him at work selling again.

The air from the heater was at best tepid, and he shivered while he sat waiting for the Maggot to come out. Everyone knew they were less than friends, so he pulled his dark knit winter cap down as far as he could, and hunched down to wait. The heater-blowers made too much noise to allow him to listen to the crackling radio. This entire experience was a giant mental step back to poverty that he could do without. He noticed that the Mag had some real sweet cars on his lot. Some expensive foreign models that looked close to new. Where in the hell did he get his jing?

The tap on his window brought him back to life and he cranked it down a few inches. It was damn cold, but his whole body was covered with a light layer of sweat—sweat, then, shiver. That was the world of a junkie, he thought, with a flicker of shame. A white packet fell into his lap and he stuck a worn copy of Arthur Miller's *Death of a Salesman* through the open crack.

The book was opened, a hundred dollar bill removed; it was tossed back inside the window. "Hey, Sambo." His tone was condescending at best.

"Hey yourself, *Mag*got." If this dirtball could call him Sambo, he could just as well call him by his more appropriate handle.

"Well now, aren't you the nervy bastard?" Maggot spit on the snow. "Nervy, for a fuckin' porch-monkey."

Sam's tires squealed as he pulled away. Maggot *did* have something to do with that car of goons that yelled at him. Maybe he'd even been in the car; that night it was late, too dark to see. Why did he allow this moron to get *inside* him now? In the past he'd always had the upper hand over slime-balls like Maggot. He knew the answer to that. Well, this would be the last time he lined fuckhead's pockets. Sam drove out on Lake Street, the small packet in his hand. He had to stop some place and do one line—

only one. The cut off plastic straw was ready and waiting in his jacket pocket. He pulled it out. If he could just open the packet and do a whiff at the next light. *Someone might see him.* He should go inside one of these businesses, maybe a McDonalds and use their can. *That would take too long.* He needed just the one snort first. Then he could stop, tell himself he was *doing-lunch.* He checked his watch. He was late for his date with Kandle. He had liked her pretty much right away. She was ditsy like his Bobbie.

The traffic light flashed red and the straw went in his nose so fast he poked himself. "Ouch." Ahh. God. A gram was such a small amount, really. Maybe he'd go on home and call Kandle. Something came up, they'd have to reschedule. He could lay out these lines and do them one after another until the pain in his heart felt fuzzy. Yeah. He turned the car around. Kandle was a nice woman. This would be the last time he degraded himself—going to the Maggot for drugs. This would be the last time he did any drugs. So, given that, he might just as well make the most of it. *What he wanted right now was blessed oblivion.*

"No problem. After all you've done for us, we'd be happy to help you. See you then." Darwin laid the phone back in its cradle. "Well. You'll never guess." The odd look on his face told Tony that something was definitely going on. "That was Law. He has a brother, it seems. An alcoholic *priest* brother. An alcoholic priest brother who is going to be staying with us for about two weeks until a spot opens up for him at that rehab place south of here—in Dundas."

"You're kidding, right?" Darwin didn't answer, but sat, pensive. Tony went to him. "Dar, will you return to earth? Land, and clue me to what's going on."

"Exactly what I said, Spike. Law has a younger brother. Funny he never mentioned him to us, but then, he's not the most open human being I've ever met. Still, he must consider us friends or he would never dream of asking to have him stay here." Darwin pulled Tony by the arm down next to him in the large recliner. It felt better to Dar all the time to be this close, to be committed to Spike. "Are you sure you're feeling okay? You're pale lately, Spike. I'd feel a lot better if you would go for that check-up we talked about." He put both strong arms around his mate.

"I keep telling you I'm simply tired. I need vitamins. Will you get off my case? Get off my case, and on my ass!" He gave Darwin's ear lobe a nibble. "You know very well how you would react if the situation were reversed. Now, tell me about Law's brother. What's his name? When's he coming?" Tony loved it when Darwin showed open affection, like now. He snuggled back, letting himself revel in the warmth of Darwin's hard, loving body.

Randolph disliked meeting at the *auto-boutique*. He could not bring himself to call it a dealership, although he knew that this Maggert fella had big-shot intentions. Maggert's Machines sounded more like a boutique to him. If anyone had the right to be pretentious, it was not this asshole. Even though it seemed risky to meet him there, he needed to move some product. It was very late; he was certain that he had not been followed. And, Mr. Pretentious Asshole had come highly recommended. Besides, Randolph had a sense of humor, and to have a car salesman peddle his particular wares gave him a good laugh.

Randolph's head throbbed. It was the strain of these past few days. He'd been surprised when Avenger-Woman had not come forward with regard to their *encounter*. Watching the nightly news made him anxious, and at the same time titillated. Either they really did not know who he was, as he firmly believed, or they were afraid he would come after Kandle. Inside he knew his identity was safe. He had not lost track of Kandle. She was not staying at her apartment, not going to her work, but he was smarter than that little twit. As he drove West on Lake Street he noticed all the blurred eyes that were barely alive. Did they owe their high to him, he wondered? Did he owe his Jag, this lustrous ebony cat that purred and carried him in such an opulent manner, to them? Right now, he could recall when a Jag meant, not this great beast, but rather, getting a load on for days at a time. The only thing that kept his personal *habit* in line, even today, was his love of beautiful, expensive things. Just driving along, like tonight, seeing how much more he had than all those shivering bodies out in the cold, gave him a boner. As he turned into the drive to the car-joint, he remembered the cop. The cop that had spoiled his good time. Randolph had discovered a great deal in just a couple of days. He knew who the slob was, where he lived, and who his friends were. He even knew that Vincent's wife was pregnant. Maybe he'd be satisfied with a waltz or two with that pretty little thing. What do you think, baby? Would you like to dance with Randy?

They don't call me ol' Randy-the-Dandy for nothin' baby.

He had seen photo's of this man he was about to meet, but they had not prepared him for the real thing. That they were not recent photographs was evident. The man sasshayin' towards him was haggard, the skin on his neck so loose it moved with the wind. He was a man that had once been handsome, but no longer. He'd given his good looks as payment to the *piper*. He'd bet it had happened fast judging from the way his filthy, yet expensive, clothes now flapped and bagged.

"You must be Mr. Randolph. I'm Larry Maggert." The wide grin showed a couple of black holes where he had recently lost molars. They shook hands like two businessmen.

Haggert-Maggert, thought Randolph. He put his hands into his pockets to quickly wipe them. Where were those moist towelettes when you really needed them? "Pleased to meet you. Our mutual friend said to say hello." The friend had called him Maddog, now he knew why. Even in the dim light outside he could see how the man's nails had been chewed to the quick. Brown spots from dried blood ridged the edges. The cuticles were completely gone, chewed off. He pictured an animal picking over its bones. Then thought of the rod and reel his Dad had given him for his tenth birthday. The reel was much smaller than the old one he was used to. At first, the size concerned him. He soon discovered that although it was small it had miles of line wound tight. That was the Maddog. To the untrained eye, there was not much left of him, he was small, *slim-pickins,* but Randolph knew that he could cast him a long ways out, many times over, before he would have to cut the line. Pay attention, he told himself, time to bait that big old hook.

Walking together to the used car shack, Maggert spoke, "They call me Maddog, you know."

He said it as if he was proud; to him it was a term of endearment. Robert wanted to tell him that they just as often called him simply the Dog.

Inside, the Dog turned on one small light, made certain the shades were drawn tight, then, stood on a chair and removed a ceiling panel. He had to step up on the desktop to reach the metal ammo-box tucked inside. Robert watched the smug look on the addict's face. The man's washed-out eyes made him think again of fish—a fish that's been too long at the market. He believes I will admire his cunning. Give the public what they yearn for. "What a clever nesting place. Most people would keep this in their safe, but you have found a spot the stupid cops would never find and made it fire proof all at the same time." Rah-rah, sis-coom-bah.

"Exacto-lee. I want you to know, I ain't no dummy. You can count on me to figure all the angles. Like, I was wondering if you knew how many of these chumps are getting into meth. We don't want to miss out on their cash flow."

"Really? You'll have to tell me all about it." Could he notice the sarcasm in his voice, or, was he simply too vapid?

The Dog opened the box and took out a thick wad of cash. They talked about quantity, and quality of product, turn over time, customer base, age, income, area—general demographics. This was, after all, a business meeting. It was necessary to have a business to launder the money from the real business. Randolph did his best to feign admiration for this low-life.

Maddog was getting edgy. They must have been talking for twenty minutes. He needed a fix. "Well now, Dandy-my-Randy, don't I get to sample the goods?"

"My name is Randolph." Randolph's eyes burned through him. He felt the heat.

"Hey, whatever you say, man." Maggerts knee shook uncontrollably. It was having a spasm. He needed drugs.

The face that glared back at him was sharp, like staring at the glistening edge of a bloody blade aimed directly at your throat. Randolph's arm knocked the stack of bills toward the other man. "You don't trust me?" The bills fell over covering half the desk, a few slowly rustled to the floor. The room was quiet, a tomb, even the furnace blower had stopped, afraid to make a sound.

Fear doesn't cut it for a junkie. He can't sit still for long, especially not while he knows there are drugs in the room. "Sure, man. Sure, I do. I just thought..."

Once he had established the upper hand, Randolph tossed an eight-ball at the Dog. "Consider this a tip." The street value for the eight-ball of cocaine, once cut, could be over a grand. It was a grandiose tip, yet meaningless to him. Wholesale, it was around $475.00. It was nothing. This slick man spilled that much every week. He took the money and began to stack it neatly in his briefcase. "And one more tip for you. After this, we'll let me do the thinking. You just do what you are told." His cold eyes moved back to the money. May as well release the Dog, and let him have his reward. He watched him stab the plastic baggie with his letter opener and take a generous portion up each nostril, then, wipe his nose with his fingers and rub the excess on his gums.

Set that hook.

"What's your position on pussy?"

"Pussy?" It took the Dog a second to decide what he was being asked, what was expected of him here, then he leered. "Got no use for an old cat. I like a kitten, young enough to be fresh and full of fight. Scrapy-like. An' when the scrapin's over, I like to tie a stone to em' an' watch as they sink to the bottom of the lake, a chokin' and a kickin'." He'd heard rumors about this man and very young girls and he wanted to make an impression of his own. Truth was, he liked a woman old enough to be grateful with enough money to pay the way.

Randolph sat back and looked at him with a new light in his eyes. But business was over and the room stank of BO and butts. Stale food wrappers spilled out of the trash and cigarette butts covered the floor. He could picture some old wretch of a used-car salesman down on his knees, a scavenger, picking through the butts to find the biggest for one last smoke of the day. We all have our addictions; we just have various amounts of money to indulge them. His hands felt sticky from whatever had been on the desk. Might a' been a Big Mac or, on the lighter side, maybe some lucky guy got his rocks off on it. Most likely both, and then some. Whatever. He got up. "Maybe we'll get us some fresh ones together some night. Sounds like you got the right idea." He walked toward the door. "Oh, did Harry tell you how to reach me?" The words came out off-handed and sly.

"No, sir, not a peep. He set all this up." And my Momma was the Queen of Spain.

"Good." Randolph nodded. "Precisely as I like it. If we should ever meet on the street, or you should see me or my picture anytime, forget you know me. Got it?"

"Yes sir." Oh he got it. See his picture? Why would that happen unless this *was* someone? He'd find out. Never know when that information would come in handy. Actually, that was a lie, he knew precisely when it would come in handy.

"Okay. Pace yourself...if you're out, you're out till you hear from me, and that's not good business, so pace yourself and string them along. Things go as planned, we'll find time to celebrate soon. You bring the tootsies, I'll bring the stash; we'll show them a real good time." Randolph adjusted his fifties-style shirt as he turned. "Show them who the man is. Do it up big-time." The black stitching on the bright yellow shirt collar amused him; it was what he would term avante garde. He'd paid three hundred dollars for this crisp shirt. He gave one last glance at the Dog before he left. He had no knowledge that this odious creature was once a meticulous man.

Chapter Eight

A voice said, Look me in the stars
And tell me truly, men of earth,
If all the soul-and-body scars
Were not too much to pay for birth.
                -A Question by Robert Frost

One line after another shot up his nose. Sam lay on his sofa and thought of the good old days. The days when doing a line gave him energy, made him feel as if he were on top of the world. Now, one line just felt like two, and two, more. In the old days he would spend a good fifteen minutes savoring the moment, chopping the rocks to a fine powder. Tonight, he arraigned the pile under a dirty five-dollar bill, then found a pen and rolled it hard and fast over the top. The thirty second preparation. He licked the expensive powder off the *nasty-with-germs* bill, tossed it aside, took razorblade in hand and began to form the lines. Sometime after the first few lines he remembered to phone Kandle.

Her voice held no suspicion.

"If you don't feel well I'll come by and nurse you. You don't know this about me, but I can cook, *plus,*" her voice turned breathy, "I give great massage."

Another thirty seconds and he was off the phone. He had closed her out, eager to return to his obsession on the coffee table. He wanted to forget Bobbie. "I'm sorry, Bobba my babe," he whispered to her, wherever she was. "But, it's just for tonight, for an hour or two."

The amusement park was open and he had a free pass. Rather than allowing him the moments of euphoria and bliss that he yearned for, this drug, as if it knew his secret desire, determined it would take him on a completely different ride.

Sam shut his eyes, then opened them wide. The darkness inside that he thought would give him comfort was a rolling screaming nightmarish jumble of colorless motion and sound; it made him dizzy. All he wanted to feel was nothing. What he felt was everything; he missed nothing—every squeak, every movement of air caught his attention.

The four walls began to move in closer, drapes shifted from side to side. His darting eyes were not fast enough to keep up with the sinister action. Fear crept over him like slime; he listened, barely able to think or breathe.

Outside his window he heard her voice—Bobbie's—and the voice of another, a man.

They were fucking. Rabid fucking.

He smelled rancid, rotting flesh, and saw the air seep in under his door from the dark winter night. How could that be? He lay in mortal terror. Terror such as he had never known gripped him, twisting his mind while he listened to her cries and sighs of pleasure, as the tears poured from his eyes. She had already forgotten him, replaced him with another. But these sounds he heard were Evil; Bobbie was never evil. She was pure and sweet and good.

He sat quickly.

He had to have another line.

The table was clean. Even the stray crumbs—gone.

Had he done that? On his hands and knees he searched the carpet for a rock that might have fallen. Nose to the floor, he heard them once again. He went to the window, parting the drapes a

SPIRITS OF THE ONCE WALKING

crack. It was as if they lay just below, out of his sight, on the snowy ground—writhing in putrid ecstasy.

He jerked. What was that noise? His entire body began to shake. Outside he could hear keys clattering; he fell back onto the sofa and stared, his body frozen, at the door.

A key turned in his lock and he wanted to scream!

In walked Kandle.

"What the fuck are you doing here?" His head was about to explode. "How did you get a key?" Sam shoved the Sunday funnies over the razorblade and straw that lay strangely alone on the table, as he stood.

Kandle had immediately slipped out of her heavy coat; his violent reaction to her made her drop it in a pile at her feet. "I didn't mean to scare you." Her face turned ashen, her voice small. "I borrowed the key from Darwin. And before you get pissed at him, I told him we'd talked an' you were sick an' I wanted to take care of you."

By this time she was sobbing. Sam felt like a fool. "Oh my God, my lady." He reached her arm and pulled her to him.

"I don't understand Sam, I was sure you'd want to see me." Her wet nose smeared his shoulder; he held her tight, afraid to let go. She pulled away, and for the first time, observed him closely. "Why you're clammy. Your skin and sweatsuit are damp. I'm sorry Sam; you must really be sick. I think we should get you to a hospital."

She listened as he protested that this was a temporary bug, took a tissue from her handbag and blew her nose while pacing and looking around the room. "It feels eerie in here. Were you having a nightmare?" She stopped and reached for something on the floor by the coffee table. "What's this?" Kandle was street-wise enough to know what the cut off straw was for. She moved the newspaper, saw the razorblade. Sam sunk to the sofa, if only he could keep on sliding right out of sight. Kandle's eyes held his while she ran her finger over the table, then tasted the finger.

Busted.

His gray sweats were not baggy enough to disguise what watching her lick that finger did to his body. Kandle's black silk pants fit snug across her stomach. She wore a rust Indian tunic that was sleeveless. As she stood upright, after inspecting his table and paraphernalia, the tunic flew back exposing a rather plain black silk blouse. Plain, but as she watched him, and what her finger in her mouth did to him, he could see small bumps protrude, pushing hard against the smooth silk.

Kandle's head whirled.

He was a recovering addict. Obviously, not straight at this moment, he must be having a relapse. But, she reasoned, she wanted him and besides, sex would get his mind off cocaine if only for a short time. Maybe it would be long enough…what if he couldn't *do it*? Failure to *perform* might make him worse, she thought. The bulge between his legs helped make her decision. There was one thing he could do for sure. Her shoulders dropped back and with one clean movement the tunic fell to rest on top of her coat. "Great massage is not all I can give, gorgeous man."

Sam felt as if he were swimming into her wet eyes. In this light the water-green of them was as shiny as freshly washed grapes. So extraordinary he wanted to roll them on his tongue, and suck in the sugar. He could see that she wore no bra. Her firm small breasts did not need one. He lifted her on top of him and kissed her long and sweet. His hands flowed like water over the soft material that covered her from the waist down—roaming the hills and curves of her, pushing her into his hardness as his mouth went to her nipples. He sucked her breasts right through the thin material, nibbling, then biting tenderly. He knew she'd meant to suck him off, but he wanted more from Kandle. One gram of coke was not going to keep him from showing her his feelings. He worked the flimsy skirt up high and felt cool, silky skin—skin as soft as the woven silk. Her panties pushed to one side with ease and he entered her, slowly at first, with only the tip of himself.

"More, Sambo, more," she begged. With a quick move they rolled to the thick carpet, pushing the table to make room, and he was on top of her, completely inside her.

From the hallway outside his door, that led to the rest of the house, came animal sounds. Sam could tell that it was his cat Bobbette playing with Pip, Elsie's Beagle. The two animals had decided they were family, too. He had seen Pip put Bobbette's entire head in his mouth while they rolled and frolicked over the floor. Was this the noise he'd heard earlier?

At that moment his mind went blank to everything but Kandle. The world, and all its problems, including the voices of Evil, evaporated.

He was hers; she was his.

Father Lawrence arrived to the twin cities to discover that, due to an emergency, Choices had no room for him, and very possibly would not have, for a week, or even weeks to come. Hardheadedness ran rampant in his family, and since he had made the difficult decision to go to that particular treatment facility, nothing else would do. He would wait. Last night he had a brief, but enjoyable, evening with his brother and wife to be, Georgia; today, since they were both hard at work, he insisted on driving himself to Darwin and Tony's. That brought him to where he was now, suitcase in hand, on their doorstep, thinking about how fortunate Gerry was to have found Georgia. What an incredible woman. He knocked softly then noticed the doorbell and pushed the button.

It seemed a long time before the door was opened. Having expected one of the two men who had been described to him to answer the door, Terrence was stunned to see the woman who stood before him. She was worth every second of the wait. It was obvious he had awakened her, for he could see red creases on her flushed face, and her fine blonde hair stuck this way and that in a way he found most becoming. She was pulling a heavy long red sweatshirt down over her sheer, pale, cotton-voile tunic as she opened the door. Her feet were still bare, toenails painted a blush pink.

"My goodness, you're early. And I've overslept. I can't apologize enough for keeping you waiting on the stoop. Come in, come in. You must be freezing!"

"And you must be Ms. Sanders. I didn't expect to see you. You have been painted as quite an elusive creature to me." A puzzled look swept her face. "Elusive, but certainly wonderful." He was still caught on her use of the word 'stoop'. He found it charming.

She extended her hand. "Please call me Elsie, Father."

Her momentary touch, the peace in her violet eyes, stunned him as if he'd been hit by a bolt of lightening. "And you must call me Terrence, or if you like, Terry."

Claudette's face was buried in the pillow under her head. It was soaked with her silent tears. Her nose itched, but she had no way to scratch it. She kept telling herself that it would all be over soon. Her arms were tied to the bedposts, as were her legs.

She had been so happy that day Randolph had her birthday present delivered. The new four-poster-bed must have cost him a fortune. Perhaps he did still love her. He was her husband. He must love her, she had reasoned. That very night he'd showed her what it was for. Her memory was stamped with the pain of it.

Now that she was accustomed to his *game*, she did not hurt as badly. She learned fast that she had to cry out and fling herself about or he would not be able to ejaculate and would continue on until he felt the depths of her degradation and pain. She would not be able to sit for a week.

"If only you were a normal woman Claudette. I would not have to secure you to the posts. You would beg for this. But, no, I have the misfortune to have married a frigid woman, a woman who has not one ounce of animal, or sexual instinct." He said the exact same thing each time as he tied her.

"Please, Randolph. Please, let me try it without the ties. I think I like it now. I know I do. I think I can do it for you." The sound of her pleading voice filled her with self-loathing.

"Like it?" He bellowed. "You are a whore. I am certain now that while I am out working hard to feed and clothe this miserable family, you have a man in this bed, fucking him as often as he will oblige you. Perhaps, there are even two men." He was inside her now, pushing hard and deep in the tiny opening. She could hear the crack in his voice that meant he would be coming soon. "Yes. I think you have two men fuck you at once, you slut. I can see it now. One fucks your face, while the other fucks you in the ass."

"It's only you I want Randolph, only you." Tears slipped down her cheeks, as much in shame, as pain. She must get away from him. It was killing her inside. It would be easier to do, but she had lost her will, lost herself.

Randolph had seen to that.

Claudette stepped into the scalding shower just as soon as she heard his car leave the garage. She lifted her face to the cleansing water and thought about finding a way out. If only she could wash Randolph out of her life as easily as her shower purified her body. Flush him out. She sat on the rim of the tub and watched the pale pink water as it swirled into the drain. The color did not faze her; she was used to bleeding. She was used to being brutalized, used to feeling a part of her wash away each day. Feeling was the wrong word to use, she was getting used to *not* feeling. Her hands rubbed over her hair—squeaky-clean. She wanted it to stay like this. For that to happen, something would have to happen to her husband. Why couldn't she watch the swill that was Randolph, as it swirled down the drain?

Slowly she moved toward his desk. He had a week or two old newspaper neatly folded on top of some papers. She saw one word—avenger. Of course Claudette had followed the trial with interest of the woman they all called the avenger, and she wondered—*was she for hire?*

Chapter Nine

He sat where she'd directed him; his presence filled the small space with the clean, soapy scent of jojoba oil. Elsie blinked—jojoba was one of her favorites. Her face felt flushed. She sat, her spine uncharacteristically rigid, in the rocker by the fireplace. The hard-rock maple rocker was a safe distance from the plush sofa that *whooshed* as he sunk into it. He was making small talk about his night with Law and Gee. She stared, thinking... brothers; they... are... brothers. The Father was inches taller than his brother, Law. What was it he was saying...? Her thoughts were not quite in sync with this Father Lawrence man. She made an effort to shut her brain down momentarily, and to somehow get her mouth to open.

"Can I get you something to eat or drink, Father?" Where were her manners? Something about him disturbed her. He wore jeans that appeared to be new, and a dark kelly green pullover sweater. The kelly complimented his deep brown eyes. She felt a shiver. The clothing—that was it. He was not wearing the starched white Roman Collar.

"I'd appreciate it if you wouldn't call me Father, Elsie." Before she could comment, he asked, "Do you have tea?"

In fact, he seemed uncomfortable all of a sudden. His thick, wiry hair was ebony; stubborn locks fell close to his eyes. Eyes so dark you might slip and fall right into them if you weren't careful, she thought. Law's hair was already so gray; did the priest touch his own up? Why did he seem so familiar? The brothers did not look that much alike. "That sounds perfect. I'll get us both some tea; be right back."

He stood. "Can't I come with and help? After all, I'll be living here for a short time. May as well learn the ropes." She felt him follow behind her, smelled that soap again. Such a clean, fresh smell. Her body tingled.

They were in the kitchen waiting for the water to simmer when she dropped a spoon on the floor. Terry bent to retrieve it. He straightened, and she saw the man in her nightmare. The man chopping wood. Elsie felt woozy. That was where she knew him from, *the dream*. Not her childhood? A flashback of her mother out on the rectory lawn that day so long ago with Father Andy gave her pause. Would history repeat itself? No. Not that this was the same. Elsie was not a married woman. Still. A priest. He was the same as married; married to God. Or was it only nuns who married God?

"A penny for your thoughts."

"Sorry I'm so distracted, Fa...ah, Terry. Not quite awake yet, I guess." Steam shot from the kettle's spout making her jump. "You know we're having a baby shower for a friend of ours tomorrow, maybe Law or Gee mentioned it. It's not the traditional women-only affair. Would you care to come? I know your brother and Gee will be there." She blurted the words, knowing instantly they were premature, then ran her hand back through her hair. She'd not bothered to comb it. But why did she care?

He must have sensed her discomfort, and changed the subject. "What kind of tea is this? I especially love the aroma." His hand brushed against her arm as he reached for the sugar.

Elsie felt her heart skip; she saw his image, in her dream, bending, to chop the wood. What would he look like without his shirt? "It's a concoction that I make myself. It has herbs that I grew in my garden, with natural fruit bits to sweeten. After I harvest the plants and roots I make a variety of teas and other things. This, has a number of herbs from the mint family; I call it Inspiration."

"It doesn't taste like tea without a slug of brandy." His eyes dropped as he stirred the steamy liquid.

Was he asking if she knew the truth; knew he was having a drinking problem? "Would you like me to get you some brandy?" Her voice was kind, but before he could say, please yes, toss a couple of ounces in my cup, she continued. "Law told us about your nickname. I'm afraid nothing is sacred with this group of friends. I like it—the name. May I call you Toast?"

His smile was warm. "Toast, it is. But, be warned, Elsie, in my mind, that makes you family." He placed his cup on the teal tiled counter, and stretched. "Want to show me where to put my things? The trip here wore me down. I'm ready for a nap. And hey, about the baby-shower, count on me." He gave her a long look with eyes that were glistening caviar. "It's a date."

Elsie swallowed, her tongue too thick to speak.

Randolph watched the petite, dark haired woman come and go. He had made his decision. His mind played the same video every chance it got. *Vinny, baby. Shame on you. You stuck your nose in my business. Stuck your nose where it did not belong. Shame on you, Vincent. But, if I were to let you get away with it, shame on me.*

Engrossed in thoughts of self, Randolph considered another recent decision. He'll stay clean for a week. Why take a chance that he might end up like one of his sleaze customers? Like The Maddog. This was day one; it had been ten hours since he'd been high. No big deal. It would be a snap. Easy does it, he thought, and laughed. How often had he fed that pap to others? He was waiting now, in his beast of an automobile, outside the small one's house. Waiting to see what time the man of the house returned home. Timing was important. His fingers shook as he tried to light a

Marlboro. He could not remember the last time he had smoked, surely not since college. Smoking was dirty. He hated to defile his car with something so mundane as regular tobacco, but his damn hands would not stop shaking, they needed something to do.

It must have been a combination of the lack of drugs, the waiting, and the way the willow trees bent, their tears weeping over the street, that made his hungry mind render back to the picture of himself in the cemetery.

He was nine years old:

It wasn't a real cemetery. No people were buried there. He'd buried five animals in this spot. Throughout his ghoulish pre-teen and teenage years, he came to visit as often as possible. He'd sit on top of their graves and play with the dirt, reliving the actual killings. Droplets of water, from rain or dew, would fall from the willow trees and moisten the earth. As a child he thought they were tears spent for the pets.

Remembering now, how he built castles in the mud, his nipples felt electric. The small bodies buried underneath his play area, were missing limbs, or at the very least, an eye, an ear, a tongue. He hadn't thought of it in years, but those were the happiest times of his life. He would lie on his stomach playing, knowing, that beneath him lay the pile of bodies. Contentment rushed over his slight body.

He was in control.

Contentment mixed with something else. He yearned to lie on that same dirt now, rubbing back and forth into the soil, until he came in his pants.

Why not call the Maddog and set up a rendezvous with a chickie or two, for an exchange of bodily fluids? No. He had more self-control than to mingle with the likes of that trash. He could wait. He would wait.

Mary was on the phone. "I'm telling you Vinny, it's the same guy, the *same* car." She listened to his response. "I don't know what kind of car." The circles under her eyes were black in the dim light. "Look. You don't believe me? Is that what this amounts to?" Her eyes squinted, trying hard to make out even one number on the license plate. It was no use. "Oh, up yours, Vinny. Let me talk to someone who doesn't think I am a neurotic woman. Now...do it now." The sound of her own voice was so shrill it made *her* believe she was a nut. She slammed the receiver in his ear with no good-bye.

Detective Vince Tonetti had found someone he could talk to. She was the new kid in homicide, and easy on the eyes. He was so damn tired. First, from working the long hours, and then, they'd had to keep trying to get pregnant; now that they were pregnant did he get some respite? In a pig's ass. He shook his head as he clicked off the phone, his eyes wandering in the direction of the little *muffin*. He was sure she'd been listening. Officer Susie sat at the switchboard, taking it all in, her mouth a hard line. But Muffin, as Vinny called her, fluttered her adoring eyes at him, as if to say, "you poor darling." She couldn't hold a candle to his Mary, she was just a piece of fluff—piece, being the operative word. What he needed was some mainline fluffing. Muffin had been coming on to him straight and hard all week, since her first day on the squad. At first he was so caught up in Mary being pregnant he'd barely noticed the new cop. She strutted past him now. Lucky for him, to get an eye full of her tight ass he had to turn his head and, that brought him into the field of Officer Susie's vision. Her glare made him reach for his Ray-Bans. Thanks Suz', he muttered under his breath, probably saved my ass. Time to get his butt home. He grabbed his jacket just as Law walked by.
"Hey Vince."
"Hey, to you."

"You look upset. What's up?"

"Nothin'." Ah, fuck, he thought. "It's Mary. She thinks somebody's stalking her. I think it's her raging hormones."

"Mary's always seemed pretty level headed to me." Law turned to watch as the new girl slinked by. His eyes swiveled between her and Vinny. Law had known Vinny a long time. "Distracting, isn't it?"

"What is?"

"The blonde rump-roast." Law peered over the top of the bifocals he now wore almost all the time at the office. He knew that he was being a pig saying such a thing, but he'd seen the way she was going after Vinny. That put her in a separate category, it didn't deserve much respect. "Don't pretend you haven't noticed." He gave a sigh. "Why don't you tell me what Mary said?"

"Well, she's sure this guy who parks on the street an' sits in his car is following her." His tone made it sound like it was the stupidest thing he'd ever heard.

"She say what kind of car?"

"Yeah. Black."

"I mean, what make?"

"Yeah, well, she can't *tell* what make."

"Where have I heard that before?"

Vinny, starting to zip his jacket, stopped. "Where?"

"The dinner party. Kandle and Elsie. The person who gave Kandle a ride maybe ten days ago?" Vince had a blank look on his face, so Law went on. "Hello-*ow*? The man she thought was going to rape her, or worse. The night you gave her a ride."

As if to himself Vince said, "They didn't know the make of car. It was black and it was small. Even Elsie didn't know the make. What did she say the other night? It's almost as if the car is trying to disguise itself. Was that it? Mary says it's a small car." He looked at Law. "I'm heading home. I'll check it out and call in."

"Yeah. And Vinny."

"What?" Impatient now, in a hurry to get on the go.

"Next time old spaniel eyes bats them at *you*," Law nodded toward the blonde. "Lift *your* eyes from her bazooms and notice how beady her eyes are. What you already got has it all over that one." He took off his glasses and rubbed his sore eyes. "Want me to come with, just in case?"

"Na', I don't think so. This guy hasn't done nothin' but sit. Maybe he likes to beat-off outside in the dark. It's a quiet street. And the streets are filled with small dark cars." As the door closed behind him he heard Law's voice.

"Let me know." Law looked over at the new female. He was counting on the power of suggestion. Her eyes were not in the slightest beady.

"Don't let the door hit you in the ass on your way out, sweetie." The door to Maggert's office slammed in his sour face. He felt the blast of wet, freezing snow hit him for just a second, or two. It felt good, 'cause he had the sweats. To the Lake Street hookers Maggert was *candy-man.* They got riled when he ran out. Like this bitch who just left. No BJ from her. Sofuckin'what? He had more important things on the agenda. Fuckin' Boodles, had an unlisted phone. Fuckin' Harry was out of town for three more days. Harry'd know how to get in touch with that Boodle-bastard. Maggert had to make a connection and make it soon.

He'd hit the shit too hard himself, not stepped on it enough in the first place. But his intentions had been good. Step-on-it too hard right away and he'd have no business to lose. Got to get these turds nailed good, before you start cuffin' them off. His plan had been to make some money with this drug deal. First give it to them near to un-cut. Then cut it, step-on-it, a couple grams. By this time, they're hooked. Now each time you can mix in more cut. They make a buy, snort it, an' bingo-bango, back for more. If they don't have the do-rae-me to pay, first they sell their stuff, then they steal, next, you get their house, or car, or, whatever the fuck they got.

They got—*you got.*

That was the plan, but he'd been stuffing all the profits up his nose. Had to slow down.

What was that?

His desk chair had rollers that were flat, it squealed like a mouse when he moved. The sound mixed with the nights strong winds made him flinch. He hated mice. Was someone tapping on his door? He went to the window to look. Sure 'nough. There is a God, he thought. He opened the door.

"Randolph! Mighty good to see ya'." He stepped back as the man nearly floated into the room. He glides, thought the Dog, like one a' them darkie entertainers.

"Yes, Maddog. I am quite certain you are happy to see me."

"Whaddaya' mean by that, heh, heh?"

"I mean, you're out of product and needing more. Am I not correct? If not, say so, and I won't waste time for either of us."

Jesus H. Christ. Could he be moving back towards the door? "Hey, sure as shit momma. You got it right, you know I need more, ah, Randolph, ah, sir." Maggert was ready to put his hand on Randolph's arm, but pulled it back just in time. That would surely have been a mistake. "Sit down. Let me get cha' a beer."

Randolph shook his head, sadly. "Beer? Do I look as if I drink beer?"

"Well, ah..." the Dog stammered, "ah, oh no, no, my mistake. What can I get cha'?"

"I seriously doubt you would have what I choose to drink. I'll take a shot of that Jack Daniels I see by the sink." Randolph paused, "Unless of course, you've poured something inferior in the bottle."

"Naw. It's the real McCoy." Maggert quickly poured, with his back to Randolph, so he would not see his shaking hands. Then, set the jelly glass on the desk in front of the man.

Not till Randolph reached for his drink, saying, "I hope this glass is clean; it has been a long, hard day," did Maggert really check him over.

Randolph was wearing an off white linen suit. White linen, for crissakes, in the dead of winter. It was those hands that gave this car-peddler the creeps. They were as white as the suit, sporting an ostentatious ruby ring, but, the fingers were puffy, and like squid, they seemed to have no bones. Soft, puffy, squid-like. Man-o-man. They reminded Maggert of something. He couldn't quite remember what.

Randolph removed his glasses. His eyes were 20/20, but it amused him to wear them as a little disguise on occasion. "Get the money. Lets get this over with. I don't have all night."

It was while he was standing on his desk, reaching for the cash box in the ceiling, that Maggert remembered what those fingers reminded him of. His old roommate had owned a small monkey. The smelly thing was constantly pissing on his shoulder. Its fingers were real soft and kind of spongy. He chuckled as he stepped to his chair, then back to the floor.

De-boned monkey fingers.

"What's so funny, Dog?" The voice was cold. This was not a man who could take a joke about his fingers, or, anything else.

"Nothin' much. Just thinkin' how surprised the crew would be if they knew all the dough that was up here." His face was purple and dripping with sweat. Once he prided himself in the condition of his body. Now, the slightest exertion made him wheeze. His quivering hands began to light the butt he'd retrieved from the floor and stuck between his cracked lips.

"I don't appreciate inhaling your second hand smoke, Dog."

Maggert noticed that Randolph shortened the Maddog nickname every chance he got. "Oh, yeah. Sorry. You're the boss." Boss. Right. He took in the way the other man's eyes sparkled when he called him boss. Sure enough, he could play that game. Right now he'd tell him he was the pope if it got him his drugs. Being called Dog did not bother him, still, Maggert thought, old squid-fingers would get his. That gleam would not stay in his eyes forever.

The money and cocaine were exchanged. This time Randolph set out 150 vials of crack and a full kilo of methamphetamine.

The Dog made a fast dive—snorting a big line of coke. He didn't give a holy-fuck what the 'boss' thought. His brain was already percolating; he spied the large baggie, "Holy shit!" He had a special fondness for meth.

The white puffy fingers were caressing the 2.2 pound baggie of meth. "I am certain you thought you were giving me some 'insider' information the last time we met. Well, on the contrary. I know my business, and I know yours. So, you seemed to think you could handle this, lets see how much product you can move." The wiggly fingers pinched at the crease on his linen trousers. "And Dog, don't fuck this up. Keep *your* nose clean."

Before Maggert could answer, the man was up and he was gone. His laughter, as he walked to his car, was garbled with the wind. It seemed to cling to the walls inside the used car shack for a long time after he'd driven away. Maggert shook off the feeling that wrenched at his gut; he had work to do. All this, he surveyed the drugs, had to be divided and packaged—ASAP.

It was hours before it occurred to him that there had been no free lunch this time. No freebie eight-ball for his own personal use. The sound of his ringing phone, just as he was about to take a piss, was harsh, interrupting his flow of urine and his thoughts. Maybe some late night business, he thought, as he zipped up, dripping tracks down the front of his filthy trousers.

"Yeah?"

"Dog?" The word cracked—a cell-phone on a windy night.

"Oh, it's you, ah, sir."

"Yes, Dog. Me. I was thinking you looked like you could use some cheer. Perhaps we should seriously think of getting a couple of dollies and having some fun." A pregnant pause. "It could get rough."

"Well, sure, I mean, if you think you can find the disposable-slits. You got access to some young puss?"

"Does a fat baby have gas?"

"Hey, count me in. In my mind, it's the only thing women are good for. After you fuck em, then's the time to really fuck em. Yeah, buddy. See ya." He hung up the phone laughing. He knew it wouldn't be long before that pervert took a liking to him, but this was quicker than even he'd expected.

Randolph's face was manic as he clicked off his cell-phone and drove into his garage; his black beast purred until he reluctantly flipped off its ignition. He noticed a slight tremor to his hand—straight twenty-two hours. He smirked. He could do it forever if he wanted to, he simply did not want to.

For the past two days he'd done little but sleep. Even the energy it took to make that phone call to the Dog drained him. Why was he so damn tired? No doubt it was the effort it took to put up with his dreary family.

Time for a small reward.

While one hand had been occupied with the ignition, and his mind tuned into how he could do any damn thing he wanted, the other hand opened the clasp on his briefcase. Ruled like a robot, he tied the piece of rubber around his upper arm and slapped the pulsing vein. With a sharp intake of breath he sucked in his gut as he readied himself for the sting of the needle. He enjoyed seeing the fluid empty and enter his vein. He stared, dazed, at the syringe. Crystal-meth—it was his drug of choice.

Life was filled with choices, hence, the name of his business.

Right now, he chose to murder his wife.

How long must he wait before the timing would be right?

Chapter Ten

In regard to man...what one must accept is the fact that the minds of other men are not in one's power, as one's own mind is not in theirs; one must accept their right to make their own choices, and one must agree or disagree, accept or reject, join or oppose them, as one's mind dictates...To deal with men by force is as impractical as to deal with nature by persuasion." -Philosophy: Who Needs It
                                                                Ayn Rand

"I do not understand why you won't see a doctor." Darwin was angry. "It's selfish, and that's not like you." He brushed his hand over Tony's ivory cheek. "I wouldn't know what to do if anything happened to you, Spike."

"Get off me about it. Listen. I have something important to talk about. We're not doing as well as we should at Silano's. I mean, do you ever look at the books, Dar?"

"Why are you so interested all of a sudden? You've always left finances to me."

Tony finished buttoning his new mustard, lambskin shirt. They were getting ready for Mary's baby shower. "First of all, you haven't hired a replacement for Bobbie. I know it's difficult to deal with, but the others in the office cannot continue to pick up the slack, they grumble constantly. Bobbie did more work than you imagine."

"I know." Darwin's voice was strained, as though he might cry at this mention of his murdered office manager and friend.

"And, we have to deal with whatever is going on with Sam. You haven't done diddly about that issue."

Darwin's eyes snapped wide. "What would you have me do, *fire* him?" Was this Tony his talking? "Spike, Sam is at least half the reason I haven't replaced Bobbie. I'm afraid of what he might do. Look at him. He's a mess."

"Right. And is it going to change by ignoring it?" Tony brushed through his curls pleased with how the exquisite mustard shirt looked with his dark hair. "Well, anyway Dar, I've an idea."

Ah. I thought so. Here comes the pitch, thought Darwin.

"I figured that if you spoke to Elsie, and explained how desperate we are at the dealership, perhaps you could persuade her to take Bobbie's place."

"Don't you mean guilt her?"

Tony put on his best smile, his black eyes little beams of hope, and ignored Darwin's remark. "Don't you see, Dar? It's the perfect solution. Els is smart. She'll learn fast. Plus, not only can we trust her, she can help watch what Sam is doing. How could he object to having her to work with? He loves her."

Darwin grinned. "And, my beloved minx, Elsie would want to keep right on living here with us."

"Well, yes, there is *that*." Tony batted his lashes.

Darwin rose, pulling on a fleece pullover that Tony particularly liked. He'd once said the material was so meltingly soft he could barely keep his hands off it. And that the contrast made Darwin look "even more rugged." It would send Spike just the signal he wanted—that he was in the mood tonight. "I think you're a genius." Leaning, he kissed Tony's lips. "I've been worried about both of these problems for way too long. I should have mentioned them to you; here you've gone and solved them with one swoop."

Tony bounced to his feet. "Let's hope it works. Will you talk to Els today? Maybe at the shower? Hmm?" Tony's hands were already stroking the shirt Darwin had just put on.

The cemetery was not that far from the river. Kandle traipsed after Sam thinking to herself that this was too close for her comfort to the junkyard where she'd nearly been attacked. *He doesn't realize,* she thought, *or he wouldn't have asked me to come.*

"Hey Wick," He'd taken to calling her that, said it was short for Kandle. "Isn't that," he pointed north-west, "where you got away from that creep?"

So much for his sensitivity, she thought. "Umhm." The carrot-orange sun was beginning to set, and they were in the perfect spot to appreciate it. Maybe he'd notice that she wasn't talking much and pay some attention to her, instead of behaving as if they were on a junior-high field trip.

"You know, now that we're here, I can't wait for you to meet Bobbie."

They walked in silence.

"Guess that sounds kind a' wacky, huh?"

"Kind a'." Her voice was small, childlike.

"Is somethin' wrong?" Sam stopped. "Wick. Come 'ere." He tugged her arm.

She tried to keep going, but he held her. "I'm fine."

"Oh. Good. You had me worried." He kissed the top of her head, and, like men are prone to do, took her at her word and continued on the path. "We're almost there."

"Why did you decide to call me Wick?" Like many women, now that she'd said she was fine, he was about to discover that she was far from it.

He turned and took her hand. "Well, let me see if I can explain it to you. A wick is part of a candle, right? It's at the center, and usually it's soft...alone, too. But when you light it, it makes everything that surrounds it glow, and all that hard wax, melts." He kissed her, a long kiss, until he could feel her body grow limp and yielding in his strong arms. "See? Like that."

"Oh."

"C'mon, Wick. The sun's almost down, and I want you two to, well, meet before it's too dark to see; besides we've got to get back in time for Mary's baby-shower."

With the sun sparkling off the tombstones and optics of snow Kandle had felt peace literally emanate from many of the inhabitants souls. Now that it was suddenly twilight the cemetery took on a somber gray aura. One thing about snow, it left distinct footprints from any visitors. Since it had snowed last evening all the footprints were relatively fresh. Kandle looked over her shoulder often as they walked. Wind blew at the snow making drifts and shadows that moved. At least, she hoped it was the snow and the wind that moved the shadows.

"This place is scary. Hold my hand. Sam?"

If Sam heard her he didn't acknowledge the fact. He fell to his knees and her heart went blip. Then she saw that he was beside a beautiful monument. Roberta. Of course, Bobbie's name was Roberta. There were bouquets of flowers in various states of decay surrounding the grave. So he came here often. *He was talking outloud, but not to her.* He said how desperately he missed her, how he loved her. Kandle felt like a voyeur. Then, Sam motioned to her; she knelt beside him.

"Bobbie, this is the woman I been tellin' you about, Kandle."

What should she do? Say hello? She chose to wait until her role here was clarified.

Sam talked about how close he felt to Kandle, how he was growing to love her, in fact, thought that he was in love with her.

Kandle did not know how to feel about him telling this dead woman more than he'd told *her* about his feelings for her. She was thinking about whether she should get up or wait this out when

Kandle felt something unexplainable. It was as if a loving presence had placed its arms around her, hugged her, kissed her cheek. Startled, Kandle's hand rubbed her cheek. *Wet.* Probably from the snow, she reasoned.

Sam was still talking. "Watch over us Bobbette. I'm glad you approve—I know it's fast, but she's so much like you. Keep her safe for me. Keep us—" The wind had picked up and his words were cut off. He'd closed his eyes for a few seconds of private goodbye, but Kandle could barely see his face through the blowing snow.

Sam stood and held out his hand to pull Kandle to her feet and yelled over the wind. "She likes you, Wick." Sam's face resembled a man just out of jail; his face lit up, he leapt in the air, and with a whoop that echoed over those who lay dead, grabbed Kandle, and together they ran.

As soon as they were out of sight of Bobbie's stone he pushed her to the snow and fell on top of her, covering her damp face and head with kisses.

She saw tears in his eyes, and if she hadn't loved him until now, she instantly fell in love. "My crazy man, I will be your wick, your center."

Holding one another tight, they rolled, laughing, in the snow. Through their laughter, she heard what she thought was the crack of boots that were breaking through the top glaze of deep snow. The temperature had dropped with the setting sun. She pushed at Sam, "Let's go. I want to go."

"Okay Wick, Wickie, Wicker." With one arm he lifted her slight body, then, at the last second seemed to change his mind, and instead, shoved her into a snowdrift. "Race you to the car."

Giggling, blowing snow from her mouth, it took seconds for her to realize what he'd said, to see that he was gone. "No!" Her voice was already too far behind for him to hear the fear through the wind. "Don't leave me Sam, wait!"

She brushed snow off her face and tried to see. Where was the cemetery; which direction was the car? She'd lost her bearings and if there were landmarks she could not see them through the blowing snow.

This was a blizzard.

Chapter Eleven

Claudette, was weary. She'd spent the biggest portion of her day on the telephone. First off, she took a trip to the library to search through the old newspaper files. The Avenger-Woman was seldom named. But, diligence paid. She stared at the name. *Elsie Sanders.* How many people could there be with a name like Elsie? Sanders would be harder, more common. After fruitless hours on the phone, Claudette was ready to admit that Ms. Sanders did not have a phone in her name, at least not one that was listed. This search would have to branch out to include Elsie's family or friends. Fortunately, Claudette had thought to make copies of the pertinent news stories while at the library.

She looked at her watch. Fifteen minutes after four. She'd done nothing about getting dinner prepared. *Screw Randolph.* Just the simple act of reading about this woman gave Claudette a whole new attitude. Copies of news articles littered the area around her; she returned to her reading. Many nights lately Randolph had missed dinner altogether. Although she was expected to have it ready on time regardless, she often sat waiting for a man who never showed.

And those were the *good* nights.

She prayed that tonight would be one of the good nights, because if he found her like this, he would very likely kill her.

Hungrily she began to read another clipping.

It was worth the chance.

Kandle's brain went blank. Fear paralyzed her. She longed to be able to run, but she could not move. She listened. Was that the muted, pounding of Sam's footsteps, as he ran from her on his race to the car? But if it was him, exactly where…?
She tried hard to listen—held her breath so that she could hear without her own breathing disturbing the sound. Right then she heard the very soft and very slow crack*unch,* crack*unch,* crack*unch. Footsteps in the snow.* The sound was barely audible, yet it was growing louder. They were coming toward her.

Closer every second. Sam? Was it Sam?
No.
She knew that it was *him.*
A thought pushed through her growing hysteria. "The creep expects that you will lie here, brainless, waiting in terror." And she remembered Sam's words, "…the wick makes all the hard wax that surrounds it melt."

She was *strong.*
Each step that she heard was an explosion! She propelled herself to her hands and knees—then, to her feet, and finally hurled into a run. A run *for her life*. It was closer, almost touching her! She heard a thunderous rumble as it's feet beat hard into the snow, hard, wham, wham, *wham, wham*! Close behind her. Her arms flailing, feet sliding sideways, she stumbled, yet managed to remain upright. Her heart roared in her chest until she felt it would burst. She felt its body heat inches behind her, felt the whack, as it flung itself, its arms, its giant claws at her legs!

Then came—reality—the weight of the sweating, throbbing body on her back as she lay face down in the snow. Her scream was a muffled squeak because her mouth was filled with snow and the icy edge of steel burned at her throat.

"I thought they were serving us dinner in less than an hour and a half." Vinny sat on the edge of their bed putting on his socks. He'd just showered and his damp back glistened.

"I know exactly when we're eating, Vincent. I'm hungry now." Mary, still chewing, took another Oreo cookie from the half empty bag on her lap. "Are you worried I'll spoil my appetite?" She gulped down half a glass of milk.

"Hardly. That doesn't seem possible." *Why the hell had he said that*? He hung his head. Could he possibly be any more *the boob?*

Her answer was loud. "Are you saying I'm getting fat?" Mary twisted another cookie apart and began to lick the white center.

"Look Mare, all I'm sayin' is you're three months pregnant an' you should be taking better care of yourself. Instead, you're eating all the wrong foods, consequently—no energy. It's no big surprise, is it?" At the last of the sentence, his voice dropped. Vinny stood in front of the dresser mirror and brushed his wet hair back. His stomach was flat, not an ounce of fat on him. He didn't like the direction this conversation was going. He'd like to be anywhere but here.

"You know I hate to be called Mare. That's a *horse*, Vinny." She shoved the rest of the cookie in her mouth and kept talking. "And, the only reason you're so concerned about my energy, is because you keep wanting sex and I'm way too exhausted."

Vinny had pulled on a red turtleneck, and was tucking it into his faded jeans. The way she said sex made his gut buzz. "Mary, Mary, *quite contrary*." He bent to pick up his black cowboy boots giving her an excellent view of his backside—what she always called his best side. "Okay, Momma Mar-*ee*, you are trying to pick a fight with me, an' I ain't goin' for it, my lady-love." He blew her a kiss. "Eat the whole damn bag. See if I care." He zipped up his jacket. "I'm going to start the car, it's ten-below zero. You finish getting ready; I don't want you, or junior, to catch cold."

Mary watched his fine butt strut through the door. She sat, her bottom lip poked out, sulking. In her best imitation of Babe Ruth she heaved a cookie at the closed door. What did he mean *finish* getting ready? She *was* ready. She forced herself to lumber out of the chair, then made an honest effort to pick up the black and white crumbs by the door. Her back hurt when she bent over. He's right, she thought. He's looking so damn good, and I'm already getting a belly. And, I haven't lost all of the last one yet. Yet. Who am I kidding? It's too late now. One thing he was wrong about. *Sex.* Her lack of desire for him had nothing whatever to do with her level of energy. It was the stalker. Or, rather, Vinny's reaction when she tried to talk about him. Whenever Vinny came home, that damn car was gone. Until he saw it himself he wouldn't believe her. How could she feel loving towards a man who thought she'd make up a story like that just to get his attention?

There *was* someone following her, wasn't there?

Sam's chest was heaving from the run to the car. Man, was he out of shape, he thought. But, as he stood leaning on the hood, gasping, he knew that was a lie. He was in great shape, until he took that first line again. "Fuck this shit," he said loud and clear. Then to himself—I've had it, I'm done. He reached into his wallet and removed the white packet. Still half left. He'd brought it with, in case he had the chance for a snort. It was crushed and ready. Sam took one corner of the packet and gave it a shake. Fifty smackers worth of blow—his gift to the night—his message to the devil that haunted him. The blinding wind burned his earlobes. He could swear it spoke to him, thrilled with him, at this choice he was making. He listened to the chortle that came from somewhere deep inside him. The wind picked up. The moon, as if it were a strobe, flicked over pearls of snow.

Sam gave a real laugh, and spoke aloud, "I'm not going ta' follow no *white-center-line* down my highway a' life." His head shook. "Nah-ah."

That settled, his breath came easier, a great boulder had been lifted from his shoulders. *"Wick!"* he yelled. For the first time, he noticed she was not within his sight.

Chapter Twelve

Her bed was heaped with clothes. This was the fourth outfit Elsie had tried. The champagne denim skirt was short. People rarely saw her legs and never this much of them. Tony had picked it out. Not for tonight, just for any time. He said it was time for her to get out and about. Elsie was sure he didn't expect to see her wear it this soon—but then he didn't know about the way her heart banged when she saw Father Terrence—or how her knees wobbled, or how her brain stopped dead. The cotton sweater, of the same color, had a large floppy collar, and sleeves meant to be rolled. This way, she could show off her new copper bracelet. It had been years since she'd worn jewelry; she'd treated herself today. After the shopping, this afternoon, she had her hair cut and colored. Tony always fixed it, so this was going to be a surprise. She'd gone to a place Gee recommended in the Dinkydome, by the University—Hannaville Hair. Elsie glanced in the mirror; she was getting a slight stomach, but what the heck. Some men thought that was sexy. Or so she'd read. The shade of her hair matched the outfit. She liked the way she looked. Her heart fluttered.

Maybe it was something she ate.

But maybe not.

Kandle was pinned to the ground.

She quickly discovered that the more she struggled the deeper she sank into the snowdrift; a mound of glittering ice. She felt a forehead pushing at the back of her neck, while hands roughly pinched and pulled at her clothing.

"No, please...please. Don't do this," she tried to cried out until the ice filled her throat. Her strength of just moments earlier dissolved and she gave up and went limp into the iced coffin.

Her mind skipped back in time and she was gone, no longer cold.

The blade no longer burned.

As a young girl, she had watched the roofers seal the new eaves on their house.

"You'd had trouble. Ya' had some squirrels nestin' in your roof." She had overheard them tell her Momma. "But, Ah'm sure we got 'em all out, ma'm."

She remembered that it had been the noise that night that had driven her outside. She was concerned about the squirrels. The rodent-family had a pitch-black baby that Kandle had trained to eat out of her hand. There had been a crackling-storm that fall night, and her parents would have wanted her to stay safe and dry in her bed. Still, she snuck out and sat on her haunches, under her favorite tree, icy water pelting her body.

Like the water that froze her face right now?
What? What water?

The squirrels were after the little black one trapped inside the new eaves. Rat-a-tat, rat-a-tat, rat-a-tat, scratch, gnaw, spatter, clack, splutter. They tore at the eaves as if it were flesh. They had to get at what was inside.

Was something tearing at her flesh, now?

Chapter Thirteen

THE DOG & THE SHEEP
A Dog sued a Sheep for a debt he claimed the Sheep owed him, and he called on a Kite and a Wolf to be the judges. Without asking any questions, they both decided right away that the Sheep was wrong and the Dog was right. Then the three of them tore the Sheep apart and ate him before he had been given a chance to say a word.
THE POINT: It's sad, but it's true, that honesty and right sometimes haven't a chance against cruel force.
          - AESOP'S FABLES

The fucking miserable cock-sucking nigger-loving bitch had tricked him!

At the last minute he'd remembered to pull on his black face mask. It felt like a pink neon sign flashing, "*See me do dirty-deeds, dirty-deeds, dirty-deeds.*" He told himself that although he would normally not be caught dead wearing this knit face protector, it was more common than not to see others wear the ugly things in this bitter cold. He would blend in. Something he wanted to do more often. Blend.

Watching from a safe distance, he'd thought the couple had quarreled! The black one *hit* her, then ran and left her. What luck to find her alone—much less lying in the snow! The whore. One minute Miss-Sugar-Sweet, the next, she's clinging to this *darkie*. It occurred to him then, as he got a closer look, that it was the same man from the house. What was that house? A fucking comm*une*? Faggots, whores, and a token *nigger*.

He was caught up in the smell of her—so fresh. His spurt would come faster than he desired; the blade was at her throat, ready to plunge deep as he came—that was his plan.

He was going to come. Soon. He was climbing—he was nearly there. *No chance that he could fail to 'perform' for this bitch.* He instantly felt himself shrink. Why think of that—failure to perform—why think of it *now?* He'd have to slice her, just a little, to get his hard-on back. His grip tightened around the knife's small handle.

The squirrels were gone—she was back in her snowdrift.
Kandle felt icy air on her ass.
Was that then, or now?
The clouds obscured the stars and moon, making the night black as the devil's heart. Tiny screechy noises turned, raucous, persistent, throbbing.
Throbbing?
Her body felt itself tear open. A small crevice made larger.
A guttural-scream.
Oh, my-god.

"Wick, Wickie!" A screaming desperate voice with matching feet was clearly pounding down the trail toward them. *Wick?* It couldn't be the wrong woman he was fucking. *Could it?*

Randolph stumbled, yanking himself together, glad the black mask that was so uncool covered his head and face— He got his balance and he ran his guts out thinking about how she laid there —there'd been no fight out of that one, not what he'd expected.

Had she hit her head? Was she—dead? No, couldn't be. She'd live to show him a far better time. But what about the name. Wick?

Light, she felt light as that floating cloud after all of the water had drained itself. The pressure of that iron weight was gone. Her clothes were being tenderly, carefully, pulled around her. Snow and frozen tears were brushed from her face. Strong arms lifted her and a strong voice murmured, "Wick, you hear me baby? Wick? Give a nod if you know it's me, know it's Sam."

Sam. Her soul said his name. With great effort she moved her head up and down to nod.

The squirrels got their little one out that roaring night. It was her step-Daddy who was left screamin'; he was mad 'cause the roofers had split town, so he had to do the patching on the eaves.
"I paid them good money," Daddy'd said.

"Sambo," she said aloud.

He'd *had* to run, he thought, as he got into his waiting car. No man fights his best with his pants around his ankles and his dick fox-trotting in the wind. Her white-hot ass had been so ready for him, wet even. Randolph almost cried to have to leave it. Once she'd settled down, accepted the inevitable, he could feel that she wanted him.
Nothing was going down the way it should.
It was difficult to think. His hard prick needed relief. But it was because of *them*. The women, mostly, but not *only* women—it was not an exclusive club—this group of people who hated him and were hated *by* him. He felt like a child. It was preposterous. A professional man like himself. Made to feel this way. Even in his confusion it was clear that he hated them all: his wife, the bitch;

this new one, this Kandle; her buddy, the Avenger-Bitch; the queers, and now, this nigger. And let's not forget that fucking cop. He wanted to hurt them all... wanted to hurt them in a way that would make them remember him forever. *Or, as long as they lived*; he gave them all the contempt he possessed.

There was time. He was beginning to loosen up. He did not wish to be parked outside the house when they came for the baby-shower anyway. So this was a fortuitous change in the agenda.

The night was young.

Young.

Young was Lola. He drove south, in the direction of Dundas, and Choices. Didn't he tell his students that life was all about choices?

He was about to make his choice.

Chapter Fourteen

Lola had been expecting him for days; by now he knew it.

Oh, he'd felt her up a few times, enough to know she wanted more. She was a clone of the others before her, that meant he had all the time in the world to set things up nicely. Seldom was the time that his patience was not rewarded.

On a daily basis Lola paraded that lush body for his pleasure, purposely dropping things, then bending, sans underwear, for their retrieval. Randolph was in a perpetual state of arousal. Was she playing a game of her own with him, he wondered? Even when he'd stopped doing drugs for that short time span—had no interest in sex—Lola could easily force him to excuse himself, mid-day, for a visit to the restroom to polish himself off. The look on her face, when he returned to the class, made him feel like her puppet. He felt twisted. He did not appreciate the feeling. She walked by him one afternoon humming, he could not place the tune until later that evening. *Whatever Lola wants, Lola gets, and little man, little Lola wants you.* The words to the tune curdled his dinner and scorched his testes.

Whatever Lola wants, Lola gets? We'll see about that.

And soon she won't think of him as a 'little' man, will she now?

He used his master key to enter Lola's room. The dim light from the open shade, and the bright angel nightlight by the bed, presented to him—Lola's bare-ass. It pointed up, an opening flower, in bloom just for him.

He pulled the shade as he reached into his pocket and took out the rubber that was marked with thick black letters, LOLA. He had a cigar box filled with these souvenirs. He liked to smell and suck on them later. Sometimes he would use one of them on his wife when he fucked her. Claudette's whine was a constant, *"are you using a condom?"* Did she somehow suspect his infidelities? He couldn't wait to tell that bitch about the variety of marinating cunt juices, tell her she was getting the leftover 'rain suits'. Save that until he was ready to end her.

But Lola. This one would be different. He had made up his mind. He wanted to show her all the things she'd never known. Together they would discover uncharted territories. She would learn to lean on him, look up to him, her mind would belong to him, he would be come her master, her teacher, her mentor. His mind rambled on and on over this, *"how it will be once she knows the truth of his power."*

Lola was about to discover the truth of lies, too.

At this point, right now, she could live a short while, adoring him, eulogizing his prowess, or live one glorious night with him, he had not yet decided what was to be her 'time of death'.

The knife was still with him—his other hand caressed the bone handle—he dared not touch the sharp blade. He felt immediately engorged—a leftover from the feast he had just been forced to push himself away from—and rolled the LOLA rubber easily up his stiff shaft.

He felt no need to rush, to worry she would cry and be heard. This was *his* place. *His* school. He did what he wanted and took no prisoners—nor advice—nor crap from the peanut gallery.

That wondrous ass moved, circled, rotated, taunting, beckoning, it told him clearly that Lola was awake and ready for what he had to give.

Lola was quite willing. Too willing. That irritated him, and he felt his member shrink as he made his approach. One rub on the bone handle and he sprang forth, returning to his previous state.

The budding ass loomed closer, filling his field of vision. He sucked in his saliva just as it began to leak out his lips. With all the force that he could muster his swollen weapon stabbed Lola's gyrating ass with enough impact, he thought, to rupture, rip, and mutilate, what he believed would be, a tiny orifice. In a matter of two short seconds he spurt inside the roomy hole and his 'weapon' turned to the size of a small wriggling worm.

There had been no need to gag Lola; that puzzled him. The girls' soft laughter grated in his ears. This slut thought she ruled.

Her chance for more than one evening of paradise was slipping fast.

Going, going, *gone*. Sorry Lola—but you're a slut—and I think you did your best to trick me.

He pulled his blade and in a putrid rage that made him hard once again, plunged the knife into Lola—maniacal frothing Demon took control—he knew not where he stabbed, or what he violated. His left hand had, at last, to cover her mouth. Minutes passed and the laughter that had turned to muffled shrieks, abated. They were joined like real lovers in hot, liquid bodily fluids, that were at first slippery, then turned to clotting, caking blood. He caught his breath, his hands roamed her hard body, thinner than he remembered—they slid making a slurping noise that startled him.

Randolph flipped her over—one last look at the face that could no longer laugh back.

He felt himself snap—the blood rushed to his head. He felt hot, faint, his head would explode!

How? How could this be?
The motherfuckingbitch had a dick! She had a dick!
A penis!

It took every ounce of self-control to keep from screaming out. Falling on the body for the coup de grâce, he set to annihilate every bit of what Lola had been. In his frenzy, he burst inside the still worn rubber—his longest, hardest orgasm yet. Disgust painted him, yet he told himself that his excitement had nothing whatever to do with the surprise that had hung on the front of Lola's body. The prize inside the *Cracker-Jack* box. Numb, his soul absent, he squeezed the severed cock in his hand and tossed it to the bloodybed. Emotions swirling, his laugh was shrill; this was one limpdick that was smaller than he. His morph-like face gave a sneer. It was not the dick that gave him a boner, it was the fact that he had the power to obliterate this aberration of life that made him rise and shoot again.

Yes. That was it. He was certain of it.

Carefully he saved the LOLA rubber, then began the arduous task of wrapping the body, cleaning the room and lastly stepping into the shower himself. He felt lighter than air—as if he could fly. How could they begin to catch a man who could fly without a plane, without wings? Why had he waited so long for this moment?

Only woman could give birth to a life. So true. A dab of frozen sperm and the man was not even needed to be the 'injector'.

But, taking a life, the real, the *actionized* event—in that regard, *man was God.*

Lola would never laugh again.

Randolph was just beginning.

Chapter Fifteen

"A feeling, for which I have no name, has taken possession of my soul—a sensation which will admit of no analysis, to which the lessons of by-gone times are inadequate, and for which I fear futurity itself will offer me no key. To a mind constituted like my own, the latter consideration is an evil. I shall never—I know that I shall never—be satisfied with regard to the nature of my conceptions. Yet it is not wonderful that these conceptions are indefinite, since they have their origin in sources so utterly novel. A new sense—a new entity is added to my soul."
    -MS. FOUND IN A BOTTLE   EDGAR ALLAN POE

Elsie felt foolish with her bare legs exposed. After all, it had developed into a serious evening. Tony whistled when he saw her; that was when she knew that she was exposing more than her legs.

Kandle was released from the ER with few outward bruises. She appeared stunned, but only slightly, as if she'd been thrown from a horse days ago and survived without any broken bones. This woman's life would never again be the same, thought Elsie. Where in the book-of-life did it account for that aspect of her calamitous attack?

What could they say?

They only knew that they wanted to be with Kandle; wanted to be with her to help her through this. And Sam, oh God, Sam, too.

They would give her time; take it slow. As close as they were to one another there would be a nurturing talk later in the evening. Right now, they sensed she needed a diversion for her mind. A little mindless chatter can go a long way if it comes from friends.

Pip too, sensed that his family was upset. He ran from one to the other for some kind of assurance that all was well, managing to get a few pats on the head. Even Bobbette was strangely subdued. She sat aloof on the mantle, her eyes slits—open enough to see, but not enough to be obvious; a soothing hum, barely audible, came from inside her furry body. It became evident that she would give the worried dog no help with crowd control; Pip took his cue from her and lay under Elsie's chair. His usually perky ears drooped down on the rug, his doggie chin rested on one paw. Unlike the cat, there was no subtlety about the way he watched them, his moist eyes were open wide, searching their faces, one to the next, for the first sign of a real smile.

The group made an attempt at dinner—not because of hunger, but because Darwin and Tony had gone to such efforts to please them.

This evenings fare was more casual than their last time together, yet it was food that took a great deal of preparation. This was one of the ways the couple demonstrated their love for these guests. The main course was a Turkey-breast Chili that was unbelievably succulent. It contained the usual ingredients, as you might guess, plus additions such as beer, grated chocolate with sour cream and diced avocados. It was served with a sausage stuffed French Bread loaf. The tantalizing foods' aromas mixed with the smell of pine throughout the house; this was every bit as glorious as the scent of the first apple blossoms in the spring.

A Spinach salad was garnished with Pumpernickel Croutons—Tones favorite, he made them himself.

An elegant Pumpkin-Ginger Mousse sat virtually untouched. They knew they were not doing any of it justice. Darwin saved them from their shameful picking. "Why don't I slide this in the fridge until later." He took the delicate concoction, laced with orange liqueur and heavy whipped cream, away. They hoped that the heart to eat it would return later in the evening.

Feeling closer than family, they moved to the living room carrying diminutive glasses of Chartreuse. The green herbal liqueur was potent.

"Perhaps you know that the makers of Chartreuse call it the formula for an *Elixir to Long Life*," Elsie reminded them as they got situated. "I suggest that's what we toast to." All glasses touched in a toast to the elixir and it was decided that it would be the drink—the theme—of the evening. Their toast made Elsie think of another Toast.

Father Terrence had been a no-show.

Sam and Kandle sat on a dusky-green velvet loveseat, off to one side of the wondrous Christmas tree. He lifted her feet to stretch them out on the sofa; it wasn't long before the warming effects of the Chartreuse, coupled with her loving friends surrounding her, did the job. Kandle's head leaned to rest on Sam's shoulder; her pallid cheeks turned pink. Hundreds of multi-colored miniature tree lights were like clear glass marbles, their colors flaming under a star-studded sky. The colors became such a light show that you could barely stand to look away. The rest of the room was aglow with gleaming red pillar candles. You couldn't help but feel like a child in the blush of this room.

"I've decided on a name for Kandle." Sam stroked her hair, then, kissed the top of her head. He wasn't asking their opinion; he'd decided.

They pulled chairs close-by, or sat on the floor around the loveseat. Tony, somewhat of a puppy himself, got as close as he could, his arm rested on the short sofa lightly brushing against Kandle's foot; not so close that she pulled back, but close enough for her to feel the warmth of his body. "Tell us!" he asked, eager for good news.

"Yeah. That's why I brought it up. To tell you." But he looked shy suddenly, then grinned. "Wick. That's her name. 'Cause that's what she is to me."

Bobbette's hum was so loud all heads turned to her. Was that a cat-smile?

Other than the purr, the room was quiet for a second or two while they considered the name. "Because she is your center." Gee's lilting voice closed in to hug them.

"Somethin' like that. Yeah." Sam and Kandle's eyes met, for those were the exact words Kandle had used earlier. "I, ah, I feel as if that wick, when it's lit, well, it will light my life, melt through all the hard stuff, you know, the shell around me."

Elsie was bent under the tree with a watering can. Sam's words gave her goose-bumps and she felt choked as if she might cry. She heard a soft sob and noticed that Mary was boohooing with no effort to disguise it.

"Sam, that's beautiful." Mary blew her nose. "I'm emotional, I know, hormones and all, but that's it Kandle, forevermore you'll be Wick to us all, right guys?"

There were murmurs of assent.

Vinny gave Law the eye when Mary said the word hormones, as if to say, "What'd I tell you?" But, he hugged her to him. This was, after all, the woman he loved; he needed to do something to show her how he felt. Listening to Sam's elegant words made him feel verbally impotent.

Sam's words had an affect on everyone in the room, drew them closer together. They hovered over their new friend, newly named Wick, and told her their feelings for her—told her how badly they felt about what had happened—told her they would take care of her, watch out for her.

"I love it...Wickie, love it...." Tony patted Kandle's feet. Pip wriggled over while they were talking and now put his paws by Kandle's hand and after waiting a short but respectful time, began to lick her hand.

Darwin and Tony kissed so long that Law kicked Tony's butt. He was not always comfortable with their obvious displays of affection.

As often was the case, it was Law who broke the spell. "Was it the man in the dark car?" He had to know. The police had tried talking to her earlier but she was remote, adrift in her private hell.

"Law, please." Gee stroked his arm and entwined her fingers with his. "Give her some time."

Kandle interrupted. "I don't mind. Really, Gee. I know why he's asking, and it's not, well, it isn't for any titillation purposes. He wants to help." She sat straighter and sipped some of the lovely green liquid. "I can't say for certain, Law. I don't know what he looked like."

"He wore a black or navy ski-mask," said Sam.

"I can't even say for sure what that man in the car looked like. He wore a hat and had the collar pulled up on his jacket as if he were cold. Well, it *was* cold. Although the car was warm. Come to think of it, the jacket was odd—like for summer." Silent tears appeared on her face making it glisten in the marble colored lights. "But tonight, I can't remember what he said, or if he talked at all."

Gee felt her gut swirl with memories of her own kidnapping—not all that long ago—the horror revisited her often. "You'll remember Wick. Give it time." Gee worried as she said the words. She hoped this tenderhearted woman would not be alone when the memories flashed back to her, as they surely would. "We can talk sometime Wick. It would be good for me too."

"I hope you don't mind, but Elsie told me something about what happened to you, Gee. You're right," she took Gee's hand, "I want us to talk, soon."

Gee seemed to shy away from talk of her abduction. "I have a therapist that is wonderful. You might want to see her. Her name is Diane. I'll get you the number."

Law frowned. "A therapist? You didn't tell me you saw a shrink, Gee." He thought she told him everything. But then he hadn't even told her that he had a brother.

Elsie's knees trembled, still close to the tree, she fell back on the floor in a state of collapse. She looked around her. Luckily no one had noticed; they were all deep in conversation. She knew this feeling well. Confusion preceded the fury. Moments earlier she'd been concerned about where the priest, Toast, was. Twit-like, she'd wondered if she was dressed in a way that he might find pleasing.

Now, Toast was already a memory. It always began the same; she was involved in a case of life and death. She knew that it had to be the man from the junkyard that attacked Kandle—Wick, tonight. He had to be stopped; she would not lose another friend.

Gee's speaking invaded her thoughts.

"We need to make such changes in our world. Changes that begin inside our hearts and souls." She brushed Law's hand unconsciously, reassuring him as she talked. "We went to a late lunch today, a friend and I from the clinic. I didn't want to eat much because of our dinner tonight, so I ordered their salad-bar. We sat for less than a half-hour. I asked the waitress for our check, I was surprised to see that she brought two."

"Two?" Tony asked.

"Umhm. We lunch there often, it's so close to work. Well that's never happened before, but it was a new waitress."

"Wait persons hate to give separate checks." said Tony.

"Umhm," Gee nodded, "I wanted to pay for both lunches, so I got out my wallet and proceeded to add the checks together. I had an odd feeling because of what Tony just said. Then I noticed that she'd written her name—like they generally do on the back of the check? That little, thank-you, signed, Tami? Well, rather than write on the back of the check, she'd written her name right over where the register printed the time of day. It was nearly three o'clock. My check for the salad-bar said 11:32, my friends check had the correct time, 2:47."

"I don't get it. That makes no sense." Darwin frowned.

"It makes perfect sense if the waitress was using the same check for all of her salad-bar-only customers and pocketing the $6.95 each time."

"No!" Tony was horrified. "Are you sure there's no other explanation?"

Law gave Tony a look that asked if he was an idiot. "Did you pay her for the check, knowing she was going to steal the money?" Law was interested in the legalities.

Elsie listened intently to the story as she let Pip and Bobbette outside for their last nightly run around the yard. They wanted to play as soon as the animated conversation told them things were returning to normal.

"Yes. I wrote her a note, telling her that I knew what she was doing and hoped she would make the last time, the last time. From the looks of her she wasn't a drug addict, or a poor person, simply a young girl without values." Gee went and squeezed onto the sofa beside Kandle, putting her arms around her. "You know that I am not trying to compare this waitress's theft with the hideous thing that was done to you."

"Of course, I do, Gee." For a split second, as she felt Gee's arms around her, Kandle could feel the weight of him on her back again; she seemed to sink into the couch, her *self* disappearing. "He was a big man—heavy," she whispered. Then, "It's all part of what you talked about before. How we as a people are backsliding. I think of it as if we were falling, tumbling—a fall from grace, right Gee?"

"His footprints were around a size 12." Law seemed to be talking to himself, then turned his attention to Sam—interrupting Kandle and Gee. "Speaking of *falling*."

"Hey, ya' yippy old-hound dog." Sam grinned. "I'll have you know, that first of all, you were dead on. I was sniffin' my way back to hell. But. I say, *but*. That's done—it's over. I tossed my stash to the wind tonight. That's what I was up to while my baby Wick was being raped. If it wasn't for that poison, I'd a' been with her." He bent to kiss her damp cheek. "Forgive me baby. I had my head up my ass and I was too much into myself. I'll make it up to you, I promise."

"It wasn't your fault Sambo." Kandle kissed his cheek. "You thought we were racing to the car and we had just been tumbling in the snow, minutes before!" She frowned. "And if it weren't for that wind, you'd have heard me calling for you."

"What were you doing at the cemetery?" asked Elsie. She wanted to get the talk away from Sam blaming Sam.

"Tell them what happened while *we* were racing to the cemetery earlier." Tony tugged at Darwin's pants leg.

Darwin smiled, happy that some of their chatting made it seem that Kandle would be okay. "Well, Gee called saying Law was on the way to the crime scene." He noticed Kandle wince at his last words. "Sorry, Wickie." He reached to squeeze her hand. "We were driving pretty fast."

"We?" Tony teased.

"Okay. I was trying to break the speed of sound. An old fart honked his horn to get my attention as he took a right turn."

"So, I obliged by rolling down the passenger window to hear what he had to say. I thought we had a flat tire or something." Tony's cheeks were flushed.

"He yelled out, "I hope you two are going to the cemetery, 'cause that's where you're gonna end up".

They all laughed, happy to lighten the mood.

Gee said, "Perhaps he was a bit psychic."

"No psychic, Gee. Just a grump. I wanted to yell back that he'd be a cemetery-resident before we would—with that nasty attitude, but I was in too much of a rush and too worried about Wick, to get there to chat with him."

"Dar! What a brute you can be!" Tony was standing by now and with one hand on his slim hip, the other outstretched waved to Darwin to come to him. "I love a man with an attitude!"

Law covered his eyes with one hand. "Jeeze-louise."

Darwin had gone, in answer to the wave, to Tony's side. "Why don't we get that yummy dessert out Dar. I think we're ready to dive in. All that sugar will make even Law sweet."

Elsie stood. "Excuse me for a few minutes. I'm feeling cold; think I'll put on some jeans." She hollered as she left the room, "Anyone want a sweater?"

Chapter Sixteen

At the end of the block the car breathed in quiet excitement; its trunk held something so deliciously evil that the dark metal shape knew its own destiny was to be forever intermingled with this man—this weapon of the unclean. Randolph felt the 'presence' surround him as it merged *with* him. Inside it, he was safe; together, they were the perfect demoniacal couple. He had the heater turned full power. The night was black, wind snapped like a whip; he felt the car sway and bounce with it.

He sneezed. A tainted smell seemed to seep in through the heat ducts. Couldn't be. This was an expensive, well-made automobile. The smell took him back to that room; he felt himself become aroused. At the same time, he wanted to get rid of it, of Lola. That was his first order of business.

What had called to him to stop at the mansion on the way? He'd simply looked out his window and there it was. The car drove itself here. No. That couldn't have happened. Get a grip, he told himself. He looked at the house, imagined the people inside talking about him and what he'd done to Kandle. Was she in there with them? Or was she still in the hospital?

The door opened. The Avenger-Bitch. Her legs bare. Never seen those legs before. Now that he knew how much power he possessed he wanted to rush at her. This murderess was a symbol of innocence. His train of thought was interrupted by the fur-ball cat and long-eared mutt that ran out of the warm, safe house, to the yard.

She watched a moment as they chased one another in fun before closing the door on the frigid air.

And *he* watched as the animals zoomed across the yard. Randolph was out of energy—drained. But the hatred he felt for the occupants of this house pulsed its poison throughout his body. The black beast tensed around him. Was he losing his mind? Metal, cold dark metal, cannot tense. He heard the motor rev; his foot had not moved toward the gas-pedal.

"Ook*eeed*ooo*k*ee." he said aloud. Let's go where the beast takes us. Already he had conjured up a little treat...a little fun...a little dance they could do without any of their bodies touching his.

The dark shadow could barely be seen in the starless night as it moved slowly along the curb and stopped dead in front of the house.

Elsie rode the elevator with her arms wrapped around herself. The house was warm; why was she shivering? She left the lights off as she stepped into her room, knowing just where her jeans were. Pulling them on she thought about how much she'd wanted to see Toast. It was a dumb idea. Why should she want to be involved, even friends, with an alcoholic? Someone to remind her of her Daddy. She sat at her desk by the window and turned on the small lamp to find her other shoe. Her journal lay open. She had been writing poetry lately. It made her feelings seem more real.

> *The elephant is big.*
>   *Will it sit on me? Smash me? Kill me?*
>   *Or, will it lead, pushing obstacles aside*
> *for me*
> *as I follow close behind? timid and afraid at first,*
> *but later, chest-swelling, I realize my new friend has*

given me its power.
I lead the parade of the elephant and me.

Pip's bark was louder, more persistent than usual. He must be extra cold. Or, Bobbette was taunting him. Elsie flipped the journal shut and went to the elevator, hurrying now, to let the animals in and rejoin her friends.

Elsie could feel tension in the room as she re-entered the party. Mary's gifts were piled around her; she was waiting for Elsie to begin tearing them open. While waiting she was enjoying a second slice of the pumpkin dessert, "with extra whipped crème and extra sauce, please Tony."

"*Extra* crème and sauce? This is rich; it's a wonder anyone can finish one slice, how can you manage to wolf down two?"

The room was quiet. No one had ever heard Vinny speak to Mary with that tone. His body language was nasty too. He'd moved himself to the far side of his chair and watched her eat as if she were some alien being. What was going on between them lately?

Mary continued stuffing it in as fast as she could. "At least I know I'll get some pleasure this evening—some feeling of fulfillment." Her usually sweet voice was snappish.

"Yeah, well, it's the only pleasure you have time for lately." Her husband looked down, his voice quiet, but reeking with sarcasm; he knew they were making a scene.

"Hey, hey. You two cut that crap." Sam eyed Vince like he'd just as soon punch him. "Don't you know your missus is eatin' for two?"

Elsie noticed Bobbette sitting on Sam lap. Someone must have let Pip in too.

Law's face was deep red. Angry. "What the hell's wrong with you, man?" He felt protective over his old partner, Mary. Rather than hit Vince, he tried changing the subject. "Speaking of *crap*," his face was a stone but to give him credit he tried keeping his eyes off of Vinny. "Has anybody seen my baby-brother tonight? I thought he was coming to this shin-dig?" He felt Gee's hand on his back, trying to soothe. She kissed his neck. Thank God for his Georgia.

Gee had not said a word. If Vinny was so concerned about what the tiny Mary ate, what must he think of *her* extra pounds? She was getting ready to ask him, when Elsie ran to Sam.

"Look!" Her voice cracked, her eyes were wild. "What's on Bobbette's nails and paws?" She pointed to the smeared red area on his pants. Her head spun around the room. "Where's Pip?"

Tony answered. "He didn't come when I called. I guessed he was doodooing."

Law examined the cat's paws. "Looks a lot like blood. Wonder if they had a fight?" He answered his own question. "No. I can't see that happening." He held her suspiciously quiet body in one arm and flipped his cell-phone open in the other.

Elsie ran to the door and Law hurried after her and grabbed her with the other hand. "No! Not after all that's been happening. You sit."

He spoke into his phone. "This is Detective Gerald Lawrence. I want a car here, ASAP..."

While Law gave the address Vinny jumped to his feet and with gun drawn and a flashlight Darwin tossed him in his other hand, went carefully outside. "Pip, here boy, come here." He yelled from a crouched position in the yard. No answering bark, no noise but the stinging wind. "Pip!" Whatever was here seemed to be gone. He stood and with arms outstretched, pivoted through the yard—one lone, stiff with cold, marionette.

Vince was back inside before the squad arrived. "Does he ever leave the yard?" Vince asked her, knowing the answer.

Elsie shook her head and cried.

Pip was gone. Snatched. For whatever reason. Tracks in the snow told some of the story. By who? It looked as if that same person had attempted to take the cat too. She had resisted and clawed her escape.

Bobbette sat very still on Law's lap, something she'd not normally do. As if she knew. They were waiting to take the scrapings from under her claws—DNA.

"Gimme my cat." Sam's voice was quiet.

Law didn't answer Sam; neither he nor the cat moved. The hair on the back of Law's neck was stiff. Something was going on, something close to home.

The room was in chaos when Toast walked in. His face was red; it was obvious he'd been sleeping off a bender. He went to Elsie, not knowing why she was in tears. "I'm sorry I overslept. A car door woke me."

Law watched, agitated, as his brother put his arms around Elsie. "Car door?" he asked.

"Yes, Gerald. It appeared to be a tall man tossing a couple of packages in his trunk, right out front of the house. I couldn't see that well from the window upstairs, and he had the car lights turned off for some reason." Toast worried that he was the cause of Elsie's distress. He turned his attention back to her. "Are you okay? Can you tell me what's wrong?"

"He had a black car, right?" Elsie sobbed. "Small and maybe expensive?"

"Mom." Elizabeth came home from school early with a horrendous headache; Claudette figured that she was coming down with a virus—some new Asian strain that was going around and was supposed to be hellish. "Mom, what is going on? You haven't been yourself lately. All you do is sit and read these newspaper stories. And Mom... look at me Mom."

Claudette tore herself away from what she was reading. Her daughter stood in the doorway, in her rattiest bathrobe, hair over her eyes as if she were a sheep dog, dabbing at her red nose and whining. "What is it dear?" Claudette tried not to be impatient, but this time of day was all she had to herself. Why did Bethie have to get sick *now* of all times?

"Dinner, Mom. You haven't even started and you know what Dad will do if he comes home and it's not ready. Are you, like, losing it, or what?"

"Your Father hasn't been home on time all week."

"Why?"

Impatient now, "How should I know, dear? Perhaps you should ask him."

"Well, I'm hungry."

"So eat something dear. There's tuna salad in the fridge. Or maybe have a peanut-butter and jelly sandwich to tied you over. Let me worry about your Father."

The body stood glaring at her from the doorway. If Claudette had bothered to raise her eyes she'd have seen Randolph's hate reflected on her daughter's face, but she was intent on what she was reading.

"You know he takes it out on us kids when *you* fuck up. But do you care?" The whining voice was a wail. "No wonder he calls you a fucking bitch."

The boom of the slammed door brought Claudette out of her trance. She knew that she would never have the guts to kill the bastard herself. Maybe she'd found a way out. She looked at the closed door. Had her daughter said *fucking bitch*? She shook her head. No. Her mind must be replaying Randolph's words. She eyed the clock, leaned back in her chair and with a sigh went over her plan.

As Randolph himself would say, no guts, no glory.

Chapter Seventeen

*"God of the machine,
Peregrine machine,
Some still think is Satan..."*
            The Mixture Mechanic   Robert Frost

Fucking-bitch-pussy. It was a damn good thing he had no more bare skin exposed. The damage was limited; she'd made her own special road-map on his left hand. Fucking cunt-cat. It hurt *bad*, brought tears to his eyes.

    He felt heat from the trunk when he stuffed the squealing mutt on top of the body. He wondered, then remembered the sales pitch about how the trunk was airtight—probably keep the body from getting stiff and unmanageable too soon. He knew it was past time to dump the corpse. Still he sat, unreasonably attracted to this house. From time to time he could see movement through the copper tinted glass walls—not people, simply movement. With pleasure, he imagined how those very people were afraid of what he would do next.

    He was sitting like this, parked at the end of the street, when he saw the squad car arrive. As much as he'd wanted to leave the area, his body would not follow his brains instruction. He'd stared at the bloody tracks on his hand, saw the blood freeze, making little mounds. Humps. In his drug induced psychosis he attempted to think the situation through. Was it the meth that made him need to stay right on the anvil's edge of danger? Or, could it be, as he truly suspected, *his car?* The last, an idea hardly worthy of consideration, yet, he believed that was the correct answer.

Sitting, waiting...time passed, first, simulating a video in slow motion, then, flipped to forward fast. His mind flittered and fluttered, barely landing on one thing before twisting itself off to buzz on yet another. A bee. Yes, that's what he was.

Buzzzzz.

He named his car.

What else was there to do with the time? The name? *Eclipse.* The car was difficult to see, because it shut out all light and became not only dark, but invisible in the night. For short, he decided on *Lips.* He giggled at the name, then glanced in the rear-view mirror. Randolph never giggled. Had he ever giggled in his life? Well, no matter. The moment passed. Right now he wanted to complain to Lips.

"Listen here, Lips," he said aloud. "I paid a pretty penny for you. What do you give me in return?" His bottom lip pushed out in a pout. He waited, as if expecting an answer, watching his breath—thick, icy, smoke. Lips had convinced him that to turn off the motor would be the wisest choice, and Randolph was definitely into choices. In this case, sure as his dick would give some new young thing pleasure, Lips was right. Why attract attention to himself? A passerby could barely see inside his tinted windows, and why would they give this damn—nearly invisible—car a glance? Only an idiot would be sitting in this cold without benefit of heat.

If not the car, then who was in control of him?

Swirls and violent colors blanketed his mind like fat, dark, leeches—he was living the chaotic madness of *Beethoven's Fifth.* Randolph tried to think. He'd brought some of the young girls here, inside this Jaguar, to impress them while he diddled them.

But he'd done the others in a variety of places. And *they* were all still very much alive. Surely he could not have been so savage as to dismember Lola all on his own. *Could he?*

"*You were not in the car when you dismembered her, you dolt.*"

He barely noticed that the voice did not come from himself, or inside his head. In passing, he thought, "why call myself a dolt?" That part *was* odd. The other problem, the question he wanted the car to answer, was even though the air was frigid, that stench still came leaking through from the trunk. "I'm asking you nicely Lips, *what's this shit all about?*"

That was when the squad car parked at the curb.

In seconds he found himself able to move once again.

Time to dump the body and finish off the mutt.

He backed around the end of the corner, drove around the block, then back to River Road and on to his destination.

His neck jerked to look behind him.

He was sure he heard someone talking.

Lips motor was a gentle hum, certainly not loud enough to mask spoken sounds, yet Randolph could barely make out the words. "What was that?" he asked, checking to be certain that the radio was off.

"*Death and Madness.*" The whispered voice seemed to be an answer to his previous—*what's this shit all about*—question.

But from whom?

The forensics people took scrapings from Bobbette's claws; spotlights shone on the yard—tainting those fantasy Christmas lights—to aid the police in their evidence search, and Mary and Vinny's baby gifts were placed into a large box—the friends vowed to get together to open them on a happier day. Elsie paced the floor while they tried to comfort her. Pip got away, they said. He would return when all the ruckus died down.

Tony kissed her cheek. "He's a smart dog. If that dumb puss got away, so did he, don't you think?"

Elsie nodded. Sam frowned.

Eric Clapton's song *Layla* began playing on the radio. It was one of Elsie's favorite songs, but now it reminded her of the old days, of her friend Lynn, and just how alone she really was. She flopped back onto an overstuffed chair, crying harder, shoulders shaking. Toast went to her quickly and pulled her to her feet. "Please." he said. His eyes showed pain she knew was for her.

Her eyes said. "I'm not dancing."

"You've got to relax; it's the only way you'll be able to think about what you have to do next." With his arm around her he led her to the next room, and in the dim light held her close, moving slowly to the music. Her head—at first rigid—seemed to give up the fight. She sunk against his chest, eyes closed; the tears stopped. This was the comfort she needed. Had he read her mind? He hardly knew her.

The Christmas lights reflected on the couple in a most romantic way. The lights, the music and the couples stressed bodies fused together. Law watched his alcoholic brother with misgivings. They appeared to be something out of a dream. Law knew it was an optical illusion, but it gave him a twinge all the same. The flame-red lights from outside twinkled on and off and lit the dancers from behind; the others, the tree's *marble* lights, shone helter-skelter, hazy, mini-colors that glowed in the otherwise dark room. The effect was seraphic—they floated together—one angel.

Toast, with tenderness that was palpable, brushed Elsie's hair off her face and stroked her cheek. Law waited for her to pull away, but to his horror she nuzzled his brothers hand like a kitten; he watched as they gazed into one another's eyes, their faces coming closer together. My God, Law thought, he's going to kiss her.

Elsie stopped abruptly. She stepped back from Toast and placed both hands on his chest. "I want to go to the junk yard. Now." Her voice was clear, the sobbing over.

"Sure. We'll go together Elsie." They were holding hands, magic connected them, as they walked to the door forgetting the group.

"Hold it." Law went after them. "We'll take the forensics van." Darwin and Tony were already getting their coats on. He kissed his lady absentmindedly on the cheek. "Gee, um, will you stay here with Sam and Kan— er, Wick, and Mary? Hold down the fort; we won't be long."

He turned to his partner. "Vince, let's have the squad lead us, but without the siren. Elsie has always had phenomenal instincts." Going down the front walk Law noticed the incredible closeness between his brother and Elsie. Why didn't he feel happy for them? He would, of course he would; it was just going to take some getting used to.

The trunk was dark enough to scare him to death. Pip tried not to stand on the body beneath him but it was everywhere. His paws sunk into the mangled flesh. He knew he was hurting it. The smell of blood, urine, feces and fear overwhelmed him. Because his mouth was taped tight, he could not lick the body he stood on to try to heal it. He wanted to help. He cried. Inside, he cried for whomever it was who lay beneath him.

First the noise of the trunk opening, then the cold wind punched him in the face.

Randolph unlocked the trunk. Sharp needles, from the ferocious winds, punctured his cheeks and hands. He had the knife in one hand—no telling what that crazed mutt would do. He lifted the trunk lid and immediately heard the dog's cries—a torment of agony. Evidently the neon-pink duct-tape he'd wrapped around its jaws was not enough to silence its cries. He heard its anguish, then was hit between the eyes with a whoosh of heat and stench from the body that was sealed so tight it was stewing in its own juices.

Why didn't he hear the mutt cry from inside the car, he wondered? Maybe the trunk *was* airtight, as advertised. If he couldn't hear, how then could he smell Lola bubbling and brewing?

"Ever consider that the fetid odor could be coming from inside your rotting soul?"

He jumped. The voice came from behind him. No one was there. Fucking whores had him losing his fucking mind. With one hand he took the wriggling—slippery with gore—frantic animal by the throat—its feet were running a marathon in the air—stuck its head under his arm, and with a fast stroke of his razor sharp knife, Randolph sliced off an ear. It fell with a plop on the toe of his shoe. He gave it a kick against the wind—an ear Frisbee that landed two feet away. The bloody dog cried as if its heart were breaking.

"Gonna let them know how you suffered, my boy." It was so cold he could feel that his nose-hairs had ice been dipped in ice, but he also felt a twinge in his groin. The ghoul that lived inside Randolph loved seeing the animal jerking and flopping every-which-way.

His plan was to cut off each ear, the tail—in small painful chunks, then the paws—that would be harder and he hadn't much time. Leave the bastards a pile of body parts.

The other ear was next. As his knife came down on the long silky ear, a belch of wind came at him like a backfire; it made him stagger. Randolph slid back and fell on his ass in the slush and show. "Fucking cock-sucking fuckers," he screamed. The dog took off running like a maniac had him by the balls and all Randolph could do was sit on his ass and watch it happen.

From a distance he saw two cars headed toward him, down the deserted road. Quickly the mutt was forgotten; he hastened to his feet, barely noticing his twisted ankle, and reached into the trunk for the body. The young girl-man was light as a feather for him. He'd parked by the rusty old Camero with its door hanging open *skreek*ing in the wind like nails against a blackboard. It took mere seconds to prop the oozing wet body behind the wheel of the dead car. The body seemed hot; why wasn't it cold, as frozen, at least, as he? The eyes, open, gave him the creeps. Why? They were mindless now.

Randolph reached back to claw down the neck of his coat with one of his blood stained hands; it felt as if something were biting him there. He ran the few steps to his car—got to get away—he was covered with blood. As the drugs wore, he was no longer the tough guy; he felt fear—atrocious fear, that made his stomach bubble up a puky bile.

"*Dead car, dead body. Dead car, dead body. Dead car, dead bodyyyyy.*" The voice behind him laughed, cackled... the words distorted, repeating themselves, riding on a tail of wind. That voice was savage, cruel, and it seemed to come from *inside* the Camero!

Randolph started his car and pulled away from the Evil rusted cars. He drove fast and he turned up the music, just in case. The cassette paused between tunes and he heard a whisper come from his back seat. From right behind his right ear. "*Dead car, dead body. Dead car, dead body. Dead car, dead bodyyyyy.*"

Chapter Eighteen

Gee and Mary cried in unison. They were worried about Pip, worried about what could be happening, but more, they were upset about their men's attitudes. Wick dozed soundly, her head in Sam's lap. Sam tried to comfort the two women.

"You saw the way he looked...I mean, they were just dancing. Why should he care?" Gee was usually the calm before the storm. They'd never seen her like this. "How can I marry a man in two short weeks who still loves another woman?"

"He's not *in* love with her. He loves you." Sam said.

Mary's face was streaked with tears, leaving lines that washed through the coral blush she'd put on at the last minute—her effort to look better than she felt. To look her best, she thought, for that asshole Vinny.

"He's always said he loves my body, but maybe he really thinks I'm fat." Gee said. "Look at the way Vinny talked to *you* Mary and you're skinny!"

"Oh God, Gee." Mary put her arms around her friend. "I'm not just going to divorce the bastard, I'm going to kill him for making you feel bad."

"Hey, my sweet ladies. You listen up to ol' Sam. First of all—you're not fat," he turned from Mary to Georgia, "and you are beautiful, beyond the beyond, you hear me my sisters? Tension is rightly high about now. Law loves you Gee—no way he loves another. He lov*ed* Elsie. We men are possessive about our pasts—be it a woman we *once* loved or a bad experience, like a drug. An' Elsie loves you, she'd never lead him down that path. 'Course you saw how she and Toast looked at each other. Law's maybe jealous." Oh, that was the wrong thing to say. "But not 'cause a' love. 'Cause a' some sibling crap stuff. Am I right?"

Gee took a deep breath. "I can't believe I've behaved this way. You are *so* right Sam." Her hands rubbed at her head. "Sibling crap stuff. I couldn't have put it any better." She turned to Mary. "But what about Vinny? What could possibly make him behave as he has?"

Sam was on a roll. "That my sweet-ones, is even easier. He's like a kite, Mary's his anchor."

"Anchor? I don't want to anchor him!"

Gee beamed and nodded at Sam. "He means it in a good way, hon. That kite takes you up, your anchor helps you both stay grounded. It's a perfect team—a perfect match. Your yin for his yang."

The door had opened, Tony and Darwin walked in on the last sentence. "You guys are just sittin' around talkin' about my *wang*?" Tony strutted past them. "Can't leave you alone for a second!"

"Now here's a good example of a kite and an anchor!" Sam was glad to see the conversation and the faces around him relax.

Gee was not about to be put off. "Where *is* everyone? Did you find Pip?"

Tony eyed the toes of his boots. "Umhm. We found him."

"Well? Tell us what's going on? He's okay?" Sam's voice was so loud it woke Kandle. She sat, blinking her eyes.

Darwin took over—it was easier for him to talk at times like this. Something about the yin and the yang, or the kite and the anchor. "A squad drove us home. They found Pip; he's alive, but traumatized. He's been cut some."

"Cut?" Pretty much everyone spoke at once. All but Kandle. She seemed to shrink into the sofa, her face sickly. "Did they catch the man?" she asked softly.

"I'm not sure. I don't think so, Wick." Darwin automatically looked out the window as he said it. They had to all be thinking the same thing. Where *was* the bastard? "There's worse, I'm afraid. There was a body in one of the cars."

"Whose?" Mary asked.

"We don't have a clue. All hell broke loose. Law had a car bring us home and called an ambulance to take Elsie, Toast, and Pip to the hospital, to emergency. Elsie wouldn't go to the animal hospital; she thinks Pip's her brother is my guess." Darwin patted Gee and Mary. "I'm sure Law and Vinny will call you two, but they're bound to be busy for quite awhile." Bobbette leapt to Darwin's lap. "Don't you worry." He stroked her while she nudged him, her purr almost a roar. "Your buddy is going to be fine."

Elsie held her shivering, bleeding pup. Toast took off his coat and wrapped Pip, then his arms went around them both.

"We're taking him to Fairview-Riverside Hospital," Elsie barked at Law.

"Hey, whatever you say, Mam'." Law was busy with a body and however much he wanted to comfort Elsie, his brother seemed to be doing the job just fine. He allowed himself about ten seconds to watch them—his faded blue eyes hard to read—they'd been through too many wash and dry cycles over the years. He started back to the Camero, then stopped at the sound of Elsie's voice.

"Law. Thanks for helping."

Law nodded, continued on to the bleak, raw, rust-bucket-graveyard; he heard the ambulance carry the three away. He remembered kids playing all over these cars when he was first on the force. He'd chase the little shits home. But that was long ago.

He thought they'd taken all this rusty metal out of here years before.

Just one more sign that he was losin' it.

Chapter Nineteen

PROCTOR: Abby, that's a wild thing to say—
ABIGAIL: A wild thing may say wild things. But not so wild, I think. I have seen you since she put me out; I have seen you nights.
PROCTOR: I have hardly stepped off my farm this sevenmonth.
ABIGAIL: I have a sense for heat, John, and yours has drawn me to my window, and I have seen you looking up, burning in your loneliness. Do you tell me you've never looked up at my window?
PROCTOR: I may have looked up.
- THE CRUCIBLE - ARTHUR MILLER

Theodore Boodles smelled of fries and burgers. Like goose-bumps in the cold, his face was covered with pimples. He knew it was from the grease and he blamed his mother. If she cooked him enough decent food to eat he wouldn't be so fucking hungry for trash. He hadn't been laid in four months. That was her fault too. Who wanted to fuck a guy who looked like if you kissed him you'd get a mouth full of pus? Who?

He slammed the door and hot steam hit him in the face. The warmth felt good, real good, but, he sniffed, what was that cooking for dinner, boiled water?

Bethie's friend Greta was over; they sat at the kitchen table. He pulled out a chair. Not because he wanted to see his sisters ugly face, but because Greta gave him a boner that was obvious to all, especially her.

"Go away, but first stir the pot, pus-head." His sister nodded at the stove. He could see the box of macaroni and cheese with the top torn off.

"Why don't I just go smoke it, lard-ass." He pushed the kitchen chair over in an effort to detract from himself.

"Oh, aren't you just the clever wise-ass." Elizabeth glared.

"Hey Teddy-bear. Are you packin' heat, or are you just happy to see me?" said Greta. The girls pointed at his crotch, at the same time, as if their moves were choreographed. Their laughter did not fade until he had locked himself in the can.

Time for a doobie-doobie-doo, he thought, as he fired up a joint. It was an easier way to relax than jacking-off every time he got the urge. If only daddy could see me now. Maybe he'd send me off to his treatment center. There'd be lots of action there. Good food too. Three squares. *Doobie-doobie-doo.*

Claudette heard their laughter and felt pleased—at least the *kids* were enjoying life. It made Randolph's abuse bearable. Not that she wanted it to continue, but it did make taking the abuse in the past, worthwhile. It was a mother's duty. It was the least she could do for the children she loved. She took her glass of wine off the table and washed down another Prozac with a gulp. The doctor was right. Her feelings of anger *had* dimmed with this new drug. But something new appeared to have replaced the anger.

She remembered sitting in this doctor's office. She was afraid, anxious and unable to leave the house without this extreme high-anxiety. She wanted him to know what was happening to her. She'd been on the freeway this morning, driving to his office, when she thought she was having a heart attack. She couldn't breathe; it felt like a huge gorilla was sitting on her chest. Waiting in his office, she wondered why her doctor was trying to get rid of her anger? It was the *fear* she wanted to dissolve. She was determined not to tell him how her stomach hurt, or to mention the chronic diarrhea. She'd been having these complaints for two years now, and he'd sent her to have all the tests; many of them very painful. The results always came in the mail—like a failed college exam score. *Once again, you are fine. You have no earthly reason to be in pain or discomfort.*

So why was she?

The last doctor he'd sent her to was the worst. He'd come to the exam room in his expensive silk suit. The burgundy vest he wore underneath was cashmere. He was nearly as young as her son. The 'new' way these days, was to go to a specialist. These specialists were often more wealthy than knowledgeable. They had one area of expertise, if you had cancer an inch away from their specialty—tough *noogies*. His 'area' was the colon. She'd been told to undress and a gorgeous young thing had told her to lie on a table and face the wall until Dr. Cashmere was ready. Lie quietly and wait for someone to come and stick something up your butt. Finally, three people came in. Dr. Cashmere was training Ms. Gorgeous and another older nurse to do this unpleasant task. Why should he risk getting something on his silk suit? She heard them all laugh. "Yes," the doctor said, "you *have* to just lift it with your hand." They all laughed again—merrily. If any of the three of them had to take this test their buttock would have stood up hard and firm with no need to give it a lift. Claudette felt Ms. Gorgeous timidly place her hand on her behind, and lift the top side of her ass in the air, and then, felt a tube inserted inside her; that was accompanied by a stabbing pain that went on for most of the test.

Through her screaming she heard him say, "Sometimes this happens, but it's rare. Her colon appears to collapse when we insert—" The rest of his words were intelligible through the laughter and her own yowls. Through her tears she thought of Painless on Mash and wished to be at war instead of where she was. She'd been promised they'd give her something to make the test nearly painless—uncomfortable for a short while perhaps, but not painful—never painful. Humiliation was never mentioned. So did this pain mean something was seriously wrong? No, the usual letter came. You are fine, there is no reason for your pain. All that it meant was that she must be a big baby.

She straightened, hearing the tap on the door that preceded doctors' entry.

"Hello, Claudette. You look great. I guess the Prozac is doing the trick." He beamed at her like a magician who'd performed a wonderful trick for her.

"Well actually doctor, I've been having some problems."

He frowned. What's this. A complaint?

He listened to her high-anxiety story and told her she was not unlike many women her age—full of bitterness and anger over things from her past—things often having nothing whatever to do with her real life today. And this is what is making her a sick woman. Her children were grown and she felt empty and unfulfilled. She expected her husband to make her happy. "I notice that your weight is up again. Could *that* have anything to do with your depression?"

Claudette began to laugh hysterically. "I don't believe I said I was depressed doctor."

He wrote down the name of a psychiatrist whom he recommended she see—right away, and also a prescription to increase her dosage of Prozac.

"We'll have you feeling tip-top in no time, little lady," he said. "By the way, how're those stomach problems?"

"Just fine, thank-you." she answered, her stomach on fire.

She walked to her car, her new prescription in her hand. She felt very small. He was a Doctor, he must be right, she must be wrong. She was fat and old and bitter and now she was even afraid to drive her car. She was more afraid now, and less angry.

She wanted to be *more* angry, less afraid. *There was only one person who might be able to help her.*

Maggert was asleep when the call came in. He was out of drugs and had smoked or sniffed or shot up a good part of the money he owed. There was nothing left to do but sleep. Before long he'd start hurtin', then he'd find a way to get more drugs—no matter what.

"Yeah? It's your nickel." His voice was craggy with sleep and the bloating he got when he was out of the shit that made him sharp.

"Dog? It's me. It's Randolph."

"Well, I'll be goddamned if I wasn't just thinkin' a' ya Randolph my man."

"Right." The voice sounded sarcastic. "Look here, have you got a shower there?"

"A what? Did ya' say shower?"

"Right."

"Sure. Well, sure." *What the fuck?*

"Is anyone there with you?"

"Naw, shit, an' if there was I'd ah," the Dog spit a green blob of a honker on his own floor, "I'd ah, get rid a' them for *you*." He could feel the excitement swell in his chest. "Ya' wanna come over, is that it?"

"Right." Randolph sighed. This was worse than a trip to the dentist.

"Hey there, good buddy, you just skip on over. 'ave us a party-hardy, we will!"

"No. That's not it, Dog. I, ah, I got myself in a fight. My, ah, my office shower is being redecorated so it's inoperative at the moment. Just so you know ah, when you see me, there's some blood. I want to shower so my wife doesn't know."

Oh there is a God. "Oh sure, hey, we're bud's. No problemo." The last tidbit—the blood—gave him nerve. "Hey, are ya' holdin' any shit?"

"You're already out?"

"Clean as a bean."

"Got my money?"

"Well, that's the problem. I, um, trusted some folk that I shouldn't ah, trusted, ya' know?"

Fuckin' asshole. Fuckin' thinks he's got me over a barrel, thought Randolph. "I'll have enough with me to give you a treat. I'll bring back more later tonight or tomorrow."

"Yeah. Tonight would be best." Cannot wait to see how much is *some* blood.

"We'll see. See you in fifteen."

Chapter Twenty

The body of the dead girl had turned out to be that of a young man, Timothy Horton Hillquist. His parents—he was an only child—lived in Las Vegas. "We've not heard from T.H.," as they called him, their voices void of emotion, "since he turned thirteen and chose to leave our home." His mother, Bea, was a retired hooker; his father—who could have been any one of dozens of Bea's 'clients'—remained unknown. Chuck, his step-father, had caught T.H. dressing like a girl and beat the beejezus out of him. They weren't much interested in hearing what had happened to 'that-little-fag.'

Nothing unique about that story.

Under the name of Lola Lord, Tim lived with a prominent State Representative. Lola was a live-in nanny. Although the politician had no, what he termed rug-rats, he claimed two children on his taxes and so was able to have Mr. and Mrs. Tax-payer pick up the tab for Lola's salary for day-care. Mr. Prominent had never been married, or audited. In his case, the cops wondered if it was who you knew, or who you blew. When the drug problem surfaced Lola was shuffled out to Dundas by her *amour*, the bills paid out-of-pocket—knowing he could easily be reimbursed by slipping the cost into the state's generous travel-allowance. Minnesota takes care of its politicians. Choices had him listed in their records as the next-of-kin—an uncle—albeit a generous uncle.

Law and Vinny spent an intense 36 hours. If they could apprehend the killer they had plenty of DNA to hang him. They had both blood and sperm samples, but the results weren't back yet. There were some unusual fibers mixed with the blood—that would be sorted out in no time. It seemed probable that this particular criminal was the same man who had attacked Kandle and was running his own surveillance of their homes. Vinny finally believed Mary's story.

It turned out that the female officer Vinny called Muffin did have a name. She followed Law and Vinny whenever she could. Getting hot coffee, oooing and cooing over them as if they were at war and she the head nurse. That was her name, Officer Head. Law grimaced when he heard it and tried calling her by her first name, the way they'd done with Officer Suzie.

"Officer Val, have they called to say when the autopsy is scheduled?"

"I'd sure prefer it if you'd call me by my last name, Detective Lawrence. I like to save my first name for my intimate friends." She breathed the words, affecting a somewhat southern accent that was a one-hundred-percent forgery, and pointed her large breasts at him. Although the words were meant for him, her eyes were on Vince—her long lashes doing a kind of hip-hop dance. Her nipples always stuck out. Did she give them a flick every now and then? "The autopsy should be starting in about thirty minutes, gentlemen."

Law stared at Officer Head. He felt like giving her a slap in the face. What she was trying to do to Mary and Vinny was Evil. She was hardly in love at this early stage of the game. At the front of Law's brain was the picture of the young man propped behind the wheel of that blob of rust. The body looked rusty too. Rust got to metal; we humans got to one another. People he loved were going to die unless he found this killer. People he loved were going to suffer and die. He felt sick with fear. And this bitch was pushing her tits in Vinny's face. Made him wonder why they let women on the force.

Law pushed away from the desk. "Jesus H., I gotta get myself a break, and check on Gee." A phone call wouldn't do it. He had to have his arms around her. "Meanwhile, why don't you do some checking on that junkyard, Officer Head?"

The footprints Randolph left in the snow were a reddish-brown. He noticed the color as he stomped through the unshoveled walk to the used-car shack. It was beginning to snow. The wind had picked up and the flakes were not-so-friendly. It was late. Unlikely there'd be any visitors. He'd shower, clean his clothes, then kick at the snow drifts to cover any of the rust that might be left on his way out. His fist was poised, ready to bang loud enough to be heard over the screaming wind, but just as his hand drew back the door opened.

The Dog stood waiting.

"Hey, good buddy." With a sweeping gesture, Maggert beckoned him inside—a long lost brother. "I, ah, took the liberty a' turnin' up the heat in the can. Got one a' them space heaters, ya' know? It'll be toasty as...heh, heh, hell, for ya' right about now." His eyes widened. "Man-oh-man. That's some fuckin' fight you got yourself into, boss."

Maggert used the word boss to attempt to give himself the upper hand. Catch the sleazy-suit-bastard off guard, then go ahead with his plan—blackmail; no sense in showin' his hand this early in the game. "Ya' know, myself, I like the kind of a gal who don't like ta' be tied down, but likes to be tied up."

Yuck-it-up, Randolph thought, waiting to see if there was a point to the asinine one liner.

"So, ah was it a chick you was ah, fightin' with, boss?"

"Why do you ask? You writing a book?" The words came out hard and cold. But Randolph had his own hand to play. He tossed a glassine on the Dog's desk. "Why don't you try some of this while

I clean up. Save the gabfest for later." He headed straight for the bathroom, taking his briefcase with him.

Maggert gaped at the glassine. "Horse? Is it?" His heart thumped as Randolph's nod said, affirmative. "Ain't never done any a' that."

Randolph, as if he'd take it back, asked, "Want something else?"

"Well, hell no, I don't. Fuckin' A—I'm up for it." He hurried, dumping a pile of white on his desk.

Can I pick em', or what, thought Randolph? "It's pure as a virgin *used* to be, when you could still find one, so take it easy—just snort a smaller line than if it was blow. Snorting H is the rage in Hollywood these days. I'm surprised a dialed-in guy like yourself isn't already into the good shit."

Randolph saw the Dog was already poised with a rolled bill up his nose as he closed the bathroom door. Right about now that powder would be giving the withered car salesman's brain a big kiss.

Smooch! Or, in this case, SMACK.

Let me plant a little smack on you, ya' hound-*dog*.

Randolph couldn't have the Dog out on the street now that the scum-bag had this on him. *Was it a chick*? The addict's words stung. What would make that fuck-head think that he was fighting with a girl? Except instinct. Blackmail was certainly in the offing. Should he kill him right now, after all, he was already a mess?

Even a dog could be useful at times—for a time. Why not control him a while longer, then get rid of him? Never can tell when you might want your dick licked. So to speak.

He turned on the water—the small, filthy room was hot. It felt like he'd stepped into heaven. He caught a glimpse of his face in the tiny mirror that hung on the front of the paper towel holder. Crusted blood surrounded his eyes like a raccoon. Chunks of flesh had frozen onto his eyebrows and around his nostrils. He bared his teeth—rusty-pink everywhere. No wonder the Dog was suspicious.

"Was it a chick?" The voice whispered through the pipes.

Humming, he stripped and stepped under the steaming water. "Ahhhh." The beauty of it all. Hot water poured over him—healing and calming—like a whore sucking him off. He felt like a million bucks. The world was his.

"Hey Dog," he yelled when he'd finished. "Perhaps you have something relatively clean that I might borrow?" No answer. He opened the door a crack and the cool air rushed in giving his skin bumps. The fucker sat slumped over. The glassine nearly half empty. "*Hey.* Dog."

"Yeah, boss." The Dog jumped as if Randolph had stuck something up his butt, instead of just called his name. "Whas' up?"

"Clothes. Got any clean clothes?" Randolph was getting a chill and his good humor faded fast when he was chilled. This moron, well, that's it...it was important for him to remember just what a moron the Dog was. He slammed the bathroom door and tried to see in the mirror. It was fogged—fog so thick you could cut it with a knife.

"You just happen to have a knife." The whispered voice came from the shower.

Chapter Twenty-One

"Now I truly believe in miracles."

Toast had wanted to help her carry Pip up to her rooms. Elsie took Pip into the living room to briefly show the others that he was alive—he and Bobbette rubbed noses for a minute or so—but Elsie wanted to hurry him to her room, where he would feel warm and safe. She felt so protective—Pip was her baby. Maybe the only baby she would ever have. The hospital had called in a veterinarian surgeon after Elsie's assurance that she was paying the bill whatever the cost; the pup had lost so much blood and was in shock—they didn't want to risk moving him. One ear was slit off at the very top of his head, the other had a cut that ran down the length of it—leaving him two ribbons of ear. Luckily the police found the ear that was severed and brought it to the hospital. The surgery took only about thirty minutes, and after they felt he was stable—three hours later—they let Elsie take him home.

They stood silent in the elevator riding up to her room. Elsie felt wary of this man. His arms around her earlier that night had felt too good, too right. While they waited for Pip to be able to come home, they talked about their lives as if they'd known one another forever.

That frightened her. It felt way too intimate.

That wasn't all she felt. She felt the heat: it made her throat swell, her tongue feel thick, her pulse race. She longed. For what she did not know. But she longed.

Only her concern for her baby, Pip, kept her semi-sane.

She looked at the frail, vulnerable doggie, as she laid him in her bed. His fur had been bathed with warm cloths; most of the blood had been wiped away, but his body was no longer black and white. It was black and pinkish-brown—matted with the residue of the blood. She put on one of Pip's favorite CD's. Billie Holiday hugged the apartment with *"I can't give you anything but love, baby."* Elsie whispered and kissed and stroked her baby until she knew he was sound asleep and having warm, sweet dreams.

She stood, and Toast took both of her hands. In the next few seconds, not knowing how it really happened, she was on her back, on the floor—his body covering her body like a placenta.

"Now I truly believe in miracles," he said while kissing her, breathing his soul into her soul.

Together they swam in and out of the world around them. It was heat so hot that nothing else existed. Like a pot of stew left unchecked their insides raged and boiled nearly over the top, slowed to a simmer, then once again began to roll with the fire. As the pot began to boil over the top, Toast ripped open her blouse, the buttons airborne, "I like it...oh God, I can feel you everywhere ...inside me, outside me," she said.

Their bodies stuck together—paste made of love?—nothing could come between them.

Pip moaned in his sleep.

Elsie put both hands on Toast's chest and pushed—lightly. He rolled off her.

"My father was an alcoholic," she said. "He killed himself, and my mother, too."

Suddenly there was space between them.

So much space.

She got up off the floor and went to find something to drink. "I'm really thirsty. How about you, Toast?"

He wasn't standing, but sitting—legs pulled towards him—head lying on his knees, eyes closed, he sighed and spoke so soft she could barely make out his words. "I'm not your father Elsie—nothing like him. Is it pushy of me to want this feeling to go on? This stirring in my gut, at my core? It's brand new to me, and yet it's something I've burned for. I knew it was…somewhere. Now that I've found it I'm bursting with it; can't you see that?"

She stood her ground. I won't be sucked into *his* needs, she thought. I have needs of my own. Those I love have needs too. "Do you think you'd like a cup of tea, or a soda?" she asked.

There were a few seconds of silence and then together, as if on cue. "Let's have tea." The same exact words were their duet.

He laughed and got up. "You see how connected we are?" He was certain she would see that they *were* connected—the missing pieces of one anothers' puzzles.

Elsie turned her back on him to put the water on. "We've really not known one another long." She kept her back to him. "I'd like to talk about the case, Toast. Can we save the personal stuff for another day?"

His eyes were liquid, hot black wells that wanted to draw her in if only she would look his way. "But what about us?"

"Us? How can you talk to me of us? You'll be leaving soon, for treatment; who knows when you'll return, or even *if* you will? You may find that your vocation in the Church, your love of God, takes precedence over these other feelings, other *desires*." She poured them Chamomile tea—its aroma immediately soothed her—making her visualize the field of daisy-like flowers that made the golden buds for this tea—picture them blowing free in the breeze, smelling oh, so, sweet.

"I don't need to go to treatment now Elsie. All I need is your love. Can't you see that?" He took her hand. "I know you feel it."

She stared at his mouth. A short time ago it had been as close to her and as hot as this gold liquid she sipped. She longed to fling her cup aside and drink from his lips again. But she would not. "I'm not your savior, Toast. Please go. I need to think about so many things. I may be younger than you but I've learned; I know I cannot save you." She pulled her eyes from his. "I do not want to."

He walked toward the elevator. "Only you can save yourself, Toast. Only you." she said.

Already she wanted his arms back, his hot breath a blanket over her neck. "You must go to the clinic," she'd said—not certain if he'd heard her words or even if she'd said them or only thought them. The elevator doors closed on his defeated, pain-filled face. How long will I remember those haunting eyes, she thought. Yet his powerful need unsettled her.

Pip moaned louder, then gave a, "Yip!" Elsie crawled into her bed next to him and wrapped him in her arms.

Pip tried not to hurt what lay beneath him but he had to get away or he was not going to be of help here, and what's more, he knew that his Elsie was in danger. His paws sunk, dug, into the mangled flesh. It felt as if he were walking in mud—although it was the pitch black of hell he could tell it was a woman—or so he thought, then no, a young man. He gave up thinking. It was a soul and it was dead. The stench was strong. It was of blood, urine, feces and fear—it overwhelmed him. His mouth was taped tight; he could not lick the body to try to heal it. He wanted to help. He cried. Inside, he cried for whomever it was who lay beneath him.

First the noise of the trunk opening, then the cold wind punched him in the face.

There stood the man with the knife. The knife that had made all the blood he'd just laid on. He tried to run fast and slip away, but the hand held tight.

Next, the grip around his throat choked off all air. He saw the knife come down on him and he howled. He felt the first cut, and his heart screamed and his feet pumped, trying to run. Pip whined, his feet spun through the cold air like bald tires in the snow. He saw his ear hit the monster's shoe and bounce off.

This monster of Evil would get his Elsie. Would hurt his Elsie! He had to escape!

Elsie held his thrashing body tighter to her breast. She sang to him while he whimpered less and less. Pip loved the water and she sang an old song about water, "Ebb Tide."

Pip opened his eyes a small crack and saw her, then closed them again. He was safe. He licked her hand—just one small lick. They were in the water together and it was warm and they were safe.

Singing the song she fell asleep.

Lots of the people in Northfield already had their Christmas lights on. The sight of the tiny colors made her skip on her way home from school. The wind made her nose red and icicle wet, but she had Santa on her mind.

She looked up to see her house. She was already home. That made her think of her Daddy. He'd been in the hospital all week and she missed him. Elsie entered the kitchen taking her snowy boots off carefully and setting them on the small rag rug by the door. Momma wouldn't be pleased if she got snow tracks on the floor. Just as carefully she brushed off her jacket and hung it on the hook by the basement stairs. She stood and listened. Nothing to hear but the hum of the refrigerator. She was alone. Her favorite time.

She took out the picture she'd made in school for Daddy. Her first grade teacher raved about how good it was and gave her an A+. Daddy was going to be so proud. Sister Irene, her teacher, let them use colored chalk, and when you held the chalk just right, almost completely on its side, you could shade things like trees and flowers to make them look almost as good as the real thing. It was all in how you put pressure on the chalk. She leaned her picture on the table against the napkin holder so Daddy would see it as soon as he came in the door.

She looked around the room. She and Momma had decorated the Christmas tree last night and the room looked like a fairyland. They'd strung popcorn with bright red cranberries on the long strings of thread. Elsie made a big star for the top of the tree out of cardboard covered with tinfoil. The room smelled of pine—of Christmas. She plugged in the lights. Twinkle, twinkle, little star. The tiny bulbs of color lifted her spirits even higher and she slowly began to skip around the room. "All I want for Christmas is my Daddy home, my Daddy home, my Daddy home," she sang softly to the tune of "All I want for Christmas is my two front teeth."

"SHUT YOUR GODDAMN FUCKING MOUTH!" his voice boomed from the bedroom.

Daddy was home. She took her coat and trudged through the deep snow around the side of the house and climbed to a tree she always felt safe in. She watched the neighbors' family build a snowman, while she waited for her momma to come home from her work at the rectory. When Momma's station-wagon drove in the driveway Elsie slid down the tree and ran to the car. Momma's hair was a mess and her clothes were all pulled around—not the way she normally looked. Elsie picked up the milk and they headed for the house.

"Is your father home already?" Momma sounded worried.

A wet nose nudged her cheek. Elsie opened her eyes.

A priest.

Just like Mother.

Hadn't she vowed never to be like her mother?

Chapter Twenty-Two

Things happened fast.

The morning newspaper carried an article about Timothy Hillquist on the front page.

The nude and butchered body of a young man was found last evening in an old car junkyard on the west side of the Mississippi River. He had been sexually assaulted, raped and sodomized, before, during and after death. The victim was a sixteen-year old Caucasian male; medical reports show that he was HIV positive. He had full-blown-aids. The victim's genitals were severed; his body was stabbed over forty times. The body was so badly pummeled that it was not possible to tell the exact number of stab wounds. Minnesota's Gay Rights Activists have started a Reward fund to help find the perpetrator and pay for information leading to a conviction. Those who wish to contribute may call...

Darwin put the paper aside to grab the ringing phone. It was a message for Law's brother, Terrence. The call came from the business office at Choices Treatment Center. They had an opening and would expect Terrence Lawrence to be ready to check into their facility by 5:00 PM that evening. "Well, yes," answered Darwin. "I'm certain he wants the room. I'll have him call immediately if there's been any change. If you don't hear from him, expect him by five." He hung up the phone and said to Tony,

"They're ready for Toast. I wonder what this news will do to Elsie?"

"Oh, I think she can handle it."

Sarcasm? Darwin raised an eyebrow.

"Do you trust him, Dar? I mean, he's nice and all, but would he be good for Els?" Tony's face showed concern. "I'm not sure I even like the man."

"You haven't given him a chance. Who *would* be good enough for her?"

"You'd love to see her 'tied-up' in a relationship of *any* kind. And for your own selfish reasons, am I right?"

"*What* do you mean? You don't think I want her involved and happy? You're being unfair Spike. I've always had Elsie's interests at heart and you damn well know it."

"Umhm. And if she fell in love, she'd no longer be our Avenger, and your little-immediate-world would be safe."

Darwin couldn't believe what he was hearing. "And I suppose you don't want her safe?" He tossed the news article in front of Tony.

"I don't mean *her* world safe. I mean us, *ours*." Tony was irritable lately. He saw the headlines and gave his attention to the paper.

They heard some rattling of dishes in the kitchen and in minutes Toast came into the room with a cup in his hand.

How long had he been there? Had he overheard their conversation, Darwin worried?

"You two birds want some coffee?" Toast asked.

Darwin, irritated, asked, "Is that short for *love*-birds?"

"Sorry. I, ah, I didn't mean to step on any toes. I'm just finding the caffeine a great injection of energy."

"Forget it. It's me that's touchy. Look. The treatment place left you a message. They have an opening and want you there to fill it by 5:00 PM. I told them you'd call if you couldn't make it."

Toast's eyes watered instantly. "I don't want to. It's not the time to leave Elsie. She wants me to go. She doesn't believe in the power of love."

"Why not respect her wishes, Terry." Darwin's expression was stern. "Love that's true will hardly crumble in thirty days, or whatever their program is."

The doorbell rang and Tony went to answer it.

Randolph sat at his desk reading his morning paper. He didn't have his mind on work today and he had a class in less than five minutes. They were getting a new man today. He disliked the time he had to spend with the adults. A waste of his valuable time. His idle, wandering eyes landed on one area of the paper.

AIDS. *Lola! That bitch!*

His eyes were wide and he saw a picture of his own face clear as a bell. A picture of his face in the bathroom mirror at the Dog's. Last night. Blood and guts were a crust over his body. He'd looked up into the mirror and pulled back his lips, and teeth stained with human blood reflected back at him. Human blood that was infected with an incurable deadly virus.

"What about your wife? Are you too chicken-shit to do her up right?" Again, the voice. The door to his office was closed. No one but him inside. He laughed. Me and these chickens just havin' a morning chat-a-thon.

The condom.

LOLA.

A murder weapon. A great murder weapon.

He would use it on Claudette, infect her with the virus and she would—*expire.* The perfect crime. He knew very little about AIDS ...but he knew how strong he was; his power was infinite. The terror that had first gripped his heart took flight when he realized the truth. That this was a sign. His LOLA condom was fate speaking—giving him a helping hand—a hand that said, go for it.

At that moment his body relaxed completely. Randolph felt utterly satiated.

Sam dropped Wick at the head-doc. While Wick was visiting 'shrink city' he was going for his own form of therapy; he was going to see Elsie. They had to talk. Tony answered the doorbell.

Sam tried hard to make it brief. He wanted to see Elsie and not chitchat in the foyer with Tony.

"Did you know that our 'Pater' Terrence has dialed Elsie in with an intercom?" Tony's whispered sarcasm seemed permanent, but he pointed to it on the wall.

"Hm." Sam was leery of the ex-priest, too. "Guess we got to admit he's quite the handyman. An intercom is a good idea for Elsie. How come we didn't think of that?" Sam put Bobbette on his shoulder, he'd decided to take his cat along upstairs to see Pip—it would cheer up the Pipster and Bobbette, too.

Tony shrugged and Sam pushed her buzzer and waited. He wanted to ask if she was busy, but as soon as she heard his voice she buzzed.

"Now what?" he asked Tony, who was clearly sulking.

"You *go* to the tunnel. Her elevator will open for you. If she hadn't buzzed it would be locked. I think Terrence thinks that her setup is so unique word will get out and she'll be in harms way."

Sam nodded. "Makes Sense." He hated saying it and he knew Tony hated hearing it even more. Sam looked around Tony and saw the ex-priest with Darwin. He raised his voice so they could hear him.

"Hey, you two. Top 'a the mornin' to ya'. And a fine idear it was, my laddie, to have this put in for our lassie." He mouthed a grin that was obviously not from the heart and gave a salute that was returned by both men. Awkward to say the least and he could feel Tony's eyes bore into his back.

No time to care. He wandered down the stairs to the tunnel. Bobbette clung to his leg, playfully batting, trying to get his attention; she was excited knowing she was going to see her chum, Pip. Sam ignored her; he was not in a playful mood. The elevator door opened as he'd been told. As it opened again on her top floor, he heard Elsie's voice and saw that she was on the phone.

"I don't really understand what it is that you want from me." Her face had a frown that matched the uncharacteristic impatient tone.

"No. It's not that I don't care about your problems. But I have a sick dog and I'm just beginning—"

Elsie was now extremely irritated. "Why do you keep interrupting me?

"Yes, I do understand that you are in a hurry, but you haven't said why?" Elsie paced.

"Well, first of all, this is a private *unlisted* line." She shrugged at Sam. "Look, ah, Claudette, was *that* your name? Why don't you tell me how you got this number."

Pip woke from his name and barked when he saw Bobbette standing next to him, nose in his face, feet kneading his tail like bread and keeping time to the purr that hummed out of her chest.

Elsie's frown turned puzzled as she placed the phone in its cradle muttering. "Whoever she was, she hung up as soon as she heard Pip bark."

Remembering Sam she beamed. "Hey. I've been wondering if we'd *ever* get the chance to talk; you've been pretty intense with Kandle." She took his arm. "Or, as we now say, Wick. I love that nick-name, by the way."

"Who's on the phone?" Sam asked, giving his friend a bear hug. "You need an answering machine. Why don't you have one?"

Tony was engrossed in reading the article. "Dar, did you talk to Els this morning yet?"

"Righto, Spikerino."

Tony threw the paper down. "Do I look as if I'm *joking?* What was she *doing?* What I mean is, Sam didn't say much, were they going *out?*"

"I believe she's trying to sponge-bathe Pip-the-pup." interrupted Toast.

Darwin and Tony were like robots, eyes first down to the paper on the floor, next up and they looked at one another. "*The blood from the body.*" They talked, both at once. "AIDS. *Infected blood.*"

They ran from the room; frowning Terrence picked up the newspaper.

She was about to open her mouth when the intercom gave an annoying, "Eeeeeeh." The noise was followed by Dar and Tony. "Hey Els, send down the elevator! Quick!" The intercom squeaked and squawked cutting in and out. Still they heard their friends... "*stay away from Pip!*"

Elsie noticed the elevator doors were standing wide open. Sam had a slight expression of guilt mixed with annoyance. "I pushed the hold button. Wanted privacy so we could talk."

They heard Pip yip and whine like he was trying to tell his friend what he'd gone through. He was buried under Elsie's covers, only his tail hung over to the side. Bobbette was now on top of the quilt and purred and padded with her feet on his back—trying her best to soothe him—and it was working, he was falling off to sleep once again.

"It's your call," said Elsie. "Should we let them intrude?"

"What do they mean about Pip?"

"Don't know. Guess we'd better find out. Look at him. He's been drifting in and out all night and all morning too. He looks peaceful now. Sometimes he looks like he's been dropped into a vat of *hell.*"

The voices on the intercom showed no sign of giving up. Glum, Sam went to the elevator and with a sigh, sent it down.

"I guess there's no use in getting into whatever you've got on your mind till we do this, Sambo-sweetie." Elsie pulled his head to hers and kissed the top of his head as the elevator opened. "Don't touch Pip, that's a good one. Pipster and me have done everything but French kiss over the past 8 hours." She giggled, almost like her old self. "I've got lots of time, so if you're in no hurry we can spend some time catching up once we find out what this is about, would that work for you?"

"Yeah." Sam grumbled, thinking of Wick's appointment. She'd be waiting for him to pick her up.

Tony was actually yelling at Darwin. "Why didn't you bring the paper to *show* her?"

"Calm down Spike. I thought you had it." The fluorescent lighting from inside the elevator gave both of their faces a greenish hue. Things were off kilter in every respect lately.

"Do I have to do *everything*?"

"Will you two quit your squabbling?" Elsie saw Darwin push the hold button again. What was going on with the elevator today? Wishing for a visitor, she often hoped to hear the hum of it—to no avail.

They talked at once—over one another. But the story became clear. The body Pip had spent time with in the trunk of that car had been infected with *the* virus. The big one. No one knew all that much about it yet, but they knew it was something to fear like the plague. Elsie was on the phone to her vet while they were still chattering.

"Tony," she said, after she hung up—authority and calm in her voice, "would you please fill the tub with nice warmish-hot water and put some Dreft in it. Lots of Dreft. It's in that cupboard under the sink—I was told to use it for his "owies." My vet's on the way. We're going to soak Pipper until she gets here. I was going to do it soon anyway." She pulled on her plastic cleaning gloves, turned back the covers and lifted her "baby" in her arms. "And send that damn elevator down."

Tony ran ahead of her to get the bath started. He heard her soft whispers to Pip, trying to wake him from his deep sleep. "You have to wake my baby boy." She rocked him in her arms. "This is going to be such a fun warm bath. Momma will be right here with you. Come on Pipper baby, wake up." She blew smooching kisses at his head.

"Els! Will you watch what you're doing?" Darwin's voice was loud and the dog jerked in her arms, frightened.

Tony, startled, eyes popping out, said, "Well now, if that doesn't beat all. With all *you* know about HIV. How can you be so insensitive? Makes me wonder why I 'named' you Darwin. You sound just like a Clarence, *Clarence.*"

"And *you* sound like a shrew!" Darwin was crestfallen. Shamed at his own words. Quietly he said, "I'm worried about Elsie, Spike. She understands that."

"No, I don't. And you're both frightening Pip. Go downstairs if you must argue." Elsie was in no mood for domestic problems—from anyone. "I know what I'm doing. It's unlikely that the blood was still able to contaminate by the time Pip was thrown in that trunk." Her face softened. "Look guys, I thank you from the bottom of my heart for telling me what was going on. You know how seldom I read the paper, but please, sit down and be civil."

On the "be civil," the elevator opened one more time; the vet came in. "Hi ya' Judy," Elsie said. She rubbed the Dreft suds into Pip's coat. "Thanks so much for the house-call. Come on in; let's talk. How'd you find your way up here?"

Judy sat on the toilet cover. "A very handsome man showed me the way. I think he said his name was Terry?"

Elsie's smile froze. Why hadn't Toast at least come to see if she and Pip were okay?

Chapter Twenty-Three

"We have a rookie male-adult, a problem drinker, checking in tonight around 5:00 PM." Randolph's office manager handed him a file. "I thought you might like to look him over on paper, sir."

"Um." Randolph didn't move. His head was on fire, each and every cell, alive and burning. Overtures of Ludwig van clashed and clanged, shadow-boxing their way around his brain; the anguish that tormented Beethoven's soul was evident. The notes singed, pinching Randolph's every nerve-ending. More and more often he felt his mind was not in his control. Yet, there were surges of power that made him feel as if he, himself, were a *god*. He was planning his next 'encounter' with the people in that house. The entire world would know what a god he was. His family, he thought, they would be the *first* to know. He flicked at the manila file for the male 'rookie' as his underling, the quasi-manager called him, pushing it to the side of his desk. Could there be anything of *less* interest to him than an alcoholic *male adult*?

"I don't think so, do you?" The voice again.

He had been certain the voice came from his Jag. That car was coolness itself—it was closer to being a living thing than most *people* he knew. But its comments came to him whenever it pleased, wherever he happened to be. Here, in his office where he knew he was alone, he felt an eel of fear slither along his spine giving his groin a painful tweak.

With that tweak his mind tumbled back in time to the cemetery under the willow trees.

He was nine again and it was as if three drive-in movie screens surrounded him, forming a triangle. Was *he* really inside the movie? His child's mind felt terror mixed with awe. For indeed his body was in the eye of a ceremonial magic fest. And as he ground his small penis into the earth beneath him (earth that covered the squirrel he had just dismembered) he swore to the demon that watched, ready to invade his soul, that if he could have this thrill of power, this pleasure beyond measure, have it forever, he, Randolph, would pay any price.

He heard his small voice beg. "What ever you want I will do. I love this feeling. I want this feeling forever."

Sitting at his desk, now, he recalled the answer—that rasping, guttural, menacing shriek as it reached in to take his child-soul. He had forgotten. All these years he'd forgotten. The terror returned as he wondered what that demon would want of him.

And quickly, the corners of his mouth came up, although his eyes remained empty. Because he knew how to please the Evil one—how to make that fear go away.

A parade sashayed along the runway of his mind. *Kandle and that black asshole. The cop and his pregnant-wife. The other cops' girlfriend. The Avenger-Bitch. And, the bitch he had the misfortune to be married to.* He knew how to please the voice. Randolph touched his intercom. "Something's come up. If I get any calls, I'll be out for the rest of the day."

"What about this new guy? The ex-priest."

"He was a *priest*? You didn't say that."

"Maybe it slipped my mind. I *gave* you his folder. I assumed you'd read it." His whine was pissy. "Jesus. I don't know what to do with a *priest*."

Hearing that tone of voice made Randolph want to see the inept fart bleed. But you can't kill everyone, who'd do the work?

SPIRITS OF THE ONCE WALKING

"Can you handle anything without my step by step instructions? Give him my love for Christ sakes. Oh, and introduce him to the young boys. I bet that'll keep the sick fucker occupied."

Putting on his coat he thought once again of Kandle. She had been the turning point in his life. Shouldn't that count for something? "Like man," he thought, trying to sound like Maggert would have, "shouldn't that give the *bitch* some kind of priority?" This time, he laughed out loud. "Kandle is a small residue of Vietnam; she's hiding in the Jack-in-the-box that sits at the very top of my toy chest."

Kandle loved visiting with Diane—the psychologist Gee had recommended. Peace and tranquillity seemed to emanate from the woman. It made her think of Georgia. Fleetingly she wondered what Gee would need to talk to a therapist *about*—she seemed to have all the answers already.

They'd been talking for over a half-hour. "He's so good to me, but he has such a temper. It brings me right back to feeling like I felt around my step-father—feeling like I'm a little girl again."

"Have you told Sam that's what he's doing?" Diane's voice was calm, soothing—making everything Kandle said seem completely rational and right.

"Sure. I told him that he couldn't talk to me that way—that he had to have more respect."

Diane nodded her on.

"Well, he said he wasn't angry, or disrespectful. He said, 'Just because I have a personality you think it's disrespect. It's not. It's me.' And then he said, 'What do you think people are talking about when they say, 'He has a colorful personality.'?"

"I said, 'I don't think they mean it's colorful. I think they're politely saying, it's mean.' And Sam said, 'Well, whatever *they* mean, it *is* colorful, it's just a little dark like me'."

Both women laughed.

"Most of the time he makes me feel very loved. He helps me grow. He takes away the fear I have of caring for someone. You know? If you don't care, you don't risk getting hurt. I think it's because I never got to know my dad." Kandle knew that her time was up. She reached for her coat.

Diane appeared to regret her leaving. "We'll find out why you're afraid to care, and why you feel small or little when he's angry. People do get angry and it's not always personal. But one thing's for certain, you're not afraid to tell Sam what you think. I like that. That's a healthy sign. A sign of a healthy relationship." Diane walked into the other room with her. "None of this is serious. We can work it out. You are a very perceptive woman."

Kandle went down the front steps with a feeling of lightness. All they'd done was "chat" and that heavy, ragged weight she'd carried was gone. Diane was pure gold.

Outside, she looked around for Sam. He'd said he might not be able to make it back in time. The cold air made her step quickly; she went to the eastside of the Art Institute. She'd grab a bus; Sam would come over later.

Chapter Twenty-Four

Law was impatient; Gee was late getting home.
But before he had the opportunity to become overly concerned Vince phoned.

"Are you ready for this?" Vince said. "Another body; I'm sure it's by the same guy. Remember how we thought that he must have thought Timothy was a dame? Well, it's another male, but kind of a regular male, if you get my drift. How weird is *that*?"

So. A guy. And evidently he wasn't wearing a teddy. This fella was the owner of Maggert's Machines on West Lake Street. Maggert. *Why was that name so familiar?* He tried to page Gee one last time. No answer. Why was his life always in a state of hurry and worry? He was sick and tired of got-to-do-it-ASAP'S. And here he was, one more time, dashing off a quick note to his love before literally running out the door. He knew Gee was upset. He knew it had something to do with his own behavior regarding his damn brother and Elsie. All those years wishing Toast hadn't become a priest; years of feeling as if he'd lost his best friend, well, it was confusing. All Law could think of now was why hadn't the a-hole stayed a priest. But it was Gee that he loved so why did he care what his brother did with Elsie?

Now that was a damn good question.

One he was sure that Gee was asking herself right this very minute.

One more cup of Godiva hot chocolate and the photographer was certain she would go into sugar shock. She'd hung the crime scene contact prints to dry and left the dark room. Something didn't seem right. Beaver had an odd urge to deal with each time she went into her dark room to develop. Negatives represented hours of work and she had a nearly uncontrollable urge to flip on the light and expose everything. Ruin the soup, so to speak. To date she'd been able to resist, but it seemed to be getting more difficult. What *was* that about?

That wasn't the problem today though.

She set her chocolate lovingly on the desk and went back inside the dark room. Seconds later she came running from the room, arms draped with damp contact sheets. Her face was a puzzle of disbelief as she studied the small prints. Even at this size she could clearly see the cops and their cars. She could see the ambulance, the filled body bag, the coroner's car. That's it. *That's all.*

What could she possibly do with this crap? These photos were worthless.

Where were the junk cars? The heaps of rust?

Was she losing her mind?

Was God really punishing her for that one hit of acid she did in the tenth grade? He was. Just like her mother said He'd do. And she couldn't do one damn thing about it. Wait it out. See what the other reporter's photographs looked like.

She sure couldn't call anyone and ask if those junk cars she saw were *there*. "Hi. Beaver here. Ya' know that big junkyard murder story? How'd your photo's come out?"

Hadn't the newspaper article talked about the junkyard? She rustled through stacks of papers. Where was a damn paper when you needed one anyway?

Ah. The light went on.

SPIRITS OF THE ONCE WALKING

She'd wrapped the grease in it from her morning sausage and egg. See Mom, I do still have a portion of my mind. It was time to become a vegetarian instead of just talk about it. Much less grease and she wanted less grease in her life.

Well, why not drive there and have a peek for herself? That's what she'd do. Beaver grabbed her coat and keys.

The 911 paramedics raced the screaming old man to Riverside Hospital's emergency room. They'd had to secure his hands to his sides to keep him from tearing at his penis. From what they could make out he'd dumped an entire pot of fresh scalding coffee on his lap. His wife said it was because he always tried to do two things at one time, in this case, pour himself a cup of the coffee she'd just prepared while looking at the newspaper.

Why couldn't he pay attention to what he was doing for once? He had trouble getting it up as it was, what was going to happen now, she said? Looked like he'd gone and shriveled his *noogies* for good, she said.

The old man (his name was Frank) was worried that more than just his sex life was ending. After all, he knew that it had been years since he'd crushed those old junk cars he'd been reading about.

Except for the Camero they'd found that body in. It was originally brown, like the paper said, and it was gutted except for the driver's seat. And it had been stolen the night before he'd crushed all that useless iron. He knew those rust buckets were no longer there on River Road. He knew it. He did.

Didn't he?

What if he'd already died and gone to hell and this was only the beginning of an eternity with his dear wife Mildred taking care of him?

Chapter Twenty-Five

The strange human being said, "Now, my boy, you are to learn a lesson. I have been guarding you all your life, but you have been careless. You shall travel to the House of the Dead and learn that life is important. The path is already made for you. You had better hurry, and perhaps you will get back before they bury your body. I am your Guardian Spirit (dumalaitaka). I will wait here and watch over your body, but I shall also protect you on your journey."
    Don C Talayesva   SCHOOL OFF THE RESERVATION

Claudette was feeling somewhat disoriented. She thought she might have taken one, or even two, too many Prozac. They kept increasing her dosage and rather than throw away the expensive pills and get stronger ones, she'd always use up the last of the old prescription. As Randolph loved to say, "Waste not, want not." She hadn't heard the children leave but they must have. The empty house seemed lonely without the noise of their constant bickering. In a daze she wandered into Theodore's room and began to pick up the debris that was everywhere.

It seemed like hours had passed. She found herself sitting on the floor of *her* bedroom holding a book she thought she remembered finding underneath Teddy's bed.
    A book on Satanism.

She glanced at her lap and read again the signs of demonic possession. Let's see. Where was she? Number six.
To make a pact with the Devil.
Well, how could *she* know if her husband had done that? The rest fit him like a condom. Each and every one of them...he did *live a wicked life*...he lived *outside the rules of society*...he made *sounds and movements like an animal* every time he made love (she shuddered at those words) to her. Was she living with a real man, or rather, a demonic *thing*? She heard Randolph's answer. *Paranoia.* That was her middle name. Just call me Ms. Prozac Paranoia Boodles. How-do-*you*-do?

Hundreds, no, millions of people took this drug. It was safe. The doctor told her it was safe. There was something wrong with her.

Perhaps *she* was the one possessed.

Dispite her fog she knew it was time to return to her immediate problem. What did it matter if Randolph was a devil, or *either* of them possessed by one? She had to get rid of him—or them. She took Theodore's book and hurled it at the whirring humidifier; the sound of it sometimes threatened her sanity. "Why buy such a cheap one?" she'd asked her possibly demonic hubby.

Replaying his answer she pulled herself off the floor.

"The only difference between this and the more expensive model is the noise it makes, Claudette. You can have it on when *you're* home alone; we'll leave it off when *we're* home together."

She spoke out-loud as she went over to the stupid thing. "Well that's just dandy, Randy. Dandy Randy." She gave it a kick. "You prickhead. You think I'm a nothing." She glanced in the mirror and saw a disheveled stranger. Running her fingers through her sticky hair she meandered to the bed. I'll *get* him, she thought. One more Prozac to calm my nerves and I'll go to the Avenger-Woman's *house* if I have to.

Sam and Elsie walked along River Road.

Pip had gone with the vet for a day or two; although no one liked that idea they thought it was for the best. Even Pip appeared comfortable leaving with Judy; he knew her and knew he was safe.

Darwin and Tony were on a roll with their bitching; when it seemed they were not going to take the hint and do their carrying on in private, Sam asked Elsie to go for this stroll.

"I've been dying to get you alone, Sam."

"Oooh baby. I've waited so long to hear those words tumble from your wine-dipped lips."

"What?" She giggled. "Are you nuts? Or what?" She scooped her mitten full of snow and tossed it in his face. "My lips have not touched wine in much too long!"

Laughing, "Just practicing for Wick," Sam brushed at the snow. He suddenly turned somber. "So what did the vet say about Pip and HIV?"

"I don't really understand how it works but I want to learn. I guess the virus dies almost immediately when it's exposed to our atmosphere. They think the victim was dead quite a while before Pip came in contact with the blood. They're doing tests, but everything should be fine. Still, it will be months before we know for certain."

"Wow. At last some news, huh? *Our atmosphere*? Makes me think of aliens; the kind with those big eyes. Look, I got to talk to you Els. I'm damn near scared to death."

"Wait. Before you go ahead with what I think you want to talk about, something's been killing me. Who visited you that other night? A tall guy who looked familiar got into a car with dealer-plates? I wanted to talk to you, but shied away when I saw him."

"Wish you'd have come on in. It might have saved me from my *slip and slide.* Know what I mean?"

Instantly her face lit up. "Maddog? That geek who used to work for Darwin! That's who it was, right?"

"Umhm."

"He didn't look like himself. More like a withered old...ah. I get it. *Junkie.* That's where you got the shit."

"That's where I got the shit. If it weren't for that prick I'd have stayed clean and I'd have been with Wick at the cemetery."

Elsie put one arm around his waist while they walked. "Excuse me for not biting on that party-line, but take it from one who's been there, you were looking for trouble Sam. It was only a question of time."

She noticed how his eyes were instantly slick, like the oil that sits on coffee that's made from quality beans. Her voice softened. "It wasn't your fault Sambo. What happened to Wick, I mean. The other, the drugs, you can beat yourself for that if you want. But I'd say you've been doing real good with the guilt. Come on. Let's get past this blame and get down to it, shall we?"

"Right you are. You're the lady. So here it is. I fell flat out in love. Fast, I know, but there you have it. She's special. Well, you know. How'd you know we'd click?"

"I didn't know. But you're a lot alike. And it's always good to meet strong, positive people. Right? You have this way of living your life with flair. What's the word? *Panache.* She's the same way. And she's self-reliant in the way Bobbie was, with heart, and she has this way of finding what's good in people. Like loving people in spite of the many reasons they give you not to love them. Don't you think?"

Sam hugged Elsie. "You've just gone down the list of why I love her. I'm scared out of my wits; you know he's after her, my Wick. You know she's gonna die less somethin's done. It's déjà vu. The cops are running in circles; like they did when Bobbie was killed."

Elsie knew what he was asking her to do. And she was already committed to being involved in the case. But did she want to put him in danger again and tell him her secrets? He was studying her face waiting for an answer.

"Look Sam." She'd gone pale. As if she'd seen a ghost.

"What? I don't see anything."

"That's the point. This is the spot where the body was found. The place Wickie and I met that night he was chasing her. Don't you remember? The cars! The junk cars!

Where are the cars?"

Chapter Twenty-Six

"Name's Larry Maggert. Owner here. He used to work for Darwin. Hear they called him Maggot." Said Vince.

The used car shack was filthy—with one big exception—the shower. Oh, there were other parts of the place that had been wiped down for fingerprints, that was obvious, but the shower sparkled. Obvious also, was that the man who'd died this bloody death was a pig. Not the chauvinist kind, although perhaps that, too. The shower sparkled yet the body was evidence that the owner had not been in that shower himself within recent weeks.

Law looked up. "You must have seen him yourself at Silano's when we worked that Eunuch case?"

"Hm. Naw. Don't recognize him. Could it be that his face is mostly gone?"

"Oh. Yeah. Guess it is." Law seemed preoccupied.

"You didn't *notice*?"

"Vince, will you get off my ass? I've got more on my mind than this pile of ground beef." Law pointed to Maggert's gored body. "Frankly, I don't know why you aren't thinking along the same lines as I am."

"What does *that* mean?"

"It means that everyone we care about is in friggin' incredible danger. Some murdering bastard is after our entire damn *clan*; I'd be willing to bet his list includes you. But for sure, Mary, Elsie, Gee, Sam and Wick."

"What're you saying?" Vinny's face was the color of an old-time black and white television screen—faded dinge-gray.

"Jesus, Vin. It's like when they were passing out brains they thought you said strains, and they gave you a head full of Rock and Roll."

Law had to grin. "C'mon. Let's get out a' here. We're done. Only important thing to see was that somebody took a shower and it sure wasn't the Maddog. Under that crust of blood there's a load a' dirt. I'd be willing to bet he died not long after our young man."

"Mary and I haven't been gettin' along too well." Vinny's voice was choked. He looked like he might cry.

"No shit." Law took him by the arm. "Let's go Einstein. What does she see in you anyway? Can't be brains or sensitivity. Got a big schlancter?"

Randolph could not clearly process his thoughts until he felt himself hugged into the womb of his Jaguar—the beast—his closest kin. He sat in a funk while the rumblin' beast warmed its engine.

His major concern was who should be next. That, was his *beast of burden.* No. They were, he chuckled, *beasts* of burden. Soon to be annihilated. He really needed to formulate a plan. He opened his briefcase. A shot of the crystal would get his mind on track.

"Why do you think they call it dope?"

This time he ignored the voice.

He felt the liquid manna feed his need. What a glorious drug! How could something so glorious be so inexpensive?

In Randolph's mind, that was what kept him from becoming a junkie. At least a major part of it. Junkies lost their family, homes, jobs—they lost it all for their *loaves-of-bread*—methamphetamine was dirt cheap.

"*Dirty deeds done dirt cheap.*"

Randolph's head snapped 'round to check the rear of his beast. Nothing there. What *or* whom ever sang those last words could read his mind. The knowledge chilled. But the *drug* warmed.

He felt that oh-so-familiar tingle in his balls, and rather than concentrate on his plan of action his mind took him for a stroll.

He'd come from money.

Randy the Dandy had been the first kid in Farmington High School to have a brand spanking new car. A red Mustang convertible. In those days that was some hunk of iron. The twitty 'hides' fell over one another trying to get to him and his car. That was when he realized what a great set of wheels can do for a man. He and his convertible were a package deal. Randolph's chest puffed out as he thought, "that backseat sure saw the back seats—almost every girls' in town."

"*If we got to take this stroll down your memory lane Dandy, why don't we stroll on down Park Avenue that night of the girl's slumber-party?*" The normally harsh voice was aluminum-siding-salesman, smooth.

He did what the voice suggested, he went there.

He watched himself on his minds' big-screen: he was standing in the rain outside Patty's house, peering in the window. The night was starless; his then plumpish body was well hidden in the shadows. What were the bouncing beauties inside doing, playing charades? Patty had stuffed clothing inside her shirt, around her waist, then cinched a black belt to make it look as though a roll of fat hung over it. She had her back to the window and stood legs apart, hips jutting forward, holding her hand in front of where her curly bush lived.

Outside in the cover of night he'd reached inside his pants thinking that she was playing with herself, sticking her fingers in and out of her pussy while the girls watched. No doubt she was telling them how good he'd fucked her.

He was hard as pipe seeing the girls watch her hands please herself while hearing about his prowess; just as he was about to shoot his wad he heard their giggles turn to shrieks of laughter. Patty turned and he saw that she held what appeared to be a tiny pale and puffy uncooked breakfast sausage. She wasn't playing with herself, she was pretending to be someone. Voices and laughter came through the window loud and clear.

"I don't think he even knows it's 'spose'd to be hard when you stick it in."

"I think, *he* thinks, it's a race! The quicker he comes and that little thing shrivels even more than it already *is*, the quicker he can qualify to run the race again!"

"But don't 'cha' think that teenie weenie looks just like one a' his pale ol' fingers? So, soft and puffy an' all?"

"Not much bigger, that's for sure."

He wanted to run, but he stood mesmerized until the one girl who had kept her 'favors' to herself threw her slipper at Patty's wiener knocking it in the general direction of the window.

As Randy ducked he heard Claudette's angry voice. "You guys are warped. You do anything Randolph asks, for a ride in his flashy car, and now you make fun of him! You make me sick."

"*Oh, oh Claudette. Prettiest little girl that I ever met's Claudette.*"

Except she wasn't, was she?

Claudette was plain. She'd tricked him by being so damn agreeable, so willing to please him. Randolph deserved better. Much better. Randolph thought about his pet cemetery. He thought about the junk-car cemetery. He wanted to fill a cemetery with people.

Enough of this. Time to motor. The beast needed to be fed. Who cares who's on first? As long as somebody is.

Chapter Twenty-Seven

"Fear gained more and more mastery over him, especially after this second, quite unexpected murder. He longed to run away from the place as fast as possible. And if at that moment he had been capable of seeing and reasoning more correctly, if he had been able to realize all the difficulties of his position, the hopelessness, the hideousness and the absurdity of it, if he could have understood how many obstacles and, perhaps, crimes he had still to overcome or to commit, to get out of that place and to make his way home, it is very possible that he would have flung up everything, and would have gone to give himself up, and not from fear, but from simple horror and loathing of what he had done."
      Crime & Punishment   Fyodor Dostoevsky

Sam couldn't get back to the house fast enough.

    He had to get in touch with Wick. He'd wanted to talk to Elsie so damn bad that he'd missed the time he was to pick his lady up from her appointment. They'd agreed that if he wasn't there she'd simply take the bus. Not a big deal for Kandle; she bused a lot. And that seemed fine at the time when he knew he'd be there. But now. Now, all this talk with Elsie about why Wick was cool and exactly right for him had ended with the discovery that those junk-yard cars were gone. What the hell was going on?

The worst was that Sam hadn't been able to finish his talk, hadn't done what he'd set out to do. He'd wanted to ask for Elsie's help in catching this man who was stalking Kandle. Had Elsie waylaid him on purpose with talk of Kandle's attributes, he wondered? She definitely had a way of doing things at her own pace, in her own way. Like right this minute. She'd refused to go home with him, literally shooed him away. Saying she wanted to be alone. Maybe she wanted to think about her own problems with Law's brother; Sam had to respect that. But what if she needed his help but would rather protect him than ask for it?

Sam went around the side to his own entrance, dialing the phone before his coat was off. "Wick?"

"Oh honey. Man oh man. Am I glad to hear your voice." Relief feasted on him, forcing a grin.

"I know I said I'd come to your place, but would you mind taking a cab here instead? I noticed a lot of our buddies cars out front and I want to find out what's going on."

She sounded so happy, it made his grin foolishly wide; he was all teeth.

"Hurry Wickie. I can't wait to lay these eyes on you. Be careful, 'kay? Real careful. See ya' babe."

The second he hung up, content that Wick was safe, he remembered Elsie back at the river. She attached some great significance to the fact that all the cars were gone. Couldn't the police have had the area cleared for purposes of their own? Sure they could have. What else would explain their disappearance?

Elsie stood by the edge of the partially frozen water and thought back to the night when she'd found Kandle. Ever since she got out of jail she'd been drawn to this area. Why? In the beginning she was certain she knew the reason. It was serene, historical, and not a part of the chaotic city.

She remembered wondering why she didn't realize the cars were there on her earlier visits. So, she was being summoned to this spot for a reason. What reason? Those cars weren't part of the serenity. Why hadn't she seen this sooner?

She had to understand who called to her here and why. Silently she asked her friend Lynn's Spirit to guide her. Elsie let herself relax, become one with her surroundings. She stood silent letting all thoughts evaporate.

Beneath her feet were snowdrifts that led to patterns the ice crocheted at the waters' edge. Her eyes felt drawn to one area; it resembles old Irish lace, she thought, what her grandma used to call fancy-work. It was like a veil made to cover the face of a beautiful woman—a face she could clearly see. The woman was sad; she was in mourning.

Why did she feel drawn to this space of ice and water? She was going to find out. Turning, ready for the brisk walk to the house, she paused, she heard voices. *Was that children crying?* She circled, as if in a dance: nothing there. Nothing but the cold icy snow and the black lethal water.

Elsie shook her head. Perhaps they were the children from her dream.

In the uncanny way they had of sometimes tuning in to one another's needs, the group had collected at Darwin's home. By the time Elsie came they were assembled. Everyone except Mary and Kandle.

"Wick's on her way. She's taking a cab." Sam answered Elsie's question.

"And Mary? Where is Mary?"

Vinny's mood darkened the room. "She left the doctor almost three hours ago. I checked the house—in case she wasn't answering the phone, you know—not wanting to talk if it was me. Doesn't look like she's been back home."

"Doesn't she have a cell-phone?" asked Gee.

Vince shook his head, yes.

"She'd surely call if there was any problem. She's probably shopping or visiting someone. Don't worry Vinny, she'll turn up soon, I'm sure." Gee wished she felt as comfortable as she tried to sound.

"It's just that I've been such an ass."

No one bothered to argue that point with him, not even to make him feel better.

"And I know she's mad. Last night we watched Tales of the Crypt. When they said the episode was entitled, Loved to Death, Mare said, "Or, the honeymoon's over." It was the only thing she said to me all night." Vince put his jacket back on. "I've got to try and find her. Sorry Law. I know we need to have a meeting of the minds, but I've got to go." He walked to the door, talking all the way, and by the time he finished the door slammed, punctuating his words.

"So much for our round-table discussion." Law snarled. "The rest of you, it's time to talk. Time to listen-up, too. We've got something going on here that I can't get a grip on. Every person in this room (and a couple who aren't here) are in serious danger."

"What danger?" Toast entered with a suitcase gripped in each hand.

Law groaned. Could this get any worse? "It has nothing to do with you. Go to Choices and get out of our hair."

Their predator waited just down the block.

Vinny walked outside. And was observed.

Eeenie, meenie, minee, mo, thought the Evil-one. *Pounce or pause, I want to know*?

Randolph's grin was menacing. *Why delay what can be done today?*

Elsie's face was red. From cold, or embarrassment?

"Law, I know you're trying to help us, and I have plenty to discuss with you, but if you could give us a minute or two, I'd like to have a word with Terrence before he leaves."

Elsie was asking his permission? Law humphed, and watched as the two, there goes that gaze again, went into the sitting room alone. He tapped his fingers on the table until he noticed the way Gee was looking at him. He forced a pleasant demeanor on himself. "Gee, I've got news for you."

"Really?"

Why was her look cool, he wondered? He knew full well?

"The Department is searching for a liaison person to help with the Native American youth."

"You don't want Gee to work with gangs?" Tony spoke for the first time.

"Well, I don't, no. You're right. But it's not only gang kids, it's others too, and if anyone could make an impact on the community, if anyone could reach *those* kids, it's Gee, don't you agree?"

"I don't know if I like the way you say, *those* kids."

Where were Gee's usual mellow tones? "And that's exactly why we need you, my lady, my love." Law tried to present to her his most endearing look. "You always tell me we need to learn to respect traditions. Here's your chance to make a difference."

"It sounds to me like a position made just for a woman like you, Gee." Darwin sounded excited. "You *could* make a significant difference. And much of the time it seems hopeless."

"Hopeless?" Gee's face showed the concern that was in her heart. Darwin knew which strings to pull. He and Gee were also kindred spirits. She pulled the serape she wore on this chilly day around her shoulders.

A blanket of past Spirits.

They sat on the sofa for minutes holding one another before a word was spoken.

"You know that I don't want to leave you?" Law's brother stroked her face and she felt herself become liquid in his arms.

Could she stay with him, forget the problems of the world and spend her time on Elsie? Feeling the warmth of his body soothe her she knew the answer. "No."

"No?"

"That's what I said."

"But why?"

"You have to go. You're no good to me unless you get yourself well. I'll never know if it's me you love, or if I'm just another escape for you, Toast."

"But *you* want me here, don't you? If you knew I was well, you'd want to be with me?"

"I can't tell you that. You're *not* well."

"But love, Elsie. *What about our love*? Don't you believe our love is strong enough to overcome the odds?"

She felt his strong arms surround her. Those arms alone could hold her, keep her from falling. Couldn't they? She looked into his eyes. Her palms placed on his chest. His body felt hard. Hard enough to take them anywhere they wanted to go.

Elsie knew the answer. "No, Toast. You have to find power inside yourself. You see yourself as a victim. *You'll make a victim of me.* I've been there; I don't want to go back. I won't go back. When you're strong inside return to me. Then, we'll see." She pulled herself from his arms and walked out the door without looking back.

Chapter Twenty-Eight

Detective Vince Tonetti was in a hurry but he checked his rear-view mirror as he pulled away from the curb. The car at the end of the block turned on its headlights just as he looked. That car, now moving behind him, gave the impression of a small dark shadow.

He saw the dark shadow, but not clearly, his thoughts were of Mary.

Why'd he been behaving like such a pig? He didn't care if she gained weight; when she was big with Vinny Jr. he'd loved her pregnant belly, *loved it*. That much he knew. Then what was it? He drove faster, exceeding the speed limit. He'd go on home first. She could be there, she could; the words were a chant in his head. Be there baby, be there. Be there baby, be there. They had an ultrasound scheduled for next week because she'd had problems with their last baby. Her first baby. Their, Vinny Jr.. Maybe this one was a girl? And maybe his daughter wouldn't have a chance to be born if he didn't get his 'ass*act*' together. Was it next week, or was it today?

The radio was playing a song that broke into his *be there baby* prayer. He turned it up. "*See the girl with the red dress on...*" At that moment his mind's eye pictured them dancing the night she told him she was pregnant again. They were so damn happy.

Suddenly Vinny turned the music down.

He had his answer.

He was worried that she'd lose this baby too. Worried that if she didn't take care of herself something would happen to the baby, and if, god forbid, that happened, what would become of them? So, if he cared a little less, created some distance between them, it wouldn't hurt so damn much when it happened.

That was it!

He couldn't wait to get to her; to tell her. She would know the truth when she heard it. She would know. And she would forgive him his pettiness, his temper, his lack of empathy. Mostly forgive him for being scared. What a weenie he was!

He pulled in front of their place and got out, running toward the house. Mary! His heart screamed her name. Be here, Mary.

Inside his locked car the phone began to ring.

Chapter Twenty-Nine

This was serious business; they all knew it. They sat around the table. Wick had arrived and Law's brother grabbed the same cab that dropped her off. Toast was on his way to Choices for twenty-eight days.

Law frowned when the phone rang. Another interruption.

Tony answered it. He put his hand over the mouthpiece. "It's Mary."

"Sure thing Hon," they heard him say. "I'm sure you'll find him. See you soon." He smacked the receiver, sending her a kiss.

Law shook his head, exasperation evident. Tony would never change. "Did you, by any chance, tell her to hurry, that we were having an important meeting?"

"She's going to try to reach Vin by phone. If she can't she'll stop by their apartment before she comes here." Tony gave him a look. "Love comes first, Law." He pinched the older detective's cheek as he pulled out a chair to sit next to him. "Tell him Gee. Tell him I'm right."

"My man, you are right on target." Sam hugged Kandle to him, almost as if he were afraid to let her go.

"I hate to say it Tony and Sam, but in this *one* case I believe Law could be right." Gee's tone and smile said she really didn't believe what she was saying—not in her heart.

Even Darwin was willing to say that love doesn't always come first. "Spike, it's well past time to unscramble this puzzle facing us—time to set love aside. For instance, how do cars simply disappear?"

Tony's face fell. "I thought we were getting together to talk about the wedding plans. You know? For Law and Gee? Even though the wretch doesn't deserve this fine woman, they are getting married in a week or two, right?"

"Not unless..." Law began.

"Cars that *disappear*?" Tony's screech interrupted. "What *are* we talking about?"

"If you shut your face a second I'm about to explain."

"Couldn't some city department looking for make-work have had that area cleared?" asked Darwin.

Law's voice was frustrated. "Make-work in a crime-scene area? Give me a break, bud. Even the city's not that stupid." To himself, he muttered, "least I don't think they are."

"Our city can do some pretty damn stupid things." said Sam while gazing lovingly at Kandle.

Elsie put her hand out. "Law, let me talk, please. Here's what's going on guys. The junkyard where they found the young man's body is no longer there. In fact, I go there often and I don't remember seeing it *before* the crime, either."

"Well, it was there years ago. I remember seeing it when I looked at the area before I bought this house." said Darwin.

"Okay, so it *used* to be there. I'm trying to tell you all something if you'll just let me finish. It hasn't been there for quite some time, not until lately. And now it's gone again." Elsie looked at Gee. "I feel foolish saying this, but I think you'll understand. Remember when you left me by the river Tone? I felt a presence there. Someone was under the water. It was a woman, and she seemed to be grieving. Then, as I started to leave I heard children crying."

SPIRITS OF THE ONCE WALKING

Kandle gasped.

"Like there's no children crying in this city." Law's sarcasm cut.

Elsie gave Law a stern look. He can have a head like a stone sometimes, she thought.

"Did you try to get her out?" Tony didn't get it.

Elsie sighed. "I don't mean that a woman was actually living under the ice, Tony."

"That piece of land was once sacred ground," said Gee.

"What?" They asked all at once.

"I was looking through some old maps given to me by a healer from the reservation. Centuries ago my ancestors used that stretch of land to bury their most honored dead along the river so that they might look out on the water for eternity. And so their bodies would dissolve into the earth, then, *through* the earth, made richer now, they would enter the gates to the river and flow to all parts of the land. It was a great honor to be buried in that spot."

They listened to Gee never doubting her words.

"I don't think the woman or the children were Native American," said Elsie.

"So now you can tell someone's race with your psychic powers? That's a bit much to swallow, Elsie." Law was always the cynic, unless it was Gee talking. This time it was the politically correct thing to do; he could see that from the slight smile on Gee's lips. His beeper went off. "Sorry. Got to call in."

Kandle was clearly stunned. After all, she'd been there and seen the cars, even touched them. She *knew* they were there. "I don't understand." Her voice was almost a whisper.

They sat trying to absorb this information.

"I 'spose you all heard that Maggert's dead too?" Tony said it as if he thought it had something to do with them.

"Who's Maggert?" asked Kandle.

"Just some geek drug pusher. He used to work for Darwin peddling cars. We worked with him." Why did Sam have such a look of guilt on his face, wondered Kandle? "The world's a better place without the a-hole." Sam finished.

"Is that any way to speak of the dead?" The corners of Tony's lips turned slightly up.

Law returned quickly, his face years younger. "Good news. It was Officer Suzie. We have a suspect. Sometimes good old police work pays off." He grinned at Elsie. "Not that we're not grateful for your insights on the Spirit life by the river. I'll get hold of Vinny an' meet him at the station." He kissed Gee. "Why don't you tell them about our plans for the wedding down at Hidden Falls? I'll tell Vince to send Mary over to help. You guys can work out the celebration details and Vin and I will work out on this creep.

Getting into the detective's apartment was remarkably easy. Randolph had never been one to break and enter, although he could see that it might have an element of the chill to it. In this case, Vinny'd gone running inside and left the door ajar. After it was evident little wifie was not home Vince went straight to the phone. That's when Randolph slipped inside. *Knife in hand.* Ready to slice. He hid in the hall closet thinking how this stupid pig had wrecked his evening with the delectable Kandle. Now fate was going to play out this movement in a twist that ends in a burst of colorful action. As Randolph waited, his head throbbed to the ring of the telephone. He thought about how dear just a pinch of meth would be while he heard the one word that was music to his ears.

"Mary?" Vinny sounded as if he were about to sob. "Oh God, Mary. I've been so worried. And I've got to talk to you, got to tell you why I've been such an ass...okay honey. I'll wait till you get here. How long?... Hurry. And, hey Mary? Love you."

Randolph heard the detective move around. Should he take him out now? Not enough time to enjoy the scene as it played. Or, should he wait and get them together? It would be more fun to have one watch while he did the other. However enjoyable killing could be you had to do it alone. No one to talk to after the event. No one left to fuck. Like the little woman. He could fuck her in spades.

"Oh, oh Claudette. Prettiest little girl that I ever met..."

What the—? Could *he* hear that? Could the cop hear that music too? Randolph barely dared breathe. At heart he was a chicken-shit. Like the voice said, like his old man always said, he was just a frickin' chicken-shit.

Standing terrified in the closet, terrified the cop would catch and shoot his ass, Randolph's own personal movie screen began playing again. Big as life, there was Daddy-dear taking a knife to his worthless stepmother and her two bratty kids. The oldest one came crying to him, blubbering for his help, saying his mommy was bleeding. He watched now, as he'd watched then—and felt nothing.

"Randy," his father's voice—out-of-shape and out-of-breath—as he grabbed the one whom moments earlier had pleaded with Randolph for help, "get that other rug-rat an' gim' 'e a hand. Gonna slit the squealer." Randy hadn't felt motivated to murder some baby no matter how much he disliked it; Dad never let him forget.

The little mind-flick got him through the fear. And the cop hadn't bust in on him. Maybe no one else *could* hear the music.

Claudette.

She was the only one who ever stuck up for him. And now here he was planning her demise. Planning to kill her. *Going* to kill her. He'd found out that the LOLA condom most likely wouldn't work. Unfortunate. The plan was so poetic. Not that it wasn't still worth a shot. But, the virus was probably gone. Dead.

Prettiest little girl.
What a laugh. She was a dog.

God but his head hurt. His hands trembled. Could the cop hear his hands shaking? Could he?

He wanted to be sure to do Claudette. If he killed them all and didn't get to her, it was all for nothing. In fact, she'd be left with all that insurance and the business. Choices. She'd have money enough to get any man. Even a barker like Claudette could get a man with all that moola.

Randolph felt the closet walls closing in on him. He had to get out. Had to. But he also had to stay extremely still. No movement Randy the Dandy. As his muscles turned into tight knots that were connected to stretched ropes of sinew, he heard a far off noise. Bells. Was it church bells?

"Mary?" An excited voice.

"Oh. It's you." The voice dejected.

Dandy realized that the bells were not bells, but the ringing of the damn telephone.

"We got a suspect?" Excited once again.

"Sure. Sure. I get it. Be there in a flash. Just got to wait a minute or two for Mary."

"Fuck-you Law. I'm not leaving until I see..."

What was becoming a heated conversation was interrupted by the door. "Honey?"

Wifie was home at last.

"In here Babe." Then into the phone. "I'll hurry."

From the closet he could hear the phone slammed. Trouble in paradise. Dandy loved that. But what did he mean by suspect? Ah, police business. It was so exciting. While the two smooched and cooed he tried to decide what he would do. Drops of sweat ran down his neck. He knew specks of his bodily fluids were right now dribbling on clothing. He smelled the leather, the hint of lavender that clung to the clothing around him and tried unsuccessfully to mask very slight body odor. Ordinarily he'd be hard. The smell would do it. But he needed. God, how he needed. From his wet palm the knife slipped. He reached to collect it with his other hand and fell against the door while cutting his thumb.

Ohgodohgodohgod.

"What was that?"

"Nothin' honey. I'm sure it was next door. There's nobody here but me. And now you." Vinny kissed her neck. "What do you think about what I've been telling you? You forgive me?"

"I shouldn't you know." Her voice was a whisper.

Dandy heard that sound and wanted her to whisper in his ear.

"But, baby, do you? Do you? Say you do."

She must have decided to put him out of his misery. "I do."

"Can I leave you then, knowing you love me? Law's probably pissing his pants right now waiting for me. And I want to get my hands on this turd that raped Kandle myself. You know?"

Dandy heard that. Heard about the turd that raped Kandle. Heard that the suspect was him. Or, they thought it was him. He also heard that the cop was leaving his sweet pregnant wifie.

"Will you go to Darwin's so I don't have to worry about you being alone? Don't know how long this'll take."

That was the last thing he heard from Vinny as the door closed him out. Out of the lives of Mary, her unborn baby, and the Dandy-man.

Chapter Thirty

Elsie was on the phone; the others couldn't help but listen to her conversation; it was unusual to say the least.

"You're the woman who called me two days ago. Was your name Claudette?" Elsie's voice portrayed a small amount of the irritation she felt. Gee, Sam and Wick, Darwin and Tony, sat waiting for her to finish and continue their conversation. And Toast was on her mind. She'd walked away from him. But not easily. She felt sick to her stomach.

"Do you believe I'm a gun for hire, is that it then? Is that what this is all about?"

"I'm sorry for the pain in your life Claudette, but I'm not the answer you're searching for. Have you considered a woman's shelter?"

"Why? Well, please don't call me again. Not for *this*, Claudette. I'm willing to try to help you, or talk to you, but I won't kill your husband for you." With that, Elsie clicked off the phone.

"What?" Gee voiced what the faces surrounding Elsie asked. "Did you say murder her husband?"

"Umm." The color had left Elsie's face. "The woman is clearly frantic. She needs help, but it's like she has blinders on. The only solution she can see is me killing her husband. I can't help the poor thing."

"Poor thing?" Sam frowned. "Are we thinking clearly here, my love? What makes you so sure her husband deserves to be killed?"

"Of course you're right Sam." Elsie sat next to him. "Let's forget her problems for now and get back to ours."

"What? You don't believe our fine police department has our problem solved?" Tony grinned. He already knew the answer to that. "Hey you guys, the boss said we were 'spose to be planning a wedding party, *not* talking murder."

"The boss?" Gee wrinkled her nose. "I guess by that you mean my betrothed?"

Darwin watched as they all smiled in agreement. Why, he wondered, did the detective and Gee seem to be heading toward trouble in their relationship lately? Was it his imagination?

Gee looked uncomfortable. "I hope the location doesn't bother anyone. Especially you, Wick. We want to have the ceremony at Hidden Falls. Do you all know where that is?"

Kandle answered. "Isn't it on the eastside of the river? Down about a mile from the junkyard (that doesn't exist), and across the river?" She smiled. "I think that's a perfect spot. It's beautiful down there.

"There's an enormous clearing in the woods right by the river. We will arrange a circle of young choke cherry trees around a blanket spread over the snow. Law and I will stand in the center of it during the ceremony. The blanket is symbolic of two people who have chosen to share one blanket throughout life's journey." Gee had tears in her eyes. Her tradition was sacred to her.

"Journey together." Darwin's voice was soft. He looked at Tony. "I wish we could have this kind of ceremony Spike."

"Yes!" Gee's entire face glowed. "A double wedding!"

"Honey, Law would never go for it." Tony didn't want this to come between his good friends. "He accepts us. But to get married together, to share *that* day with us? Gee baby, please don't even ask him to do it."

"Why not?" Elsie asked. "Law's a big boy. Besides, he'll come through for you on this one, I'm sure of it." She saw some doubt on the faces around her. "He wants to do what's right. Some days that's harder than others. But it's time for him to step up to the plate."

"It will be a wonderful wedding!" Kandle's eyes danced.

Sam whispered something in her ear and she giggled and gave him a shove. "Sir, I hardly know you."

"What about the lady under the ice?" Sam was serious once more.

"I don't know." Elsie caught his mood. They could communicate like two fax-machines. "I want to find out. I think it has something to do with all of this. We need to know what, if any, multiple murders happened in that area."

"Where's Mary? Mary could check. She must still have her contacts at the precinct." said Tony.

"She's probably enjoying a few minutes alone. Look I got to know a press-photographer when I was in jail," said Elsie.

"Remember the name?" asked Sam.

"It'd be hard to forget. It was Beaver. Gloria Beaver." Elsie was already on her way to the phone. "Let's get the Beaver, as they call her, working on this."

Mary lifted her face to the hot sprays of water from her shower. She could feel the tension flow out of her. Her hand rubbed the soap over her tummy. Her baby was in there. Please God, don't let anything happen this time. Let her be healthy. Mary'd gotten to thinking of it, as a her. Why, she didn't know. It was just a feeling. But, she'd learned her feelings were often right. Vinny was on her mind too. He loved her. He'd never have said those things if he didn't; never have opened his heart to her.

She sang off key a song her mother used to sing to her, "*A tiny turned up nose, two cheeks just like a rose, she's mine from head to toes, that little girl of mine.*" She hummed the verse, what would they name their little girl?

Suddenly, chills raced over her bare skin breaking through her daydreams and the warm mist.

There was no noise.

Only a feeling.

Trying hard to listen, so afraid of silence, Mary kept up her sporadic humming while she scanned the area for something sharp, or hard. Nothing.

Then she remembered. She heard Vinny's voice months ago on her birthday. "You never know when you might need it to protect yourself."

She'd been mad as hell. How could he bring her a can of mace for her birthday? She could get all the damn mace she wanted. If she wanted. He'd put it on the shelf beside the tub right that very day and lectured her; while she hummed she searched for it.

Randy the Dandy's stomach clenched. The hand that held the knife was shaking so badly he wondered if he could slice with it. She was in the shower. It was classic. And Dandy loved classic. Anthony Perkins would be proud of him. He inched forward, his knife ready to slit the pregnant bitches throat, his eyes ready to see the flood of red spread down her bare breasts and thighs until it swirled down the drain. A stain for the drain, he thought as he reached out to pull the shower curtain aside.

"AAAAAAEEEEEEEHHHHHH!"

The noise assaulted him first; while he was wondering how she knew he was there, his entire face felt as if it were burning off. He heard the sound of an aerosol spray, but not in time. Not nearly in time. Falling over his own feet, he fled.

How could he kill her? He couldn't fucking see!

With one hand she pulled the shower curtain to cover her body and with the other aimed the can of mace and sprayed for dear life.

The sound of metal hitting the bathtub screamed in her ears. Had she dropped the can of mace? No. It was in her hand. She saw red. Her blood in the water. Could he have cut her and she didn't even feel it? Mary blinked; then saw clearly. He'd dropped the knife! On the way to the tub it'd nicked her toe.

Her finger, as if stuck on the mace, continued pressing down.

She heard the door slam, running footsteps, a car start and screech away. He was gone. The can fell from her hand to the floor, rolling until it hit the base of their toilet. She was a cop, at least she used to be; she knew she should go immediately to the phone.

Cold, shivering, she slid to the floor pulling the plastic curtain from its hooks and wrapping it around herself. She laid her hands over her stomach, over her baby, and cried.

Then, as she pictured the flowers she'd wanted on her birthday, pictured her beating the assailant over the head with dried roses, saw the petals float around the room landing in a pool of her own blood. She began to laugh out loud, hysterically, as she chanted to herself:

"Thank God for my Vinny. Thank God you're so frigging anal Vinny...."

Chapter Thirty-One

CHRISTMAS EVE 1993
"Silent night, holy night, all is calm, all is bright..."
This, would be the night.
"Ta da da boom de ey, I'll cut your throat today..."

I cut my finger in their closet; my blood is now a smear on the sleeve of the cops' work shirt, or tiny specks on the toe of her *shoe. It's all right there for them to find—me—I'm right in their damn closet.*

Sooner or later they'd figure out where he'd been hiding and they'd discover droplets of crusted-rust.

Wouldn't they?

Whatever. It was smart to proceed as if they already knew who he was. And Randolph was smart. But then, there were times when the Dandy in him surfaced; Dandy was less than intelligent.

Ruled by his cob.

"The old stiff cob she ain't what she used to be, ain't what she used to be, ain't what..."

Who said that?

Randolph shivered.

Knowing he wasn't alone in this endeavor did nothing to comfort him. Every so often a sliver of fear, of, what-will-it-do-to-

me-when-it's-done-using-me, slipped between the cracks of his doped sub-conscious.

"Why do they call it dope? Have you figured that one out yet my Dandy-man?"

Randolph felt its hot breath spew across the back of his neck. Goosebumps, big as small tits, spread—a flash flood, over his skin. This time he did not turn to see. This time, he was busy piercing his arm with the needle, feeling the warm rush that meant more to him than life itself.

Where to begin?

I know the answer to that. My family. At least that bitch I married. Maybe I'll do the kiddies if they're home; if not, well, lucky-duckies.

"Ain't that a shame, do-do-wop, do-do-wop...tears fell like rain, do-do-wop..." Sarcasm spiked the singing voice that came from everywhere and nowhere.

In his daze he wasn't certain. He checked the radio.

Off.

Randolph reached for the syringe that lay beside him, discarded on the seat of his beast. With one swift swing, accompanied by a tight wheeze, his right arm clutched the needle and stabbed behind the seat.

Empty air.

Was all that was there.

Fucking miserable voice. He was tired of it reading his mind. Tired of it knowing more than he knew himself about his own thoughts. "You fucking dink." *Randolph said the words out-loud and immediately felt foolish.*

Some tough guy he was. Dink. That'll put the fear of God into the Demon.

In black-and-white he saw his father's arm as it swung, stabbing at his stepmother. Funny, but recently he seemed to have little control over his own thoughts.

Maybe not so funny. Maybe predictable?

Of all the things I do not want to be, pride myself on not being, predictable is high on the list.

"Stop it!" *Again, his own voice spat, filling the car.* "I know what you're trying to do to me. Do you think that I'm so stupid I'll fall for your cheap smoke-and-mirrors trick?"

No answer.

He'd thought he could provoke the Evil-one. But, no.

Or am I, Randy the-Dandy-Randy, really the Evil-one?

"I never think of myself as Randy-the-Dandy." *His voice shook.*

Well, who cares? He swiped the greazy oil from his brow and started the engine. Time to head on home.

The lonesome voice of Hank Williams came to him from the rear seat, singing, without benefit of the radio—but by now he barely noticed that small fact. "Take these chains from my heart and set me free-e-e."

Why sure darlin', laughed Dandy. I got much better use for chains than your fucking heart.

It was their third bottle of White Zinfandel. Not one of the expensive brands like Darwin stocked, but it was doing the job and going down with ease. After spending the early part of the evening at the hospital with Mary and Vinny, Law and Gee were in shock. Hearing how their friend had narrowly escaped death, they made a promise to one another: to make the most of every minute they had together.

When they stopped at the liquor store for the wine, they walked down the aisle clutching hands. "I'm never leaving your side again." Law said.

"That could make some of the things I do every day quite difficult—not to mention your police work." Gee smiled, holding his hand tighter still. This was getting too serious for the evening

Gee had planned. But Mary's shower scene dictated serious. It would be difficult to shake that mood.

"Don't care. Only care about you."

She'd been waiting to hear those very words.

Later, the attack on Mary, coupled with a wine-induced glow, got them talking. They talked over everything that weighed so heavily on their minds: about their mutual friend Elsie; Law's brother and *his* relationship with Elsie; how Law used to be in love with Elsie and what his feelings were for her now. That was a big one, but the liquid-spirits helped them through it. Law talked about the interrogation of their suspect, before Mary called sobbing and they realized they had the wrong man and released the poor sap to his frantic family. Gee told him about their telephone call to the reporter that Elsie called the Beaver.

Hours and wine passed between them.

"Wanna toast my bride-to-be." Law kissed Gee's hand.

Her answer was first a giggle, something this serene woman rarely did. Then, "I do believe we've already made that toass." Her words were slurred. "Sir, are your intentions honorable?"

Lights from their small Christmas tree and a pine scented teardrop shaped candle were all that lit the living room. The couple sat on a blanket carefully placed in the center of the floor by Gee.

It was their special pre-nuptial celebration.

"Do you want them to be?" Cocky now, he stood and took her hands, pulling her up and into his arms. Music in the background was Billy Holiday's sensual *"You go to my head..."*

The moment was right.

It had been too many days since their minds had let their bodies relax enough to come together.

"In this Christmas light your flowing, wild hair is like a river of autumn leaves," Law paused, weaving slightly, "sunlight skips over the water... flickers through the leaves. I am blinded by your beauty." Law had made what he considered a feeble attempt at eloquence; for in his eyes she was much more beautiful than that.

To Gee, he was the earth, the stars and rivers all in one. She swayed, too woozy to answer. Her moon-face was the shade and smooth texture of the belly of a copper shell; it tipped back and beamed at him.

She wore a thin tunic that matched her skin.

Law grabbed it in both fists and heard her gasp.

She wanted him!

With a swift motion he ripped the material down the front.

My Lord, I'm a virile beast, he thought.

My man, such an animal, she thought.

Right at that moment, in one another's arms, their bodies began to slip downward; they crumbled to the blanket on which they hoped they would soon make their vows to ride forever together.

The wine had knocked them out.

Chapter Thirty-Two

Dressing was an ordeal.

Claudette moved as if a video played in her brain; periodically it was set on pause. There would be sparks of rationality now and again, but when too much time passed without movement, the pause button simply clicked itself off—unnoticed, it made an automatic flick returning to whatever channel was already on TV—Hollywood Squares...Wheel of Fortune...she saw without seeing, mindless viewing, mindless thinking.

She got up and pushed her face at the mirror, lipstick in hand, for what seemed an eternity. Her skin was puckered meringue left too long in the oven.

In the background she was jolted by sounds of her children arguing. Just smear the damn stuff on your lips, she told herself.

Do it.

It was some comfort, hearing those nasty tones of her kids, because it was normal. She stared in the mirror looking over her shoulder at the pile of books and papers on the bed. Proof. Not real proof. But it was all she had. This woman, this Elsie, this fighter for justice, she would have to help once the story was told. Thinking of Elsie, Claudette's movements stalled once more. What was up with her? She thinks I'm a kook, is what's up, she thought. "I'm going to do this." This was now her mantra—those five words; her lips moved, but no sound came out while she dressed.

She was buttoning her slacks when she remembered it was Christmas Eve. "Oh God, no. No, NO!" *He* would be home. Well, he might be. Either way, there were the children. How could she leave her children alone on Christmas Eve? What kind of mother would do a thing like that, she asked herself?

While she thought about the answer, the video inside her clicked off.

Her movements stopped—a freeze-frame.

"I wanted to wish you a Merry Christmas."

His voice was soft, filled with tenderness. Did the treatment center allow them to make telephone calls this early in their stay, she wondered. Maybe they made a special allowance because of the Holiday season. "It's good to hear your voice. I'm pleased they let you call."

"This joint's all but shut down. You wouldn't believe it; half the staff, *more* than half, is partying."

"Surely not the kind of party you infer."

"Yep. Got me signed in, gave me some propaganda to read, papers to fill out, and disappeared. But I can hear them carrying on; I know the sound of drunks, 'drunking'." Toast spoke just above a whisper. "I didn't call you to complain about Choices. It does seem an odd place though. I haven't seen a person over fifteen, except the man who showed me my room."

"Maybe they sent them all home for Christmas."

Toast paused, considering. "Wouldn't they be more likely to send children home...? Oh, forget that. I wanted to try to talk about us. I thought now that I was a safe distance away..." his words trailed off.

"Safe? I never thought of you as unsafe."

"Are you being coy?"

Was she? "Oh," a deep sigh, "Maybe so. Okay, so. The truth is I've been invited to go to kind of a gala downstairs with the guys, and I've been dragging my feet hoping you'd call, knowing you couldn't."

"That right? Hm." He chuckled. "And my stomach did flip-flops as I dialed, sure you'd cut me off. You sounded very final when I left. Well, thank-you, this is the gift I wanted for Christmas, Elsie."

She twirled a strand of pale blonde hair around one finger while she listened; then, tugging her black terry robe tight, she sat on the sofa and tucked her feet underneath herself. She'd been sipping Drambuie and nibbling at some wonderfully lace things Tony called Parmesan crispies. He'd been visiting with her when the phone rang, trying to talk her into coming to work at Silano's. He heard the tone of Elsie's voice when *she* heard who the caller was and he quickly, and rather obviously, made himself scarce.

As Toast described what he called flip-flops, she felt her own stomach quiver, but tried to ignore the feeling. She cleared her throat. "That woman called again. When the phone rang just now I was afraid it was her. Remember my talking about the Beaver? The reporter? I'm having her check out the name."

"Umhm. What was that again? Afraid I was not concentrating on what you were saying so much as hearing the tones in your voice, your scent...how your breath smells like toothpaste, and how much I was going to miss all of it."

Elsie felt dizzy with desire, yet plodded on. "Claudette. Her name was Claudette. I forget her last name, ah, hm... wrote it somewhere. Some kind of dog. I know, like poodle-something."

"Poodle? Oddly enough, that rings a bell, don't know why."

His deep voice made her tingle. Why was this so hard? She swallowed. "Do you remember seeing old rusted-out cars in the area where we found Pip?"

"Sure. It's a grave yard of filthy brown-orange tin along there. The rats have taken over."

SPIRITS OF THE ONCE WALKING

In a flashback she felt his breath on her neck and tried to concentrate on the conversation. "Not really. They're gone. All gone."

"The rats?"

"Probably them too, but I meant the cars."

"Who cleaned up?"

"Hm. Don't know. I don't think that's what happened."

"What?" He laughed. "They talked it over and decided to move by themselves to a better neighborhood? Let's see, did the rats drive the cars or the cars transport the rats?"

Elsie laughed too. "I can see you're not about to take this seriously tonight. We can talk about it later—you can give it some thought before we talk again. I just wondered if you remembered seeing them." It felt comfortable to her to think about talking to him again.

"Or, are *you* going crazy? Is that it?"

"Something like that."

"It's great hearing you laugh. I can see the smile on your face ...your eyes." His voice dropped low. "Els, I want to wrap my arms around you while you tell me about these disappearing cars...I want you."

"I'm not worth all that much on today's market, Toast. Pound for pound."

"You know what I mean."

"How's it going without the brandy?" Maybe talk of his addiction would upset him and make this conversation, and the way it made her feel, go away.

"I'm intoxicated with dreams of you...want to have babies with you... spend Saturday nights worrying if our children are behaving at the prom and someday have you call me Gramps."

His voice was low and as slow as she remembered his hands as he'd slid them over her. "I know. I want you too." What *was* she saying? She felt heat spread, blanketing her. "Is that what you called to get me to say?" Her feet came out from under her and she stretched them straight ahead; they were pink, warm.

"No. I want more."

"Like?"

"Like love." His voice was barely audible. "Forever love."

"Hm. I think you just might have that coming your way. So, yes."

"Yes, what?"

"Yes. It's time for me to have my own life. I've been running from love too long."

"Christmas just keeps on getting better and better."

Chapter Thirty-Three

Tony stood in the doorway watching the man who'd changed his life. Darwin's face glowed with contentment. His hair was down tonight, literally, and he looked like a Greek-god to Tony.

He must have felt Tony's eyes.

"Hey, Spike. What are you doing lurking there in the foyer?"

"Trying to figure out what could be making you so happy." Tony bent at the waist, put both arms around Darwin's neck, and kissed him long and hard.

"Well. If I wasn't in a good mood before, I'd have to be now." Darwin pulled Tony down next to him on the small sofa.

"So, tell your baby."

"I was thinking about the gift I got you for Christmas." Darwin uncharacteristically grinned from ear to ear. "You, my darling, are going to adore it."

"It's got to be fabulous. I can count all your teeth."

"Do we want to wait for Elsie? Was she almost ready?"

"My goodness Dar, one question at a time. You *are* in a tiz!" Tony ran his fingers through Darwin's flowing hair. Might as well keep a good thing 'up'. "Elsie's on the phone with Toast. And, she's not dressed yet. I say, lets open our gifts to one another, by that time she'll be down. I think she's feeling blue. I don't want to be too lovey-dovey tonight in front of her."

"Whatever you say, Spike." Darwin eagerly shoved a small box under Tony's nose. It was wrapped in red and gold foil with an exquisite wired bow the color of a flaming peach. "You first."

Darwin, who was normally a man of few words, was visibly nervous. "I thought of it after our conversation with Gee about Hidden Falls," he continued.

In that second Tony knew what was in the tiny box. As he opened it, tears clouded his vision of the two gold rings nestled in black velvet. Side by side. *Together forever.* "Oh Dar. They're beautiful. You're beautiful. I love you more than words can say." His mouth found Darwin's.

"Red and yellow, kiss your fellow!" Elsie's chirping voice broke the mood.

Like teenagers caught in the act of feeling one another up, they quickly pulled apart. "Elsie! But you're not supposed to be ready yet—you weren't even dre— Oh never mind. Hey. We've got great news to tell you! And don't you look like the you just discovered Elvis? Come. Sit. Spill your guts. We insist." Tony scooted over and made a place for her beside them.

Elsie felt a calm she hadn't felt in years. When? She couldn't remember. "I think I'm in love." She began slowly, then, like a runaway train picked up speed. "And I think I'm ready. This time, I'm ready. Do you think I'm ready?" She gave a little giggle while they hugged her. "Wait." She pulled away. "Tell me your news."

A frown changed Tony's laughing face. "But Dar, have you already talked to Law about this? Is he willing to share his big day with us?"

Elsie saw the velvet bedded rings and let out a whoop! "You're getting married too!" Her eyes misted. From Darwin's expression, she knew he hadn't mentioned this to Law. "Don't you worry. I'll speak to Law."

They both knew that would do it. It was a done deal if Elsie told him it was.

Busy trying on the rings, Elsie interrupted their moment. "I'll want something in return."

They looked at her, surprised.

"This time," she said, "I want *you* to help me catch this murderer. This horrible man who raped our Wick and almost killed Mary. We've got to get to him before he gets another of us. I want a life with Toast. I can't do this alone."

Tony was quiet. "You really are in love. What is it about him?"

"I don't know. Maybe it's just time."

"No. I was worried your time would never come. It's something else. The man has some hold on your soul. And it must be stronger than your need to save the world."

"Hold on my soul?" She seemed stunned. "Like soul-mates?" It was rhetorical; she nodded. "Like Lynn. I feel for Toast what I feel for Lynn; first when she was my best friend and now, my angel."

"Then, that's it," Darwin said. "Lynn's returned to your life in the body of Terrence Lawrence."

Randolph took a detour on the way to his house. He needed a lift, an emotional high; seeing the area would give it to him. He drove along the river to the scene of the crime. Not the scene, but the spot where he'd propped poor Lola's body behind the wheel of that old Camero.

They, Randolph, his beast of a car, and the beast within his soul, pulled over to the stretch of dirt in front of the battered cars; he climbed out.

The Camero was gone.

Pity.

Evidence, he supposed.

The vivid yellow and black crime-scene-tape was gone, only a remnant, a yard or so, clung to a branch of a barren tree. Caught in the wind—a windsock to remind those who ventured by of his dirty deed.

"Dirty deeds, done dirt cheap..."

He ignored the voice that followed him. At least it could get some new material, he thought. What if it did read his mind? What did that prove?

Randolph sat on a rock, his back to the river, thinking of how most people who came to this spot would probably turn and watch the Mississippi, while he much preferred to concentrate on these old rusty automobiles. Something about them soothed him, took him back to his childhood, to a time when he felt very much in control. But wasn't his Dad the one who'd been in control? No. He realized that once he had what he had on his Dad, it was all a pretense.

From out of nowhere came the sound of children crying, sobbing. Randolph hurried back to the dark beast. He hated that sound. And it was all too familiar. Time to get home to Claudette.

"Oh, oh Claudette. Prettiest little girl that I ever met is Claudette."

"Oh, shut the fuck up." Randolph said aloud, trying to sound as if he believed the voice would do just as he commanded. All the same, he drove over the speed limit. If he was to hear children crying it might just as well be his own little darlings.

"*Little darlin' oh. oh. My little darlin...*"

Christ, thought Randolph. What would he have to do to get some peace and quiet?

Chapter Thirty-Four

Bobbette's hum, coupled with the scent of bayberry from the room filled with candles, lulled them into another space, another capsule in time. Sam enjoyed her flocked crème colored spruce tree with the oversized blue lights. Lights that didn't move. Steady, the blue hue brought home to him the peace of the season. Wick had a collection of candles and made a ceremony of lighting each of them while Sam clattered around the kitchen area.

"Sit and sip that brandy," his voice carried across the tiny apartment. "I'm makin' my specialty for our after dinner treat."

"But we haven't had dinner."

"So? It's Christmas. We'll have the after dinner first, later if we're hungry, then I'll cook the dinner."

The brandy made her flush. "Or, maybe the main-course won't be food?"

"Well, we'll see about that, my lady, we'll see."

Thirty minutes later, Bobbette lapped at her dish of vanilla tapioca pudding. Kandle sat yoga style in the center of the old braided rug; one hand held the ceramic bowl, the other spooned the heavenly potion between her lips. She savored the flavor. Vanilla was her favorite. It was the scent she wore, the candles she bought, even her favorite icecream. "How'd you know?" she asked as she rolled it over her tongue.

"How'd I know? Are you serious? Even your Christmas tree looks like vanilla pudding." Sam knelt behind her, brushing her hair. Long slow strokes. He'd eaten his pudding in gulps. It was his favorite. Took him back to childhood Christmas Eve when Gram made it for them. Always saved extra for him. But tonight his stomach came second to Kandle. He buried his nose in her short, soft hair and felt himself grow light headed. He wasn't going to push her. Since the rape he'd given her space; tonight was no different. "C'mon Wickie. Lean back, relax for me." He propped pillows behind her, filled her tapioca bowl and brandy glass.

Kandle giggled. "What're you *up* to?" She watched him gather this and that and settle by her feet. He had a bowl of very warm water and first he bathed her feet. She could see her nail polish, nail file, buffer, and vanilla oil. With a sigh she slid against the pillows and gave in to a feeling of utter contentment. In the warm candle and blue Christmas lights she let her mind lift off. All that was real was the feel of warm oil and Sam's hands pampering her toes. Bobbette stuck her nose in Kandle's brandy glass and purred even louder, then set about grooming herself while Sam groomed Kandle's feet.

"Hold your toes very still, little Wick."

His voice slid on the air—almost a whisper—more a caress, but the smell of nail polish made her nose tickle. Kandle opened her eyes ever so slightly. This was a picture for the cover of Vanity Fair: His large dark hand was cupped around her pale pinkish heel; with the fingers of his other hand he held the tiny brush dipped in pearly white. Sam's face had an expression of love coupled with concentration. The brush was too small for his big hands.

A single drop of white satin landed on Sam's thumb—a dollop of custard floating on a sea of dark rum.

Wick's smile was musical, a tribute to the mood in the room. For the first time since the rape, she forgot it completely; her spirit sailed on a calm sea.

She gave her mind over to Sam.

Claudette shook her head and looked at the clock in her room. Whatever had held her captive seemed to have released its hold. She took a deep breath. The children would have to wait for her. This errand was something she had to do; she had to leave immediately. Adrenaline surged through her at last; she threw her coat around her shoulders.

Where could she put the stack of papers?

Papers of proof.

Take them along. Her purse was small. Randolph had the only briefcase in the family. She didn't want to stray too far from her room. Her mind raced. Elizabeth had a backpack. Claudette had seen it on the hall floor earlier. It was never filled with schoolbooks, but Bethie carried it every day. Claudette looked out her bedroom door, and sure enough, the small teddy bear bag huddled against the baseboard. Like a thief she slipped half her body out the doorway, leaned, and clutched the bag to her stomach. She paused. It was Christmas Eve, yet where were the smells and sounds of Christmas? No wonder the children were angry. Guilt bathed her. She was the mother; it was her duty to see to these things. The only sound was that monotonous screaming rap music that usually tortured her senses; tonight it was protection. Beth and Teddy were enjoying themselves. They must be enjoying the music.

She made a mental note to try harder to understand them.

As she stuffed the paper clippings into her daughter's bookbag, Claudette felt herself unclench, relax. She was nearly out the door.

Chapter Thirty-Five

"Ah, Lips baby. Why aren't you speaking to me? Saving your voice for some later concert?" Dandy laughed out-loud. He'd forgotten the night he named this dark beast, Lips. Here he was back in the driver's seat. He felt smug. The damn car was silent for a change. Probably caught up in total respect, knowing where they were headed, knowing what he was about to do. Because of course it knew, it read his mind.

What *was* he about to do? All of them. Ha!
Hey. That would make a nice knock-knock joke.
Knock-knock.
Who's there?
Lips.
Lips who?
Lips who? Why Lips, born of the Eclipse. Lips who came out of Eclipse to bury all of you beneath the shadows for the rest of time.

Well, if not a joke, at least a point for philosophical debate. Like: What makes a man, albeit a man of power, take on the personality of the Demon?

Suddenly, Randolph's laughter went stale—his good mood went pale.

There it was. The voice again. The wind beat against the car making a sporadic rocking motion; it blocked out some of the words...the tune so familiar. Was it from an old TV show?

SPIRITS OF THE ONCE WALKING

"dum, dum, dum, is the place to be. Da, da, da...the place for me..."

That damn wind again. This time he wanted to hear the words. What *was* it saying?

"darlin' I love you but give me Park Avenue."

Park Avenue? Dandy heard that loud and clear. Lips, or the Demon, or whomever the hell, wanted to take him down that lane to Park Avenue. His street. The street where his promise was born.

"Oh my darlin' oh my darlin' oh my darlin' Clau-ah-dette. You are lost and gone forever..." the wind beat at the beast, wham! It felt like an earthquake. Lips swerved. "Clau-ah-dette." it sang.

"Clemantine." Dandy yelled. But his head was stuck on Park Avenue—where his promise was born, his fate with Claudette cemented.

Damn it! HE was in control. He. Randy the Dandy. He checked the Rolex. Wifie should have Christmas dinner complete. He was hungry. The least he could do for the family was have a nice dinner with them before he slit their throats. Ha!

Toast roamed the halls of Choices, unnoticed and ignored. He couldn't rest; his mind, no, his body, was filled with Elsie. He felt caged. The only sounds were coming from the large meeting room. Sounds of the party he'd mentioned on the phone. He'd seen some of the participants stagger in and out on their way to the restrooms. Was it his imagination or could he really smell the booze? Why would his imagination be that vivid, when all he wanted was his Elsie? It was booze. *In a treatment center*. The doors to most of the rooms were closed. He longed for an adult person to appear; Toast would pour his thoughts out. Where was a confessional when you needed one?

At the end of a long corridor, he noticed a small light under one of the doors. It was unmarked, but he thought he remembered the man who checked him in saying the room was off limits—that it belonged to the owner of the center.

Okay. He had some questions for this owner. No time like the present. He knocked firmly.

No answer.

On an impulse, he turned the knob.

It was unlocked.

Chapter Thirty-Six

Officer Head was in a nasty frame of mind. Here it was Christmas Eve and she was handling the desk. Suzie was having a family Christmas in Ohio, or some damn place. Those that were working were, on call, up on the second floor having a precinct party. The Lieutenant considered her fair game simply because she didn't have a family or significant other. Well, she was trying to work on getting one. Trying her damnedest. With little help from her friends. She fumed, thinking of the time when she started and Vince called her Muffin. Been a while since he'd called her anything but officer. Even that, only when he had to speak to her about business. It was that grumpy old Detective Lawrence that had scared Vinny off from her. Him and Officer Suzie, that bitch.

She went to the locker room and got out the packet of cocaine she'd taken from evidence. On her salary she couldn't afford to buy the stuff. Why not take advantage of the Holiday? The powder went up her nose like it knew the territory. It did. Whenever her boyfriends had been able and willing to afford it she had made her position clear; if they wanted what they all wanted, she wanted candy—and not Godiva. Good shit made her feel like she was on a trip to Key Largo. In the distance, Val heard the desk phone ring and ring. She could always say she had an emergency on the other line, a crisis that had called the precinct instead of 911. Most likely it was nothing anyway, she thought as she sniffed more of the powder and then took out her cherry red lipstick.

"Yeah, yeah. I'm comin', keep your panties on." she said mostly to herself.

Claudette's heart was pounding as she opened the door to the garage. She shrieked when she saw someone in the shadows of the doorway. Her heart nearly stopped beating when she saw who it was.

Randolph?

Ohgod. It *was* him. But she always heard the car. That music the children loved was blaring so loud she'd not heard the car drive in. Ohgod. Worse than the alternative. An intruder, a stranger, would be far more welcome.

"Going somewhere, my little dumpling?" Sarcastic as ever, he pushed past her—literally shoving her aside. "Change of plans, Claudette. Dandy's home and he's hungry."

The white of his eyes was red and yellowish.

Demonish.

"I, ah, wasn't feeling well earlier. But, of course, I knew you'd be hungry, you work so hard; I was just going to run to the store." Her face was hot, burning as she followed him back inside as far as the doorway. Her mind flipping fast, going over excuses, options—survival. "Why don't I make you a drink, ah, darling. A nice drink, then while you relax, I'll hurry to the store."

He watched her. Something was wrong. "Fix the drink." He nodded. Why was she still standing in the doorway? He sniffed. "I don't smell *any* dinner. You don't mean to tell me that it's Christmas and you've prepared *nothing*?"

He surveyed the room. "Where are Humpy and Dumpy?" The music answered. He proceeded to inventory the cupboards and refrigerator. Just as he'd expected, there was plenty to eat right here.

"And when he got there, the cupboard was not bare."

Dandy's head jerked; he watched his wife carefully. She hadn't heard the voice spout off about the cupboard; of course, she hadn't. "I don't know what you're trying to pull Claudette, but get that coat off and get your ass in the kitchen and make a dinner worthy of this family. I'll expect it to be ready in," he held out his wrist, even though there was a clock on the wall, "shall we say twenty-eight minutes?"

She dropped her coat on top of the teddy-bag and hurried to the refrigerator. "Theodore...Elizabeth...come in here please." She raised her voice trying to be heard over the noise they called music. There would be safety in numbers, she was sure. Besides, it was Christmas. Randolph was right. The family loved spaghetti; she had meatballs and sauce already in the freezer. As she bent to take the saucepans from the rack she saw her coat. One plump fuzzy brown teddy-bear leg protruded from its nesting place.

Chapter Thirty-Seven

The telephone rang over and over until at last it woke him. He waited at least ten more rings to see if the caller would give it up. No such luck.

"What?" Law's voice was gruff. Last thing he wanted on Christmas Eve was an interruption from the world outside. He'd had to stumble over Gee to get to the phone; no doubt she was awake too. He couldn't concentrate, felt dizzy; it was Elsie's voice, but what was she saying?

"Hold on."

He dropped the receiver and lunged for the kitchen sink—the closest drain. The wine tasted so much better earlier in the evening. "Eeah." He wiped his chin on the kitchen towel. Stubbed his toe on the way back to the phone. "Damn." This better be good.

"What's up?" He tried to sound civil—knew he failed.

"Sorry Law. Look, I'll make this fast. I found the last name, I'd written it down, of the woman who's been calling me."

Silence. "So?"

"You remember my telling you about her? How her husband beat her and her children and she was afraid he was going to kill them?"

This was Christmas-for-criss-sake-Eve. "And?" Law's voice was testy.

"And," This time Elsie's voice changed, too, giving it right back at him. "The last name is *Boodles*."

He frowned and tried to think. "Why is that vaguely familiar?" His tone curious.

"Lola. Or Tim. Whomever. The boy who was murdered had been a resident at that treatment center. Choices. The place Toast's at right now."

"Yeah?" Soon, he knew his brain would kick in.

"I have the letter right here in front of me. The administrator, and, I believe, owner, is a Mr. Randolph Boodles."

"No."

"Jeesh, Law. What's *up* with you? Are you sick?" Elsie was beginning to wonder if she'd dialed a wrong number.

"Sorry. Too much celebrating. Wine."

"Oh. Well, why didn't you say something? Listen. I tried calling the number Toast gave me. He said he'd be waiting to hear back from me, but there's no answer. I'm going out there."

"You can't go alone."

"I'll say I'm his sister. Family. They can't refuse family on Christmas. I want to warn him, maybe get him out of there until we know more."

"I'll pick you up."

"No way. Haven't you heard? It's a holiday. Go back to Gee. I just thought it could be important for you to know. Maybe this guy's the one who attacked Wick and tried to get Mary."

"Stay where you are. I'll send a squad to pick Terrence up." Law was finally fully awake.

"Nope. I'm outta here. Don't worry."

The click in his ear infuriated the detective. He dialed her number, punching at the numbers, taking out his frustration on the telephone.

"Hello." It was Tony.

"Lemme talk to Els." Law noticed that Gee look away.

"Whom shall I say is calling?"

"You know very well, smart ass."

"Merry Christmas to you *too* detective. For your information, you're too late. She and Pip ran out of here, oh, ten minutes ago." Tony smiled and winked at his pal as she closed the door behind her with her finger over her lips in the *shh* signal. He didn't know what was going on, but it was fun to give Law a hard time.

"Shit." Law slammed the phone not saying good-bye to Tony. Els must have called him from her car. Cell-phones. He hated this techno-age.

Theodore and Elizabeth had been busy.

Claudette instantly began to sob when she saw what they'd done.

The two struggled into the room with the small evergreen; from the smell of pine, it was a real tree. Shy smiles on their faces. They'd made all of the decorations; chains of colored paper, popcorn and cranberries and more chains, silver, made of crumpled foil. A cardboard star on top was crooked, nearly falling off.

"Merry Christmas Mom and Dad." they said it together.

All this had been done under the guise of loud teen*rage* music.

"And Mom," this time it was Teddy who spoke, "you don't have to make dinner. I went and got us Subs. Remember when we used to have submarine sandwiches?" Although he was speaking to his mother Ted watched his father, his voice hopeful.

"Well, what a grand idea! My children. Aren't they smart as whips, Claudette? A tree, or is it a shrub? Fit for a king, and sandwiches for our Christmas feast!"

"We knew you'd been depressed Mom. We wanted to cheer you up." Elizabeth looked to her Mom for words of approval.

Claudette was speechless. What could she say that would not upset her husband. Her tongue would not move. Her frightened eyes...darting.

"Depressed? What earthly reason would your mother have to be depressed? Unless of course, it's because she and she alone is responsible for the two of you turning into such sterling silhouettes of these past years of her life. What an accomplishment!" he boomed. His yellow eyes were slits, squinting in the stark light of the kitchen. "Why would you be depressed Claudette?" He grabbed the top of her arm and yanked her toward him, pinching the tender flesh as hard as he could.

At that moment Elizabeth's eyes fell to the teddy leg under her mother's coat. "Oh. Mom. Sorry I didn't put away my book-bag." She bent to retrieve it, feeling guilt for making her mom look bad by not picking up after herself. Mom tried to teach her.

"...he knows if you've been naughty or nice, Santa Claus is dah dum to town."

Randolph watched. Evidently the voice continued to only serenade him...giving him clues...naughty or nice. Then he smiled as he pictured his wife earlier, standing with her coat on in the doorway. She'd been holding something. Something she'd wanted to hide.

The book-bag.

"I'll take that." Swiftly he grabbed the soft bag from his daughter's hand. He looked at Claudette. Just as he thought. Naughty. Unlikely that wifie was lugging Beth's books to do some textbook reading at the market.

"To market to market, to buy a fat pig. Home again, home again, jiggity-jig."

As he unzipped the bag Claudette moved to Beth's side and held her arm.

Speaking of pigs. "Must be a few Twinkies inside, am I right lard-ass?" Randolph laughed at his daughter. His mean laughter stopped dead as the papers fell around him. His voice became a blade.

"Well, well. What have we here?"

Curious, Teddy went to the table to see with his father what was inside.

Chapter Thirty-Eight

"Nature always adopts the simplest modes which will accomplish her end. If she wishes one seed to fall only a little to one side from a perpendicular line, and so disseminate its kind, perhaps she merely flattens it into a thin-edged disk—with some inequality—so that it will "scale" a little as it descends." Faith in a Seed - Henry David Thoreau

Elsie could feel her heart pound, bam, bam, bam.

The road was icy, the wind hit the car with force and blew the snow so that the view surrounding her was nearly blind-black, but her mind was on Toast. She was warm despite the cold. Pip, however, shivered by her side, poking his nose under her leg. "Won't be too long," she tried to comfort him, "before the heater kicks in." Of course, in this extreme weather, they'd be lucky to feel heat for miles. She remembered a blanket stuffed for just such a night in her trunk and pulled over. Being in a hurry was no excuse to neglect poor baby Pip.

She heard his whine when she slammed the door. He'd not been himself since that monster had cut him. Tucking the old wool blanket around him, she was glad she'd taken the time to stop. Pip licked her hand to show his gratitude. Beagles didn't have much hair; he was always cold and shaking lately, not fully recovered from his ordeal. "I just had to have you with me baby," her right hand patted him while she drove off again. "It's hard enough to be alone on Christmas. Plus, I missed you while you were at the vets for so long." Elsie tried to concentrate on the road ahead, a road she could barely see. Christmas lights lit the houses—teeny fireflies veiled in snow. It made her think about the celebrating going on inside those warm, cozy homes. "We haven't had much chance to talk," she scratched the top of Pip's head—she knew he missed her, too. They'd been a team for many years.

"I'm afraid, Pipster. Now that I knew I'm in love—well, something's sure to happen to Toast." Pip licked her arm. "Sounds silly? Sure, I know it does, but it's always been that way for me—my track record isn't the greatest, is it?" These were irrational thoughts and she knew it, but her instincts caused her to feel queasy all the same. Was this Boodles the killer? She reached for the chain around her neck, the tiny brown bottle was there. At least she had protection.

Elsie thought about the herb that rested inside the brown bottle—for a minute she wondered if it had been the right thing to do—bringing the poison. Doubting herself was not a good thing—not now, not with the danger that she was certain lay just ahead.

The herb was called Amanita, or, as she liked to call it, *Death Angel*. This was the most deadly mushroom. There were several versions, but the one called Death Angel was the color of new fallen snow. She made a tincture of the mushroom caps which was so deadly that just one drop would bring agonizing death. She'd decided on it while she sat all those many months in jail. Not wanting to ever return to any kind of prison, she'd searched her memory for an herbal poison that would give her time to escape. Death Angel's symptoms did not begin for half a day, and it normally would take four or five days for death to arrive. Elsie could be far away before the killer even began his terrible ordeal that would ultimately end in death.

Death Angel would carry him and dump his sorry carcass right at the gate of hell.

But when she chose the white mushroom she wasn't planning on one thing—her, falling in love. She had not considered that the Demon might kill *her* before the poison killed him. She felt fear. The fear of love lost, life lost, her soul mate lost to her forever.

What if the killer was this man who owned Choices?

What if he had his knife? As surely he would.

Her bottle of Death Angel would not save her life.

Nor would it save the life of the man she loved. It would save the others, but this time was different—she wanted more. And because she'd not dreamed this could happen, she was unprepared. The evil monster she hunted would not die for days!

Chapter Thirty-Nine

When the knife is razor sharp, thought Dandy, it's like cutting yourself; you don't feel it until you see the blood. With one slick stroke he'd sliced through the jugular of this young man called Teddy.

Randolph's son's blood flooded, gushed, as his head and body fell back.

"*I caught you knockin' at my cellar door, I love you baby can I have some more... Oh, the damage done.*"

Randolph listened to the Demon's song while the red spread itself into a moat across the kitchen floor. The sack of submarines sucked the liquid and stared at him, bloated and pink. His stomach growled; he was hungry. He lunged at the sack and stuffed a turkey sub at his drooling face. "Ahh," his gratification sounded almost sexual; blood dripped on his chin, the wrapper floated to the tile floor.

"*...baby can I have some more... Oh, the damage done.*"

Why was the song about damage?

This was no damage; it was only Humpy, that pimply kid he found so annoying. Then he noticed how the pool seeped onto the news-clippings of the Avenger-Woman and Lola and more. Thoughts of Lola, and Lola's dick, made his face burn.

"*...Oh, the damage done.*"

That was when he remembered Claudette and the girl, his daughter, Dumpy. He looked. They appeared to be gone. *Gone?*

"I'll fucking find you, you bitches!"

His voice was no longer smooth as silk, it was the Evil one inside, bubbling, churning, screeching for more blood.

Beneath his feet, beneath the floor, mother and daughter huddled. Randolph had built a room under the kitchen for the day when the U.S. would be invaded—as he was sure it would be. A bomb shelter, no less. It was stocked with canned goods and powdered food. The cement floor was freezing cold; there was no window, and the one ceiling bulb was burned out. It could be padlocked from either side and Claudette locked it quickly, fumbling in the black, icy room. It was nearly sound proof yet they heard his scream. They knew he'd find a way to get in. But their tears were for Teddy.

"Mom. I've got my cell-phone." Elizabeth talked through the sobs. With no tissue she blew her nose on the bottom of her flannel shirt.

"Thank god you live with that phone, Bethie. Give it to me."

The first call she made was to the police precinct. No one was answering; how could that be? She noticed the batteries were very low and was about to click off when it stopped all on its own, mid-ring—dead. Why hadn't she tried 911 instead? Through the thick cement over head they heard sounds of things falling, or being thrown. Randolph was invincible. He'd find a way to get to them and their lives would be over.

They held one another in despair.

"I hit the city and lost my band. I watched the needle take another man... gone... the damage done."

Randolph never knew when Dandy took over him completely. He never knew when he'd stopped hearing the song and wondering and instead felt it a part of him, as if they were a team.

Fuck Randolph.

Dandy needed the needle. Fuck Claudette and little lard-ass, too. He had bigger fish to fry. He was inside the black beast, a needle in his arm, before it came to him. The, *"I caught you knockin' on my cellar door,"* had been his pseudo-partners way of clueing him.

The cunts were hiding in the cellar.

"Get 'em yourself, if you care so much," he sneered out-loud, never noticing how much his voice was changing. He sounded more like the Maggot, and less, far less, like Randolph Boodles. For himself, he'd lost interest in the girls inside. He'd be back, and they'd still be cowering in the cellar.

It was time to settle the score.

Which one first? *Who's on first?* His unique sense of humor cracked him up and he began to laugh hysterically. The plan, as he saw it, was to get each one of the women and take them to the junkyard; if he kept them all secured, he could do one at a time while the others watched and waited for their turn.

"I watched the needle take another man...gone...the damage done."

Chapter Forty

"Mary baby. Hi. I'm gonna stop by the precinct for a sec'—left part of your present there—in my desk. You know me." Vince was happy.

"It's okay Vin. Just hurry. This's our little tadpole's first Christmas! We can talk to him, you know? You lay your head on my belly and tell him how wonderful his Momma is." Mary sounded excited. The mad was long gone.

"I'll fly. See you in a jiff. And Mary...love you—love you, love you!"

"Me too, Vin—oh! Vinny, I'm gonna make you glad it's you an' me, babe! Just hurry! Bye."

Vinny was pulling into the precinct driveway when he hung up his police phone. He could hardly wait to be in his woman's arms. What did she have planned for him now? More than he deserved, he knew that, for sure. Hardly any cars in the lot, he noticed. Pretty deserted. Even criminals wanted to enjoy Christmas Eve. Well, good. Not much chance of getting waylaid. He rushed inside, went straight to his office, and began digging through his desk drawer. He could hear someone coming up behind him and turned.

"Well. If it isn't Minneapolis Homicide's hunkiest-hunk."

Officer Head looked like she'd been expecting him—or someone—maybe anyone. Her jacket was off, just a thin white blouse underneath, the top three buttons undone. The material was stretched tight over her breasts—she'd bought it at least two sizes too small. He could see her nipples, maple morsels, poking through the thin material; without his approval he felt himself stir.

"Yeah. Hi Officer. I'm kind of in a rush. You'll have to excuse me. Wife's waiting." He turned his back on her, which was a mistake.

Val reached inside her blouse and pinched her nipples to make damn sure they stood at attention. He wouldn't miss them now. Then she slithered around side him. "'Member how you used to call me Muffin? Hey. Look at me. What're you 'fraid of?"

Vinny started to sweat. Where *was* everybody? It'd been way too long since he'd had sex—although he was darn sure that tonight was the night. Still, he couldn't seem to keep himself from getting boners at times like this; he needed to get his ass out of this situation and home to the woman he loved—and right now. All the while he was thinking this, his eyes were on Val's body. She had the kind of body that looked as if he might have designed it himself. Him and every other guy on the planet. So much round, pink flesh, a man would barely know where to begin. This was a body made for sex. Nothing else. But he loved Mary. He had to leave this on his plate—push away from this table. Fast.

Val had taken his silence for assent, and there she was rubbing herself all over what was now embarrassingly hard. She took the wrapped present with the translucent bow away from him and placed his hands on her lush oyster colored breasts. They were glazed with the oils of her desire for him.

"Oh Vinny, I've waited so long for this." she breathed.

God but her nipples were hard. And it was the wanting *him* that made them that way, he thought. She lifted her rear up on the edge of his desk and in what seemed seconds he felt her legs around his waist, pulling him against her.

"Oh no. I gotta go." He could barely talk with her tongue in his mouth. "Get off a' me Val."

Mary was in the bathroom when she heard the message machine.

"Vinny?" The voice was loud, excited. "I just tried the precinct and Val said you were home. Look, I know it's Christmas Eve but we think we have a line on the junkyard killer and rapist. You want in on this one, don't you, Vince?" From his voice it was evident he thought they were listening. "Call me right back."

Mary grabbed the phone, but got a dial tone. Why would Val say he was home? What if Vince had come home and been attacked outside? She ran to the window. No car. No Vinny. Not the *black shadow* either. Mary pictured Val. They'd only met once or twice and it wasn't pleasant. A woman knew when another woman was after her man. All out, no holds bared, after him. Either Vinny was in trouble and needed help, or, Vinny was in another kind of trouble. Either way, Mary had to know. She couldn't sit and wait. Their house was less than five minutes from the police station. Where *was* Vinny?

As she went down the stairs to her car something deep within told her he was dead. She started to run. Her hair was still damp from the shower and she'd forgotten her coat, but she didn't realize the cold. Vinny needed her.

While she drove, her eyes surveyed the side streets for his car, or a black car. It hit her then that she had no gun. Some help she'd be.

Outside the precinct sat Vinny's car. Mary felt stupid. Should she turn around and head home? Obviously the killer was not here. She was about to do just that when she remembered the look in Val's eyes. Why not go inside and say she'd run to get a bottle of wine? Well for one thing, she reasoned, there was no wine in the car. Okay, she was going to get a bottle of wine when she saw his car and thought she'd see what kind he'd prefer for their big night. It was weak, she knew, but why let him spend any more of this evening with that slut Val?

She got out of the car and started inside—slowly, afraid of what she could find, yet hopeful that Vinny wouldn't let her down.

The place was much darker than usual. Stop your paranoia Mary. Why turn on all the lights when you don't have a full crew, right? She moved toward his office, then stopped. Through the window she saw them. Val's breasts were bare, glistening melons; she had her hands cupped under them, holding them up like a present, an offering to Vinny. Vinny's hands were holding her by the shoulders; Mary couldn't see his face, but she knew that Val saw her.

Had he really planned on coming home as if nothing had happened and laying his head on her stomach while they talked to their baby?

Why disturb the lovers? She turned on her heel and ran.

The sound of running made Vinny push harder; the bare breasts were tempting, but he was a man in love. He pushed the sweating body away; Val fell to the floor.

"Christ Vinny.!" She screamed at him. "So somebody saw us. Do you think it's the first fuck they've ever seen?"

"This was no fuck, Val. This was *you* making an ass of yourself."

Vinny ran to the door; he arrived in time to see the tear streaked face of the woman he loved, and no doubt thought he'd just betrayed, just as her car drove away.

"One pill makes you larger, and one pill makes you small... and the ones that mother gives you don't do anything at all... feed your head."

Ah. A tune he'd loved as a teen.

SPIRITS OF THE ONCE WALKING

Feeling the need for more and more, better and bigger highs, Dandy-Randy did what he'd sworn he'd never do: popped some acid—d-lysergic acid diethylamide—LSD. Before long he'd be seeing a room full of white rabbits. Still, the song made him feel young again.

Thinking of rabbits brought his mind to the animal cemetery of long ago. Time to make a cemetery out of that rusty iron on River Road.

The beast drove; he was cruisin,' on total cruise control.

"Well, sport. Where the fuck're we goin'?" asked Dandy.

No answer. Yet the beast moved slowly down a familiar street.

Ah. The cop. The cop and his cute little pregnant wifie. Wouldn't they be having a nice Christmas dinner? He belched onions from the few bites of blood-bloated submarine. Dandy's hunger had evaporated—poof—into thin air.

Alice was taking him to Wonderland.

Taking him on an *embryonic journey* to find his *plastic fantastic lover.*

Find her, grind her.

The black shadow came to a stop down the street from the cops' house. "What have we here?" In panoramic splendor he watched the cute preggie with no coat run up the stairs to their door; she was crying, she was. "Well, I'll be damned." Going after her was that prick cop. The expression on his face was tragic. He looked as though he'd just lost his best friend, or maybe a man on his way to his execution. Ha!

"Listen to me, Mary. I was pushing her away! You didn't see what you thought you saw! Please Mary, I want you, I was coming home to you! You gotta believe me!"

The knife slid into Dandy's hand as he swung his legs out of the dark beast.

"Mary...baby...you've got to listen to me." said Detective Tonetti.

Poor pig-boob. Never know what hit him, thought Dandy man as he gained momentum. Although Dandy was running fast the cop never looked back, all he could hear or see was the little woman he chased.

"Tag! You're it!" he yelled.

"Mary, I was pushing her away, ba—"

With one fast jab Dandy punched his knife cleanly between the cops' shoulder-blades. The body folded—a pair of threes against an inside straight; Dandy kicked it over the side of the small porch. Before he opened the door to go up the stairs and get the woman he looked at the cop. All that red blazing through the snow made him want to go on a carnival ride.

"Time for a strawberry snow-cone!" He could hear carousel music.

With thoughts of red-berries and snow-cones he labored up the stairs, his breath coming hard. Adrenaline had moved him, but halted him just as quickly. The drugs sapped what energy he had left.

What he needed was more excitement, thought Dandy as he opened the door to the cops' living room.

"*Milk...blood...to keep from running out. I've seen the needle and the damage done.*"

"Been here, done this." he said a loud. This time the Demon was along to help. There'd be no escaping him this time. Them. Be no escaping them.

Chapter Forty-One

"Though amid all the smoking horror and diabolism of a sea-fight, sharks will be seen longingly gazing up to the ship's decks, like hungry dogs round a table where red meat is being carved, ready to bolt down every killed man that is tossed to them.... If you have never seen that sight, then suspend your decision about the propriety of devil-worship, and the expediency of conciliating the devil."

MOBY DICK - HERMAN MELVILLE

Sam hung up the telephone.

"Who's that?" Kandle giggled. She'd been having too much fun to stop and eat the dinner he'd prepared. Leftovers were just as good, he told her.

"I don't know. Said it was from the third precinct, calling me for Law. Been another murder and the detective wants my help."

"Another murder? Who?" Kandle was on her feet.

"Don't worry, Wick. No one you know. Some young man. I, ah, got the address. I don't mind going; it kind a' seems strange that Law didn't call me himself, is all."

"But Sam, I don't want you to go." Kandle stuck out her bottom lip.

"Me neither, baby."

"Why does he want you there?"

"Don't know that either. I know he's been a damn good friend to me. I'll go and ask questions when I get there." He smoothed back her hair and kissed her brandied lips. "You'll be okay for awhile? I'll leave Bobbette to keep you company, Wickie." He kissed her again. "Take a nap and before you know it I'll be back to finish that massage. Gonna do your hands too. I'll hurry." With that, he was out the door.

Dandy's eyes shone with a yellowish tint as he walked across the creaking bedroom floor; she was face down on the bed, shrieking with some kind of pain. Evidently, the cop had been a real bad boy. Her body was an invitation, but he kept himself in check; they were going to a party; he was not about to settle for just this one woman.

She spun her entire body over on the bed with fists flying, thinking he was Vin. Her beloved. It happened so fast. Before she knew it, he dragged her by the neck, gagged her, then cleverly pulled a ski mask down over her head so the gag would not be visible to passers-by. He yanked up her coat collar and shoved her over the threshold.

"Check out the debris lying in the snow."

Mary'd been praying that Vinny was waiting outside to jump this bastard. It was the creep who'd tried to *get* her in the shower;

Even though she'd seen what she'd seen at the police station, Mary knew that her husband loved her. She also knew how that slut Val was after him. Vinny's hands *had* been on her shoulders. Pushing the bitch away? Seeing his body in the snow bank shattered her. Her hands were tied together, then around her waist; he'd buttoned her coat over it all. She placed her hands on her stomach and thought about their baby.

"Behave and maybe I'll let you go." The very words made him laugh hysterically.

They were going to a cemetery, he told her. "Cemetery made of rust and steel."

"No cops around to save your cute little ass, Missie. Time to party. You'll be the first to arrive at my party."

The black ski mask she wore was stiff with frozen tears. *Her hopes were dead.* How long would it be before she and their baby joined them?

Nothing about this night was going as planned. He'd been in the bathroom dressing when he heard the door bell and before he could get there the bell had turned to pounding. Law tripped over his work shoes trying to get to the door so that the banging wouldn't disturbed all the neighbors. It was early yet, but still...

"Where's Elsie? Is she here?"

Law glared at his brother. Gee had heard Elsie's name just about enough for one Christmas Eve. "Why would I know where she is?" He noticed then how frantic Terrence looked. "Far's I know, she took off by herself to go get you."

"Get me where?"

"Hey look. It's Christmas. Can you give me a break here? Figure out your life tomorrow. I don't have the answers for you." Law's face was stone. "And, I'm just on my way out. On a case."

"Gerald," the strain Terrence was under was obvious. "Let me in." He pushed on the door and entered. "Excuse the interruption, Gee." He tried once again with his brother.

"Where did she go to find me?"

"Where you *were*, Terrence. She went to the place they put alcoholics—you know the name better than I do. Patterns?"

"*Choices.*"

Law couldn't even meet Gee's eyes. He was being rude and he knew it.

Georgia took Terrence and led him by the arm. "Come in and sit. Let's figure this out." She gave Law an angry glance that told him to shut-up and follow. "Now. Law would you please tell Toast what Elsie said when she called?"

"Said she was worried. Something about the owner of, ah, Choices, being a guy whose wife had been calling her—calling Elsie. She figured he might be the killer we're searching for, that junkyard killer."

"Why did she think that?" Gee was curious and fuming inside. Why hadn't he explained this to her when he got off the telephone?

"Guy has an odd name. Boo something."

"She mentioned the wife, Claudette, that her last name was like poodle." Toast interrupted his brother.

"Yeah?" Law was too pissed to put the pieces together for him. Why? he wondered. No doubt Terrence had valuable information, they should work together to solve this. The thought that crept into his head next was not welcome, but it came anyway. First, he thought, he works on this with Toast, and then Toast and Elsie could go around killing off the bad guys and solving police problems, off into the sunset together. So. That was it. If he'd just figured his hostility out you could damn well bet Gee had a good idea what was going on, and if she did, he was in deep shit with her.

"So I went to look around and found his office. It was open. His name is Boodles."

"That's it. That's what she said." Law's voice was lighter, helpful. "So she was coming to get you until we could get the whole thing figured out." They looked at one another.

"Why didn't she show up there?" asked Gee.

"How would I know? I'll call Tony, get her cell-phone number and give a call." Law reached for the telephone. "You two probably just passed one another. Why'd you leave?" Law asked as he dialed.

"After I found out the name, I tried to call her; there was no answer. She said she'd wait for me to call her back before going to the celebration downstairs. I already called Tony and Darwin."

Law missed the last of what he said because Tony answered the phone. "Hey buddy. Sorry I was short with you before. Look I need Elsie's cell-phone number. Got it handy?"

"What's going on? Your brother called and asked for the same thing. And, as I told him, she didn't take a phone with her." That last was said sheepishly knowing what Law would come back with.

"But you told me—"

"I know," Tony cut in. "She was standing right here and didn't want to speak to you. Cuff me, officer tuff-guy."

"In your dreams. Say, we're not getting much of a Christmas in tonight, none of us, mind if we come over? We can toss this around. She'll probably get there before us."

"Sounds like you're hangin' a bit low, detective love, come on over, the wine is flowing."

"Forget the wine. Had my quota. See ya."

Maybe she was already dead and dreaming this.

All she could think, well, she couldn't think, she could only picture her Vinny lying in the cold snow, the huge red growth soaking the icy substance. If the gag had not been so tight, a mournful wail that would tear at your guts, would be heard for miles around the old car. Mary tried her best to think of the baby that would be born if she could only get to safety; she worked at the ties that bound her wrists. He'd been clever, the Demon-man; he'd wound another rope around the car seat and tied it in back where her hands couldn't reach. Her bra was soggy. Blood trickled down from the slice he'd made on her neck. Just to show her that he could—that he would. That she was his. Somehow, the thought of her breasts damp with blood made her think of Val. Earlier Mary'd hated her. Now Val was a nothing. An empty *nothing*. Meaningless.

Oh Vinny, my love, her heart cried for him.

She could see. She watched an occasional car drive along River Road to the dead-end, then make a U-turn and head back toward the city. There were battered cars everywhere around her—old, rusty pieces of crap. Her head was tied down so she couldn't turn around to see the river, but she knew it was there, behind her. Mostly frozen except for small puddles of black inky water. Ice. Like the ice Vinny bled in. She remembered the conversation with Elsie and Gee and Wick. These cars were not really here, were they?

Then, she thought, why am I so cold and afraid if this isn't real? Am I already dead?

Why do I hear those children crying?

What? Children crying?

She listened, and sure enough, over the sound of her own torment were, what? Babies? Oh god, what's happening to me? And, again, her mind returned to Vinny.

Vinny in the cold scarlet snow.

"Wait for me baby," Demon-Dandy said when he left her. "I'll make it worth your while. We'll party when I get the other girls here." He'd wheezed this out at her, as if she had a choice in the matter; as if she were going to enjoy what was to come.

Madness seeped from his pores and choked in her throat.

And so she sat, she waited, her mind a spinning Ferris wheel, a twirling top, filled with the cars that couldn't be, her unborn baby, children crying, the Demon-man and his golden eyes, and *her* man, her love. Love lost. *Forever.*

"It's a long drive to Dundas. That's where the treatment place is, right?" Tony was beginning to pace and was making an attempt at rationalizing.

Toast nodded. "Seventy miles at least."

"I don't get it." Tony was clearly close to tears. " She'd just told Dar and I how we had to help her solve this murder. Help her work the case. She didn't want to do it alone anymore."

"She said that?" Law seemed confused.

"Umhm." Darwin answered. "She said she was in love. She wants her chance at life and love." He studied the detective carefully.

If the room had been unlit, Toast's glowing face would have been all the light they needed.

Conversely, Law seemed upset by Darwin's words. "If that's the case, and we'll have to take your word I guess, why didn't she tell you what she was doing or take someone with her?"

Gee had been silent until now. "Elsie is following the pathway to her destiny."

The ringing telephone stopped her.

"Hello?" Tony's voice was anxious. "Oh. Hi. Law, for you." He handed the receiver to the detective and sighed.

"Law here."

"What's up Sam? We're kind of in the middle of something here."

Law listened. "What do you mean? I didn't have anyone call you." His voice was puzzled.

"Of course I'm sure." Now he sounded testy.

Everyone in the room listened, rapt.

"Sam, listen to me. I don't know what's going on. As soon as we hang up I need to find Vinny, we'll contact the detective in charge and find out what we can—did you say it's a teenage boy? Give me the address...got it. Okay, meanwhile go get Wick and head on over here."

Law ran his hands through is thinning hair, worried. "Someone called Sam. Said they were calling for me, from the precinct and that I needed him to help me on a case."

"What case?" Darwin asked.

"I'm not sure. He went and found the police there. A teenage boy'd been murdered. Throat cut."

Gee stood. "Call Wick." Her tone told them she was in charge.

Darwin dialed the number and held the telephone while it rang for minutes. "She could be asleep."

"Go there—now." said Gee. Her very core told her that Kandle was not sleeping.

Law grabbed his jacket. "We'd better stop at Vince and Mary's on the way. There's no answer at their house either."

"I'm coming with you." Gee, making a quick decision, wrapped the wool serape around her.

"Me too." said Tony.

"Count me in." Darwin reached for his coat.

"What about Elsie and Sam?" asked Toast.

"We can leave a note. They can meet us. Tell them to call my car phone." The group followed Law and Toast began to scribble a note to his love and Sam.

The doorbell rang.

Kandle ran to it, excited. "Sambo! Get in here! It's not like you to leave a job half done."

Kandle opened the door with a giggle, not bothering with the chain or the peephole. "My fingers are waiting to match my toes..." her words hung there. It wasn't Sam. She felt silly for she was standing barefoot wriggling her toes and shaking her fingers in the air. Silly preceded fear.

She recognized the handsome man on her doorstep and froze, jailed by her terror. Toes that moments before were dancing at the prospect of Sam, stuck upright in the air, corpse-stiff. He looked different—worse, if that was possible.

"Aw. Is that not sweet? I *ask* you. You were expecting the dark one were you not? Unfortunately, he was called away—

presumably to help a friend? Guess what, Missie? I, am the genuine *dark* one."

She cringed, shrinking from a blow that had not yet been delivered. Demonic laughter pelted her psyche leaving only panic for the horror that was certain to follow. Her brain said, *scream now!*

She opened her mouth.

He moved fast.

Towering over her, he covered her mouth to stifle the scream almost before it began its escape from her frozen lungs. Bobbette flew through the air; a tickle of fur grazed Kandle's cheek. She heard the Demon curse as the projectile pounced on his hands, raking sharp claws down his skin.

The enraged cat *screeched* and attacked; razor claws raked into him. Yet all the while his hands stayed on the core—on Kandle—his focus primal.

Mere seconds were a tortoise-paced vertigo—whirling her, petrified, dizzy, while he stuffed her mouth full, *a pig for roasting*, she thought, *readied for the spit*.

Trussed and stuffed, she was yanked by the hair out the door. She saw the red trail of droplets that seemed to follow her out.

Blood.

There was blood on the kitchen floor, too. She remembered seeing it as he shoved her inside the sleek black familiar beast that was his car. Was it her blood, or his, she wondered? Not that it mattered.

What could it matter?

What could anything matter.

"You're going to love this." The voice that was once silk was different now, too; crammed with evil, it was the voice of her death—not only death, but the pain that would precede it.

She thought about that pain.

"Have I got a surprise for you. *A party*. We were rudely interrupted before, do you remember? Twice before. Did you know it was me that second time? I assure you we will not be interrupted again."

The beast purred; it carried them down toward River Road.

"*I sing the song because I love the man. I know that some of you won't understand.*"

Randolph felt her eyes on him. Out of the corner of his eye he watched her.

She'd heard the song!

Why wasn't she upset? Or curious, even. Certainly she'd seen that his lips hadn't moved with the words of the song. Why could *she* hear it?

Kandle tripped back in time on the Neil Young words; her mother was singing to her when she was a babe. "Momma?" She tried to speak, the word clutched in the fist of the gag in her mouth. Oh, to return to her momma's arms.

It seemed to know that its audience had grown by one. "*I've seen the needle and the damage done. A little part of it in everyone, but every junkie's like a setting sun...*"

Kandle realized that death had come to take her.

What she was hearing was the voice of death. The profound, the awful truth of it saturated her. Sam. Sam was part of another world now; a world she was leaving. Her chance to be with Sam had slipped through her fingers.

She'd crossed over, then, hadn't she? She was falling, slipping, down... down, frantic, she sucked air through her nose and felt the terror of her life left to live, terror so real, so awful, it filled her veins. It filled her veins and now it was about to cause her mind to implode.

Chapter Forty-Two

"Is it not crystal clear, then, comrades, that all the evils of this life of ours spring from the tyranny of human beings? Only get rid of Man, and the produce of our labour would be our own. Almost overnight we could become rich and free. What then must we do? Why, work night and day, body and soul, for the over-throw of the human race!" ANIMAL FARM   GEORGE ORWELL

Elsie was tired but she was excited all the same. She parked right in front of Choices. Easier to grab him and run, she grinned to herself. Pip was asleep, she leaned down and whispered to him. "Wait here. I will only be a minute Pip. I brought an extra key so I'll lock the car and leave the car running."

She stood at the front desk and frowned. "But how *could* he be gone?"

"Pardon me, 'Mam?"

"I said, how could he be—"

"Oh I heard what you said, nothin' wrong with my hearing. What do you *mean*?"

She glared at the clerk. He was giving her a hard time on purpose. "I just spoke with him on the phone and he knew I was on my way. That's what I mean." Her fingers tapped on the counter. "Have you checked his room?"

"Mam. He's signed out."
Exasperated and worried Elsie turned and walked out.

The man watched her and then picked up the telephone and dialed.

Kandle was securely tied in the seat of the old car. She could barely move her head and the stocking mask had such small eye holes that it blocked her peripheral vision, but she noticed a slight movement in the old car next to her and began to fantasize that someone was in there, hiding, waiting to help her. She focused on the area. There! It moved again!

What had he said as he slammed the car door?

"I'll return my dear, and the fun will begin. Let the good times roll, yeah, yeah, yeah."

His voice was an echo in her brain. Fun, return; fun, return. *Good times roll*. Roll-yeah; roll-yeah; yeah-yeah.

The movement again.

It was as if someone were tied just the same as she. Trying to move their head. Trying to show *her* they were there. That's it! You need more than two people for a party. This monster was gathering the party participants—bringing them here. Who was it—in the dirty powder blue Ford Escort? The movement had to be a head—it was all she herself could move—

She stared and tried to concentrate. The wind blew and the sliver of moon lit just right and she saw a figure; it was halfway down the seat, like a child. Someone small.

Oh god no.

Mary.

It had to be the five foot tall Mary. Demon, for he had become simply Demon in her mind, had tried to attack Mary too. She'd be on his party list. Of course she would.

SPIRITS OF THE ONCE WALKING

Kandle tried hard to keep her mind busy; sitting alone in the freezing cold she remembered Sam. What would happen to him when she left him the same way Bobbie'd left him? Murdered. She had to try harder. It wasn't over yet. Now, seeing the short waggling motion that was most likely Mary's head in the dark ahead of her and although it seemed hopeless, she knew she couldn't give up. Mary and her baby's lives were at stake here, and who knows who else was coming to this party?

Why hadn't he tied them in the same car?

To make them feel alone and powerless.

Kandle's tin-coffin was a crashed and dented Trans-Am. The hood came toward her, an aqua-blue accordion with a huge broken bird painted on top. The window beside her was smashed out and the wind swirled around her shivering body. Only the gag kept her teeth from chattering.

Sam called her his Wick, his center, she thought; he depended on her. She told this to herself over and over again.

The only warmth came from inside the mask; her breath melted the frozen tears and snot that had stiffened the black knit. Warmer than her breath was a growing resolve, a heat that brewed and boiled from within her soul. At that minute, she channeled her power.

It was a ball of burning fire. Her power was a generator.

Kandle screamed out *"Maaary!"* The gag held most of the sound inside her own head, but she saw a shaking in the abandoned car. It *was* Mary and now she knew that Kandle had seen her.

The moment was joyous. Connecting like this, they both still existed! She knew that she had transferred some of her heat to Mary.

In the background the children cried; Kandle heard their pain. But then, she heard the strong voice of a woman:

"It may be that some part of this sacred ground still lives."

The drive all the way to Dundas was bad enough, but then to discover that Toast had left. Why would he leave, Elsie wondered? She kept touching the bottle that hung around her neck. Maybe things were better this way. She needed to mix up a different herb, one that would do the job instantly. Whatever caused him to leave Choices, Toast must be on the way to Darwin and Tony's to see her. She pressed her foot on the accelerator and checked her rearview mirror. Not many cars on the road tonight. This was, after all, a night to celebrate; a night to be with friends and those you loved. She smiled. Soon, very soon, she would be doing exactly that.

The headlights came up fast. She'd been watching her rearview mirror and they seemed to come out of nowhere.

"Hey bud. Dim those lights." she said out-loud.

Pip cocked his head to one side. Was she talking to him?

The light made her eyes burn. Then she laughed. The lights were flashing; it's a signal, she thought. It has to be Toast. He'd recognized her car, which was quite a feat from that distance behind, but of course now he was practically on top of her and could see her license plate.

Why didn't he dim his high beams?

She rubbed Pip's head. "First I'm gonna yell at him," she confided as she pulled the car to the shoulder of the road, "then I'm gonna kiss him!"

A bit of luck was all he needed and here it was.

There weren't all that many cars out tonight.

His wimp of a manager had proved useful after all, calling to tell him about the ex-priest who left, or as they thought of it at Choices, escaped, and the blonde woman who'd come searching for that man-of-the-cloth. Elsie Sanders, said the manager. And Randolph laughed until tears ran down his cheeks.

"Dandy loves candy." He hummed to himself while snorting a big line. No time for the needle, a bit of nose-candy would hold him until he got the real thing. There was only this one direct road to Minneapolis; he knew if he hurried he'd catch her. The beast was capable of overtaking anything on the road.

"Oh Dandy boy, the dah dah dum is cah-ah-lin."

Demon's tune reminded him of when he was a boy. His own Dad had sung the Irish song to him, changing the lyric from Danny Boy to Dandy Boy. The scenery along side the road went by as quickly as film fast-forwarded, while inside, his thoughts rewound until Randolph saw himself standing at the edge of the river. Dad was dragging the butchered bodies of Randy's stepmother and her two small children.

"Don't just stand there and gape. Help me you little fucker." The voice was clear; Dad was really here—here in the car with him! "Help get these asshole's under water where they belong."

Dandy had kicked each of the small bodies in the face, he could see that although they were helpless they were not dead...not until he pushed them and held their bleeding, pleading, whining, mugs under the icy water.

That memory gave him pause. It wasn't Dad after all!

He'd been the one to kill the brats!

Of course! He remembered now how they'd squealed. Like pigs—small squealing piggies! Dandy's head was encased in a bubble of laughter; again, it came from everywhere, it came from nowhere, but there was no escaping from it. On the edge of madness he covered both ears with his fists while Demon drove Lips. The road had disappeared for him; he saw a man across a threshold motioning to him to enter. The man stood midst flames that licked his bones clean, but it was quiet on that side, no squealing, no laughter; Dandy wanted to go there.

Questions, as large as his ego, remained; who then, had been holding the power when he was young, Dandy, or Dad?

Why had he believed that Nam was his first taste of murder? He saw the children's bloody faces, heard their begging cries, saw their blood on the toes of his shoes. Through laughter that was a siren in his ears he heard Dad's voice. "Aw, leave the blubbering fuckers be. Let 'em alone Dandy boy."

That was when he saw her car; he dropped his clenched puffy white fingers and began to flick his lights. He couldn't believe his eyes! Why in the world was she pulling *over* for him?

Because right was on his side, and he, Dandy, had the power—had always had the power!

Hearing the sirens coming from all directions made Law think of the National Anthem; these sounds signaling various degrees of disaster were the criminals' anthem.

"We've got a pulse!"

Law heard the voice of the paramedic cut into the chaos around him and especially in his mind; it gave him no real hope. Finding Vince face down in the snow had been Law's moment of truth. He felt sharp pain in his chest. Nothing to talk about; it was secondary to the real pain in his heart. Vinny was on his way out, Law could see it. Mary was gone and there was evidence of abduction. They'd yet to find out where Wick and Sam were, and Elsie was missing, at least not back home.

"We have to hurry Law. Go to the junkyard." Georgia wasn't going to let him do his job, was she?

"There *is no* junkyard. Can't you get it into your head? The cars are gone. Removed. I don't know by who, but I know they're gone." Had he ever raised his voice like this to her?

"Law. Listen to me." She took his arm; he yanked it back. "It is the *woman under the ice.* Don't you remember when Elsie saw her? That woman's Spirit made a connection with the Indians whose sacred remains live on, *in that ground, in that river*; she's asked for their help, for justice. Their Native American Spirits are much like you Law, just one more force helping, longing for justice."

He looked at her smooth butterscotch skin, her wide chocolate eyes; he wanted to run with her, run to a place of safety where there was no real world to come between them. But where? And could they? To run, was to give up—to let innocent people die.

Chapter Forty-Three

Mary drifted in and out of consciousness. She prayed for death before Demon's *party* began. And yet... what would happen to her dear friends if she wasn't here to help them? And she knew who he was planning to have attend his little *get-together*.

She heard a car door slam. At first she thought Wick had managed to free herself and she was going to be rescued! Here you were planning to give up, die off, and not help anyone at all, she reprimanded herself.

But no, it was no rescue. It was the sleek black car, Demon's car. And coming toward her was Demon pulling along another trussed body.

Elsie.

Avenger-Woman.

Avenger-Woman, Elsie. The one person she'd thought might just be able to save them.

Demon stuck out his tongue—a very long tongue and licked it up the side of Elsie's face. Elsie didn't move, didn't blink; a muscle in her jaw jumped but her face stared at him like a stone.

That lick of his tongue killed Mary's hope

Kandle watched the same scene, but she saw it with a hopeful, stubborn heart. Her inner Spirit stormed to keep her feet on life's road. Inside her was the forming, the birth of a structure; her Spirit was drafting its own plan—for an edifice of steel. Kandle was determined that she would be the Wick, the wick that would destroy this distorted, twisted, hideous Demon.

"Ah, my ladies," he stood midst the rust-heaps and roared, his voice guttural and stoned, eyes flashing a putrid yellow, lips sneering: *he was a mimeograph of his soul.*
   "Boodles, party of four!" The grin came just as he cocked his head. "No." The voice squeaked high for that one word, then dropped low, "we won't be having dinner. Dandy's not interested in food tonight."
   They watched as he ran that same awful tongue over parched, cracked lips. Lips caked with white. Was it foam? Was Demon foaming, frothing, poison creeping-seeping from its pores?
   He swung open the creaking Trans Am's door, and crammed Elsie in behind the wheel. She and Kandle were going to be together. Kandle's mind raced.
   That meant that Mary was chosen. He would kill her first. It *did* mean that, didn't it?
   Her answer came as he cackled. "Just like a drive-in movie for you girlies. Sorry Dandy doesn't have popcorn to offer."
   Kandle saw the first sign of fear in Elsie's eyes. Fear? Elsie? Was this what had love done to her? Kandle wanted to scream at her, "get a grip girlfriend!"
   Demon came around the car and opened the other door; he leaned inside, checked to make certain Kandle was secured. "Is what they say about fuckin' a nigger true?" He stuck out his tongue and wiggled it in her face. "Dandy's gonna show you a real man, little girlie. Too bad your *boy*'s not here to watch. I wanted him here. Wanted the fags here, too. Can't have it all. But don't you gals worry, I'm gonna kill every last one a' your happy immoral incestuous cult of a family."

Kandle wrenched with all her might and managed to move her body enough to get his attention.

"What?" His face right in her face showed green lettuce stuck between the once impeccable man's teeth; the porous nose appeared greased. "You have something to say to Dandy?" The insane monster laughed, he pulled the mask off her face and wrenched at the gag. "Tell me darlin'. Tell Dandy what's so all fuckin' important you'd bother a *creator* at his task..." His nostrils flared, the laughter gone, "an', risk makin' him angry... risk makin' what's comin' to you that...much...worse."

A rush of cold air filled her lungs. It felt good. Free. With all the loathing in her soul she spit the words, "A Dandy, is simply a word for a *faggot*."

Inside she prayed to Dar and Tony for forgiveness, but knew they'd understand. She'd said the words, but only to inflame this creep, her heart was pure.

The foul stench of his breath in her face was gone in an instant; he raged and flung himself about. His face distorted, morphing right before their eyes—from murdering beast, to murdering-child, to Dandy-man, to Randolph the businessman drug-dealer, corrupt father, perverted husband, drug-addict and family man. In a frenzy of activity he opened the tailgate on the battered pickup truck that sat in view of their windshield. He spun to the blue Escort and untied Mary. Her eyes flashed at the women—panic filled and frightened, a deer.

Still bound, he heaved her with super-human strength into the rear of the pick-up; he wove in front of the Trans-Am, head back, arms outstretched. "Let the movie begin." His contorted voice came from beneath the ground and shook the car that imprisoned the women.

Kandle turned to Elsie as they saw him climb up onto the tailgate. Kandle's head was free.

In his fury, he'd forgotten to replace the gag and head ties.

Chapter Forty-Four

Sam knelt beside Vince in the deep pink snow. "You're gonna make it man, hang on there, for Mare, for your baby." He looked at the paramedic. "What's he tryin' to say?"

"I don't know. But whatever it is, it's important to him; he keeps saying the same thing over and over."

Sam put his ear to Vinny's lips and listened. "Tell me man, say it once more."

"That's it. Got to get him to the hospital." The paramedic was already moving Vince inside the ambulance.

Darwin put his arm around Tony. "Spike, I'm going to ride in the ambulance with Vinny. We can't leave him alone. Why don't you come too?"

"You go, love. I'll stay with Gee and try to find the others."

Darwin kissed the top of Tony's head. "Be careful."

"What'd Vince say to you?" Law asked Sam.

"Don't know. Sounded like, *thinks I cheated*. Who thinks he cheated, and at what?"

Gee interrupted. "Law, you're not listening to me. The most important words come on soft shoes."

"Don't give me still waters run deep crap. My friends are dying."

"You're not hearing me! I didn't say anything about *still waters*. And they are *my friends also*." Gee was yelling. This was a first. They all stared. "You wanted me to advise the police, to take that job with the department; do you now think so little of my insight?"

"I'm not going to argue with you Georgia! I'm going to Boodles's house. That's where I believe he's taken them. I have my own insights, Gee." He turned his back on her. "Tony, take her with you to your house and wait for me." It was a command. He ignored his brother and Sam and went with two other detectives.

Sam hesitated, torn, then ran after Law. "Hey buddy, wait up. I got to find Wick."

Toast put his arm around Gee's shoulders. "C'mon my friend. Law doesn't know what he's saying. He's already grieving for Vince, and he's scared to death he's failed us all."

The passive nature Gee always maintained was gone. "Midst all the spectrum of colors," she said, "his heart is beige."

"Hey sweetie," Tony kissed her cheek, "beige is beautiful."

"I'm not speaking of skin color, but the color of his heart."

"If you're right, it's only because his fear for us has choked off his blood supply." Tony kissed her again.

"You are wise beyond your time." She touched his face. "Drive us to the river—quickly."

"Gee, I promised to take you home with us."

"We're going to go home. But first we're going to save our friends."

She'd been thinking about when Demon had snatched her from her car. At least he hadn't seen Pip inside, and Pip had that blanket to keep him warm until help arrived. She'd heard him barking as she'd struggled with the man, but the wind was loud and Demon wasn't thinking about dogs. She'd heard glass shatter; the bottle from around her neck was flung hard, landing on concrete and stone.

The poison, she thought.

The poison was gone.

The glint from Wick's eyes *transfused* to Elsie the fire she needed. Time to stop feeling so damn sorry for herself; to stop thinking about the feel of Toast's arms around her. If they were to ever get themselves out of this mess now was the time to be strong.

"Toast, wait. Do you have your roman-collar or any of your priestly robes and vestments with you, back at the house?" Gee stopped the two men just as they'd begun to drive in the direction of the river.

He seemed remote, off somewhere, as he answered. "Well, yes, I'm sure I have them packed away. I bought a few things myself when I visited the Vatican in the late eighties—things that were mine, not belonging to the Church. The lace, the hand embroidered silk, all hand made in Rome. I couldn't resist." He opened his face to them; the pain was evident. "I haven't touched them in a long time."

Gee kissed his hand. "Toast, I'm going to ask you to do something very difficult, but so very important. I want you to wear your priestly garments. Hurry to the house. We must fly."

'Why the garb?" Tony asked what both men were thinking.

"I'm not certain I can explain what I don't understand myself. You must trust me. I follow advice from the Spirits of the Once Walking."

"Once walking?" Toast was speeding toward the mansion.

"She means dead, I think, am I right?" Tony asked.

Gee smiled. "Yes, but not exactly."

Chapter Forty-Five

"The train was pounding near. Already it had emerged from the canyon, and momentarily the headlong flying locomotive loomed blacker and larger. A white plume flew upward—Whoo-oo, whoo-oo."

TRAIN TIME (1936) D'ARCY MCNICKLE

Elsie's hands fought desperately to stretch, twist, pull, her to freedom; the side of her hand hit something, she moved her fingers to get a grasp on the object.

What?

Although her eyes could not reach behind the seat to see what she held in her hand, she could feel the shape of the tiny bottle, the cord it hung from was still attached.

The white mushrooms, Death Angel!

But how did the bottle get here? It should be lying broken, its potion seeping into the road from Dundas.

Elsie could feel the car shaking as Kandle continued to bolt to set herself free. Elsie thought of it as bolting, because in the truest sense of the word, with each lunge of her friend's body Elsie could feel the power of freedom surge throughout the creaking car. She remembered something else. Gee's statement about this stretch of land by the water having once been a sacred burial ground. Bones, blood, and Spirit, of the great ones, soaked this ground beneath them.

While they watched, Demon crawled down from the bed of the pick-up and slunk off a few short feet to where he'd parked his car. Mary's limp, motionless body had failed to interest him sufficiently, or, he'd needed more fuel for his fire. He left the car door open, reached up and flipped off the overhead light, so that he could see them without giving them the same opportunity to view his movements.

He thought.

Kandle alone heard the voice of Demon's master as it sang an old ditty her momma had sometimes played. Kandle remembered the title because it used to make her momma laugh; it was called *"The Dope Fiend Blues."*

"You know you could fool with wine and reefer too... you'd never get in trouble nor be the ruin a' you...but you had to have that itch for the big an' better rush...you just need to get higher no matter what it was."

"He's dopin' Els," Kandle whispered. "I can hear the devil sing his damn mood music, urging him on."

Elsie's eyes asked, "You can *hear?*"

"Yeah. Weird I know. Can you hear it sing, too?"

Elsie shook her head, no.

"Guess I'm special."

Elsie's head said yes. Quite special.

"But look, Elsie. Take a look at his eyes."

Glowing amber eyeballs sautéed with crystallized ginger; manic eyes that soaked them like rain, yet the brain in charge danced over them without seeing—this is what they saw. Eyes filled, overflowing, with heroin, cocaine, crystal methamphetamine, and the drug that took his mind on a journey into another space, acid (LSD).

Only Kandle could hear Demon's master sing—well, Kandle and Dandy could hear.

"*I caught you knockin' at my cellar door. I love you baby can I have some more...oh, the damage done.*"

Elsie could barely breathe; she knew from the look on Kandle's face that something was happening. She thought of Gee's words, and she thought of the woman under the ice. That face, the tormented face, was here. It would help them now.

"*I've seen the needle and the damage done. A little part of it in everyone, but every junkies like a setting sun...*"

A setting sun. Was it Demon's master who sang so that she could hear, too, or some other, kinder Spirit? Kandle wrenched her wrists.

This time the ties broke free.

Chapter Forty-Six

You could see the crime scene tape around the yard from a block away. Law knew he'd made a mistake as soon as he saw the deserted house.

If he was honest, he'd known it as soon as the squad car drove him away from Gee. Sam's nervous, frantic chattering kept him from concentrating, or he might have turned the car around and headed back.

He dialed again.

"*We aren't home, or we are. Leave a message at the tone.*"

He'd been trying to call Darwin's to no avail. Gee would answer if she heard his voice.

Unless she was too pissed.

Where *were* they?

The more he thought the more he worried. Of the three, Toast, Tony and Gee, who had the strongest personality? Would the men be doing what Law wanted, even though Gee told them otherwise?

No. A resounding no.

"Go to the river," he told the cop who drove the car.

"Fuck Law. I thought you were sure they were *here*." Sam was going off on him. "I got to find Wick."

That was about the one hundredth time Law'd heard Sam say those exact words.

"Shut the fuck up. We're gonna find them, Sam. And I'm doin' the best I can."
He saw the fear cloud Sam's face and thought of Bobbie. Sure Sam was piss-in-your-pants scared. He tried to joke by nudging him and adding, "Sam I am."

Chapter Forty-Seven

"As I rapidly made the mesmeric passes, amid ejaculations of "dead! dead!" absolutely bursting from the tongue and not from the lips of the sufferer, his whole frame at once—within the space of a single minute, or even less, shrunk—crumbled—absolutely rotted away beneath my hands. Upon the bed, before that whole company, there lay a nearly liquid mass of loathsome—of detestable putridity.
     The Facts In The Case Of M. Valdemar - Edgar Allan Poe

Demon had moved from his car and returned to the truck bed. Mary lay stone still.
    "Look," Kandle's voice was a whisper. "Is she already dead?"
    "No. She can't be. She's pretending." Elsie felt an adrenaline rush—the time to act was soon.

    "...I love you baby can I have some more... oh, the damage done."
    Demon leaned over Mary and began to rip at her jeans with the hand that held the knife while the other opened his belt. "Time to party. Hey, wake the fuck up." He gave her butt a kick. "It's show time."

"Look at him! He doesn't care if she's alive or dead, just wants to find an opening." Kandle spit the words. "We can't let him do this."

"...*can I have some more... oh, the damage done.*"

"Can you hear that yet, Els? The dirge from the one who drives him?"

Elsie shook her head, no.

Cries of children, those unknown and unseen children, swirled throughout the junkyard. They grew louder.

"...*oh, the damage done.*"

And louder, still.

"I hear the children though, and they are upset. They are trying to drown out—"

Elsie stopped, she felt a sharp wind hit her side as the driver's door opened a crack; the interior light came on, blinding them, it sent a shock of fear that hit like a lightening bolt. In a split second Kandle's now free hand went to the light and punched it out. The closet of dark returned. The murderer's back was to them. He hadn't seen the flash of light from the car.

"We're here. Me and Terrence and Gee. Dar went in the ambulance with Vinny." Tony's voice was a whisper from the ground by Elsie's side.

Demon raised his knife over the limp body. "Save yourself, bitch. Live another minute or three by having this party with me."

Kandle, frantic, tried to untie her legs and feet in time to save her friend.

"*I've seen the needle and the damage done. A little part of it in everyone, but every junkies like a setting sun...*"

Cries from the children, angry cries, reached a crescendo.

Demon raised his arm higher and the moonlight transformed the metal blade into a silver fish swimming mid-air, about to dive and land in Mary's pregnant belly.

"*...but every junkies like a setting sun...*"

A tall figure appeared out of nowhere, stepped from out of the shadows and around the left side of the pickup. It was a man dressed in black with a thin embroidered veil of white sheer material laid over the top.

An angel?

The children's cries became a hum, almost disguised with the kinetic energy that filled the junkyard.

From the right, came a woman, her long robe—was it a robe?—was a flutter of feathers—all lengths, brilliant hues—they entwined, they swam, feathered arms, birds, caught in a current of flux and reflux—*sail, plunge, sail, plunge*. Her face was hidden behind a painted wooden headdress of eagle feathers and foxtails; around her neck hung a necklace of charms—charms that gave glorious and *hor*ious sounds—rumble, hiss, growl, clang, boom!—all of it done to evoke the help of the Spirits—to summon their help.

"*...like a setting sun...*"

The charms, or was it those screeching birdlike sounds along with the constantly rotating feathers, that drowned out the voice of Evil. Buried Evil's voice with their band.

The man held a prayer book; his voice rang with the power of his words. He began. "*Kyrie eleison.*" The small black rosary beads, that were wrapped around his hand, jangled, accompanying the Kyrie chantings.

Why could you hear the sound of the small beads? They were but a whisper inside this roar of motion.

"It's Toast." Tony's whispered words came from beneath the women.

"No." Elsie answered. "It's Father Lawrence."

"Lord have mercy." The woman translated the priest's Latin.

"Gee's with him." Tony again.

"Hush." Kandle was working on untying Elsie without being seen. The action on both sides had stopped Demon—but for how long?

He stood, half up, half down, his eyes bugged as if he could not believe what he was seeing. And in fact, who knew what he *was* seeing.

"*In omnem terram exivit sonus eorum, it in fines orbis terrae verba eorum.*" The priest chanted—his words rode through the swirls on the ice flakes.

"Their voice has gone forth through all the earth, and their words unto the ends of the world." The translation came from behind the wild painted mask.

Gee wore a sacred Healer's shirt, long and flowing. It had been a gift from her great-grandfather. Called an Arapaho Ghost Dance shirt, it was hand painted with stars, a turtle, magpies, crows, all symbolic of protection; all asking for help from the Spirit world.

Gee began to dance, "eeeaahh, eeeaahh," feathers and bones flew—clatter-clatter-clatter—around her. She sang in a chant as she danced; sang of the dust beneath her feet, dust made of the blood, flesh, bones, the very hearts of her ancestors.

"I am the mouth," she sang, "I am here to tell you that this ground, these trees, this river, still live. Reach out and remove this demon from our midst."

"*Dominus vobiscum.*"

"The Lord be with you." Gee said.

"*Et cum spiritu tuo.*"

"And with your Spirit." she threw her words, calling to the Spirit of the earth, and the Spirit that guides man, and the Spirit that has the *power* over the universe.

Kandle and Elsie's eyes met; the power that Gee spoke about traveled through them, one to the other.

Elsie, free now, thanks to Kandle, grabbed her bottle of Death Angel and ran to the truck.

Mary saw her coming and moved like a flash.

With both legs tied together, she lifted her feet and pushed with all her soul and kicked Demon, *Randolph*, in the balls. His body fell backward.

Kandle leapt to grab Mary, pushing her body like a rolled carpet into the arms of Tony, then, without hesitation, Kandle sprinted toward the river.

Elsie, bottle in hand, blew the bubbles mixed with deadly mushrooms into the air around Demon-man. The translucent bubbles tossed to and fro, riding the gusts, until they landed on his hands, and clung to the red trails that Bobbette had made earlier. The open scratches accepted the liquid as if it were a healing ointment.

"*Gloria tibi Domine.*"

This time Gee was silent. The Latin was made into English by the unseen children's voices. "Glory be to you, Oh Lord."

Their crying had stopped.

Part of him knew what was happening around him. His razor sharp knife was clenched in his fist ready to cut...what was it again he wanted to cut? The throb of the wind held him, rocked him back and forth, as if he were a babe in its arms. He could not seem to focus; his vision was clouded, figures swirled in and out. The dancing beast with the colorful feathers; the angel reading of Christ and goodness—where was Lips? He couldn't see Lips in the dark, yet the moonlight seemed to spotlight a figure standing out on the ice. A woman. It was a woman!

"*Randolph!*" she called to him her arms open, stretched wide.

Dandy cried "Momma!" For he'd never known his real mother, his stepmother had raised him, until of course, he'd killed her and her brats. His brain lurched—jolted. Killed them? He? But it was Dad who'd killed *her*, right?

Suddenly he saw the red and blue flashing lights. Those rolling lights behind the truck were where the devil waited to take him down, down to hell. Dandy was not going to be sucked in. They were beautiful, fantastic lights, but he was too smart to follow them. He turned back toward the river and the woman.

The chanting around him was growing louder; he hated their words!

Lord have mercy!

Spirits of the earth unite! Reach out for justice! Justice for the innocent!

The children's voices had joined in making the chantings louder.

He could no longer bear the shrieking sounds of the wind; the trees screamed; the earth opened itself and thundered to Dandy to come forth to accept his sentence; his hands covered his ears. The slippery, silvery fish squirmed from his grip falling to the ground; it skipped against a rock and bounced, landing under the pickup.

"*Clamaverunt justi, et Dominus exaudivit eos et ex omnibus tribulationibus eorum liberavit eos.*" Father Lawrence no longer read from the prayer missal. His eyes were on fire as he bade Demon listen to those he had injured, those who begged for justice.

"The Just have cried out, and the Lord has answered them and rescued them from all their distress." Only the children translated this last, this truth.

Randy the Dandy ran as fast as he could. His feet tripping, he ran straight into the arms of the ice woman who pulled him to her breast and held him close.

A glow of heat encompassed the two bodies.

Slowly descending through the melting ice and into the frozen water, holding his flailing body in her arms, they went down, down, down.

They never came back.

"Wickie!" Sam's scream searched for her. Was she under the ice?

Face ghost white, she stepped from behind a tree down close to the rivers edge. "Here I am Sam...I'm here."

"Oh baby." His arms covered her. Funny, he thought, her body's hot, not cold, not freezing like he'd have expected. "I was so damn worried, Wick. I'm sorry I left you alone."

Kandle watched the river and wondered for just a second. She knew that it was she who had stood on the edge of the ice, her arms outstretched, and called *"Randolph."* But as he ran toward her she'd ducked behind the tree. And unless she'd seen a vision, some woman had held Demon and taken him down under with her. Sam chattered away; what was he saying? Her mind was on fire—it glowed with the ice woman. She saw Gee and Elsie come toward her as the squad car pulled away with Mary inside—taking her to Vinny. Kandle slipped out of Sam's arms and went to the women; she took their hands.

"The woman under the ice," said Elsie.

"W-O-M-A-N," said Elsie, Gee and Wick in unison with barely perceptible smiles.

It was that perfect moment you live to experience. If only Mary had been here with them, thought Elsie. But then she *was* here, wasn't she?

Tony came running. "Mary's okay," he said. Had he read their minds? They all laughed. "What about Vin?" asked Gee, serious again.

Tony looked down, then, met their eyes. "I don't think he's gonna make it."

Toast had come to join the group and heard Tony's remark. He took Elsie's hand. The warmth of it in this cold wind surprised him.

"Let's head over to the hospital," said Elsie.

The glory of the moment had passed.

But it had been there, however fleeting.

It was a moment the women would always remember. They'd see to it that whatever happened to Vince, Mary got to share this feeling with them.

They were sisters.

And together they had the power.

Chapter Forty-Eight

"Vinny," was the first word Mary spoke when the ties and gag were removed. Law had been holding her in his arms.

Law took her to the emergency room using all the lights and sirens available for a speedy trip.

Vinny was conscious when Mary reached his bedside. He opened his eyes, saw she was alive.

"I forgive you sweetheart," she whispered. "I know it's me you love... me and our baby."

She saw relief in his eyes. He knew his stupidity hadn't been her death, knew she loved him still, and with one movement he laid his hand on her stomach, said "Baby girl, my daughter," and slipped off to another place.

The next step of Vinny's life, was his death.

"Oh god, Vinny!" Mary, his wife, his love, the mother of his child-to-be, cried.

Chapter Forty-Nine

Law had already said his good-bye. He watched them through the glass door with wet eyes. This time was for Mary and Vinny and the baby yet to be.

He thought about the scene at the river.

Nothing really left to do by the time the police cars arrived.

His driver'd said, "Pull over by the junk-cars, sir?" What's he talking about? Law'd thought to himself, as they headed down the dead-end—when he was close enough to see, there were no cars in sight. Just as he'd expected. Then he saw the people gathered. Law was just in time to see the man's head sink under water. It was evident that the madman was gone. Would divers be able to rescue him?

The women didn't seem to know or care; he'd overheard Elsie say something about her bubbles having made contact with Bobbettes handiwork.

Would Gee explain that to him later? Would she even speak to him?

Law hadn't seen the woman that pulled Randolph under the ice. And how *could* he be pulled under the thick river's ice?

Her body would never be found.

EPILOGUE

NEW YEARS EVE 1993 HIDDEN FALLS

The new blanket was spread—a doily on the mantle of snow.
Tall, barren trees were sculptures, statues of tribute to the Spirits that created all. Around the blanket was arranged a circle of young potted choke cherry trees; attached to each tree, a stream of long colorful cloth waved in the almost still clearing—colors of yellow, white, and red, adorned them. Tiny smoke bundles were bound with string and placed around the exterior of the trees. They were connected with more of the plain white string. Around this connecting circle was a larger circle of many small bonfires.

Between the fires and the cherry trees gathered a handful of intimate friends.

Gary Holly Bull, a traditional healer, or if you will, medicine man, his wife and six children, who ranged in ages from four years to adult, had come on a long hard journey from South Dakota to preside over this special occasion.

Holly Bull's voice was quiet, yet could be heard clearly inside the circle of fire. "I will ask you," he said, "that no alcohol be brought inside this sacred circle and that you take no pictures until after the wedding ceremony." He held the hand of his wife whom he referred to many times during the evening as his life long friend and partner. In fact, that's what they called one another.

Elsie felt a chill when he said it.

Goosebumps visited her entire body. The thrill of having a life long friend and partner brought tears to her eyes and this beautiful ceremony had only just begun.

Holly Bull and his wife, his friend and partner for life, wore faded jeans and long shirts made of buckskin with symbolic signs—birds, rivers, trees, painted on them in many vivid colors. He spoke of his life, his problems with alcoholism, and his triumph over the problems of the flesh; life's journey with his family had not always been easy or pleasant. He confided that for the first twelve years of their life together he had abused his family the same way he had been abused as a child. He had continued the circle. Now, he said, the circle of Evil had been broken.

The couple was, at last, invited to walk first around the outside of the connected cherry trees, then to enter and stand together on the blanket on which they would agree to travel throughout life together.

Gee and Law held hands, looking out at their friends. Already united in love. She wore a flowing butter-cream colored gown covered with tiny beadwork. Her hair was in long braids with a crown, a circle, of twisted flowers and herbs. Gee was an Indian princess. Law wore jeans and a blue shirt with similar beadwork; his long gray hair blew wild with the wind. He was a warrior, a man in love.

"What you are about to enter into, is an awesome responsibility." said Holly Bull.

Fires played in the wind as it began to pick up, blowing snow into the flames that crackled while the sacred man spoke. He talked of what each had brought to this day: the bride, an owl and sharp knives; the groom, a small bow and an arrow he had carved himself. These, he said, were symbols of the tools that they would need to forge a life together.

"We are all one color, one people, but the women have more power, for they can create children."

Mary's sob could be heard by all.

At some point the couple's changed places. A new blanket covered the same spot of snow and Tony and Darwin took their place in the center. The men had been dressed by Gee in jeans and beaded shirts that were decorated to please the Spirits of the earth. Darwin's shirt was the color of honey, Tony's a darker ginger-spice. They clutched hands as if they would never let one another go. The state would not recognize this ceremony as it would Law and Gee's, but the Spirits of the world were here to welcome them as partners for life.

Holly Bull had two bundles made of hide and some sineau that he'd wrapped around herbs such as sage and cedar. Both couples were placed inside the circle and the bundles presented, one to each couple, so that through their years together they would hold it between them and pray in times of trouble.

"I love you Gee," Law was on his knees—traditional himself, "I'll love you forever."

Sam and Wick held one another close and openly cried.

Holly Bull chanted and then, "Now, please, I ask you all to pray with us to whomever you pray to—pray as a group to make their walkway out of the circle—onto a holy ground that will forever change their lives. We can do this together."

Holly Bull's "lifetime friend and companion" chanted to the women and he, to the men. He picked up the white string, the chain that tied the smoke bundles together.

The smoke bundles were removed and Holly Bull said, "Our couples have been united with the Spirits and now they invite you, their friends for life, to enter this circle and present them with your wishes for their futures together."

There were no dry eyes at Hidden Falls this New Years Eve.

This was the first time Elsie had seen Toast since Christmas Eve.

She offered her hand to the priest. "The Spirits are all here tonight, don't you think so Father?"

"Yes." He smiled. "*Gloria tibe Domine.*"

"Glory be to you, Oh Lord. Right?" She smiled, too.

He nodded. "Do you understand my decision, Elsie?"

"To return to the Church? Of course. I could see that night by the river that you had never really left it. You did not need treatment, Father. You needed to discover, to rediscover, why you became a priest years ago."

"What about us? You must be angry. I was so sure you were what I was searching for."

Elsie kissed his hand. "Dear Toast. I admit I was angry. Well, not angry, hurt. But then I realized that I was what you were searching for, don't you see? Love led you to that river, to that night, to the realization that all the world is your parish." She touched his face. "What I did for you, you did for me. It was a fair exchange. You have a mission much the same as I."

Mary saw the pause in conversation and came to say hello. It was strange for her to see Father Lawrence in his Roman collar and black suit. She hadn't really seen him Christmas Eve, only heard his voice. "Thanks for your help." She held out her hand.

"My pleasure. I'm sorry about Vinny. Sorry I could not stay to visit with you after the funeral Thursday. I felt I had to return to my diocese to attend to some things."

"Hey everybody, let's get some pictures of these happy couples!" Sam broke into the conversation. They'd been talking with Law about how Val had lost her job for dipping into the evidence room, and Claudette and Elizabeth were in a counseling program and doing well. Kandle poked him in the rib and whispered. "It's time to forget the serious stuff and celebrate!"

"No, no." said Law. "First I want to know what happened to those damn rusty cars." Law's eyes met Gee's. "Would you mind telling me that *Mrs*. Lawrence?"

"I thought *you* had all the answers *Mr*. Fairbanks."

"Seems I don't."

"They were the product of evil. That ground had already been sanctified. It was holy. And it won the battle. We won." Gee looked regal, like the princess she was. "That's all I can tell you, my love. Beyond that, *you* figure it out."

Laughing, the friends gathered around the fires and poured a bottle of champagne into plastic glasses. "A toast." said Elsie, with damp eyes. "To our two happy couples who now have a friend and partner for life, to our dear friend who will, in six months, bring us a baby girl, and to a new dear friend who has returned to a mission of leadership and guidance. May our Christmas experience make us all closer to one another, and to the Spirits inside each of us, and the Spirits of the world." Elsie put her arm around Mary's shoulder. "To Vinny, who is beginning a new journey; watch over us Vinny."

Pip barked; Bobbette purred.

Tony's eyes shone with love for Darwin, but his heart ached for his good friend Elsie. Would she ever find her love? "I'll drink to that, my loves," he said.

And so they did.

Are you interested in more of the Spirit books?

Contact information:
Babs Lakey
3039 38th Ave South
Minneapolis, MN 55406
Email: babs@suspenseunlimited.net
Website: http://www.suspenseunlimited.net all books for sale on authors website's online store

Spirit of the Straightedge: ISBN 1-928857-03-5
Spirit of the Silent Butler: ISBN 1-928857-04-3
Spirits of the Once Walking: ISBN 1-928857-05-1

All three available in Spring of 2002—more to come soon.
Order Spirit of the Straightedge now at:
http://www.suspenseunlimited.net
http://www.booklocker.com

Ask babs to read or speak at your writer's group—regardless of size—contact her directly.

For other appearances, signings, interview requests:
Contact Joe Birchhill President of Full Tank Productions talent agency
952-474-0808 fax 952-470-2033
birch@fulltankproductions.com

FULL TANK
PRODUCTIONS

Futures Mysterious Anthology Magazine

Short Tales For Story Lovers
by Writers & Artists with the Fire to Fly

http://www.futuresforstorylovers.com

If you enjoy short mystery fiction try Futures Mysterious Anthology Magazine, a hardcopy quarterly magazine with the best short fiction available today (from writers around the world) published by author babs lakey. You can visit the *F.M.A.M.* online website at:
http://www.futuresforstorylovers.com
or email babs at babs@futuresforstorylovers.com